PRAISE FOR ALESSIA IN ATLANTIS:
THE FORBIDDEN VIAL

"Pulses with action right from the start in a unique tale with a magical setting and a fun plot with lots of twists and turns. The characters are wonderfully quirky and well-developed... This is a page-turner, a book you won't want to put down." — READERS' FAVORITE, ★★★★★

"Aquatic and exotic; a fun and fast-moving tale of friendship." — KIRKUS REVIEWS

"Imaginative and colorful, *Alessia in Atlantis* is a page turner from the very first moment." — THE CHILDREN'S BOOK REVIEW

"For young readers looking for a new fantasy world in which to get lost, *Alessia in Atlantis* may be just the ticket... A cute, creative, and occasionally scary world full of magical creatures and mysteries just waiting to be solved." — INDIEREADER

"Alessia's magical journey to the lost city of Atlantis... will enrapture middle grade fantasy readers." — BOOKLIFE

ALESSIA IN ATLANTIS

THE FORBIDDEN VIAL

NATHALIE LAINE

ATLANTIS

THE FORBIDDEN VIAL

NATHALIE LAINE

First Edition, 2021.

Cover design by: Alessandro Brunelli

ISBN: 978-1-7361704-2-7 (Hardback)

ISBN: 978-1-7361704-7-2 (Paperback)

ISBN: 978-1-7361704-8-9 (eBook)

Library of Congress Control Number: 2020923262

Publisher's Cataloging-In-Publication Data
(Prepared by The Donohue Group, Inc.)

Names: Laine, Nathalie, author.
Title: Alessia in Atlantis. [1], The forbidden vial / Nathalie Laine.
Other Titles: Forbidden vial
Description: First edition. | [El Centro, California] : [Nathalie Laine], [2021] | Interest age level: 010-013. | Summary: Twelve-year-old Alessia is attacked by a giant frog monster and plunges into the underwater realm of Atlantis. Upon arriving in Atlantis, she learns that her long-lost father may have been from there so she is determined to investigate. With the help of her newfound school friends, Alessia will have to steal evidence from a grumpy teacher, escape from rebel merfolk and make rhymes with menacing blue people of Minch to discover the key to her past.
Identifiers: ISBN 9781736170427 (hardcover) | ISBN 9781736170472 (paperback) | ISBN 9781736170489 (ebook)
Subjects: LCSH: Atlantis (Legendary place)--Juvenile fiction. | School children--Juvenile fiction. | Missing persons--Investigation--Juvenile fiction. | Mermaids--Juvenile fiction. | Fathers and daughters--Juvenile fiction. | CYAC: Atlantis (Legendary place)--Fiction. | School children--Fiction. | Missing persons--Investigation--Fiction. | Mermaids--Fiction. | Fathers and daughters--Fiction. | LCGFT: Fantasy fiction. | BISAC: JUVENILE FICTION / Fantasy & Magic. | JUVENILE FICTION / Legends, Myths, Fables / Greek & Roman. | JUVENILE FICTION / Action & Adventure / General.
Classification: LCC PZ7.1.L234 Alf 2021 (print) | LCC PZ7.1.L234 (ebook) | DDC [Fic]--dc23

Alessia slipped her hand into Mr. McCrum's satchel, fumbled around until she felt three prongs, and snatched back her cherished fork.

"Hey, what are you doing back there?" Mr. McCrum called out when he saw her behind his desk.

"Just looking at this 'Rules of Poetry' poster. Sonnets, haikus, cinquains... fascinating," Alessia fibbed.

"Alright, class is starting. Back to your seats – all of you," he groaned.

Alessia hid her fork up her sleeve (thankful that this was Scotland, and it was long-sleeve weather in early September) and went to her desk.

It wasn't ideal to start the year at her new boarding school by lying and stealing from her teacher. But then, it wasn't ideal that Mr. McCrum was a *completely unreasonable* teacher.

He'd inspected all of their backpacks and pencil cases for potentially 'dangerous objects'. And which 'dangerous object' had he seized? Not their very sharp scissors. Not their even *sharper* compasses. No. He'd confiscated her fork.

She'd tried explaining why she needed to keep it with her, but there was no way to convince him that a fork could be her greatest treasure – even if it was prettier than the average fork, with its blue gemstone, and engraved symbol. She couldn't blame him. It *was* an unusual thing to treasure. If she could have chosen what *one* object her late father would leave her, she also wouldn't have picked a fork, but there they were.

"Welcome to secondary school," said Mr. McCrum with the enthusiasm of a cat that's been forced to wear a party hat. "I'm Mr. McCrum, your form tutor and English teacher. I trust you've all had lunch, and been shown to your dorms. We'll spend the rest of the afternoon here for induction."

The sea breeze whistled outside the thin windows. Even though the school had only opened recently, it was housed in an old, gothic seaside manor. The result was a classroom with vaulted, blackened stone ceilings, and tacky teal-blue plastic desks. Alessia glanced around wondering which of her new classmates might be her friend, and hoping they weren't doing the same. (If they were, it was unlikely they'd pick her – the short girl, with deathly pale skin and roughly cropped mousy-brown hair.)

"You may have noticed we're starting on a Friday afternoon while the other lucky year groups only start next Monday morning. The idea is for you to settle in, make friends, etcetera etcetera," Mr. McCrum continued. "And we'll kick off this hippy dippy extravaganza by making a time capsule. So get a piece of paper and write down your name, and something unique about yourself, like your favorite hobby. You won't look at it again until the end of the year, when you can marvel at how much you've evolved between the age of eleven and the ripe old age of twelve."

He was so disinterested, he couldn't even bring himself to smirk at his own sarcasm. Alessia decided to keep it short and wrote:

'Name: Alessia Cogner

Something unique: my favorite hobby is sailing.'

Of course, that couldn't be further from the truth – her stepfather George would *never* let her on a boat after what had happened to her mother. He hadn't even let Alessia go to the town pool to learn to swim.

But she wasn't about to write the *real* 'unique' thing about her.

Back home in Inverness, Alessia was famous – and not in a good way. She was the running joke of her primary school because of her wild overreactions. She had burst into tears when a boy in her class told her his pet hamster died. She'd have uncontrollable laughing fits whenever she saw classmates laughing, even if she hadn't heard the joke. And when the class soloist forgot the lines to "Silent Night" at the Christmas concert, Alessia became so anxious she fainted. She was bizarrely oversensitive, and couldn't help mirroring the emotions others were going through and making a spectacle of herself.

No need to immortalize all that in this time capsule. This was her new start. She wasn't going to be a drama queen anymore.

"Alessia, your paper?" Mr. McCrum stood over her holding out an expectant hand. She froze midway through the fingernail she'd been biting. He was collecting them? Good thing she'd stuck to 'sailing' as her 'unique thing'.

He finished gathering the students' papers, then turned over the pile and handed them back out to other students.

"You're each getting someone else's paper and reading it

3

out to the class, so we get the introductions over with too," he announced lackadaisically.

A boy at the back burst into laughter.

"Please, sir. Can I start?" he said.

"Sure," replied Mr. McCrum.

So naïve. It didn't take a genius to work out that that boy wasn't giggling with glee at the idea of making a new best friend.

"I'm Iain and I've got someone called Calum's paper," the boy started. A boy sitting next to Alessia dropped his pen and his face blanched.

"Hand up, Calum," said Mr. McCrum indifferently. The boy next to Alessia raised a trembling hand. The class spun around and stared.

Iain cleared his throat.

"So Calum says 'Something special about me is that I love doing... ballet!'"

Iain's squeaky pantomime imitation had the class roaring with laughter. Calum's face strained to attempt a smile. Alessia winced.

"It makes me feel light and free," Iain continued reading, getting onto his tiptoes and making a mock spin.

Alessia's throat tightened and her cheeks burned. She tried to swallow back the sensation. She wasn't going to create a scene on her first day. She had to stop thinking about how Calum felt.

"I hope one day I can be in Swan Lake!" Iain continued in a falsetto voice, holding his arms up and wiggling his fingers.

Calum buried his face in his hands and Alessia felt like a load of bricks were crushing her chest.

"AREN'T YOU GOING TO STOP THIS?"

Silence fell. Alessia was standing, shouting at the teacher like a lunatic. She'd done it again.

"Uh..." Mr. McCrum seemed startled. "I beg your pardon! No shouting at teachers!"

Alessia turned to glare at Iain. "And what's wrong with you? Do you *like* making people feel bad?" she said, hating how shaky her voice sounded.

"Lighten up! Can't you take a joke?" Iain answered. Then, he gasped and swooned to imitate how melodramatic she was being, and laughter rippled through the classroom.

"Now, now, children," said Mr. McCrum, exasperated.

Iain took a bow and sat, a wicked smile curling his lips.

So much for new beginnings. Alessia had barely made it twenty minutes before getting back her old reputation. Mr. McCrum weakly shushed the sniggering students. Thankfully he collected back the papers and moved onto explaining dinner logistics, so she was able to make it through the rest of class outburst-free. As soon as the bell rang for break time, she dashed out before anyone had a chance to badger her about her display.

She raced out of the building and across the vast moorland school grounds towards the shore, wet mud flecking up her legs. She stopped at the edge of the metallic grey sea, panting.

Maybe she could still leave this school. She could call George from a payphone and ask to move to Germany with him. George was the one who'd raised her, since her mother had died when she was a baby, and her father had died before she was even born. And George wasn't a *bad* stepfather, just a little distracted. More 'kooky scientist' than 'caring homemaker'. In their house in Inverness, the roof was leaky, the window frames were rotting, and her bedroom filled with smoke every night for some reason they'd never understood. It was kind of a miracle that she'd survived, but she had. She could definitely move with George.

But even as she thought it, deep inside she knew she wouldn't. Being here was about more than the boarding school. She finally lived in South West Scotland, next to the village her mother was from – and, for all she knew, where her *father* was from too. This was her chance to find her roots. That's why she'd found this boarding school in the first place when George announced he'd gotten a job abroad.

She stroked the prongs of her father's fork under her sleeve and looked over the edge of the small cliff at the thrashing waves. Even if she didn't make any friends here, she would stay and find out about her parents – and she'd start by taking the bus to her mother's village that very weekend.

Rain began drizzling and she was about to head back to school, when she heard a whisper. At first, it was just a faint murmur, buried in the husky laughing sound of the waves rolling in and back out. But then, it seemed to float up from them. It tingled her ears, like a fly brushing past. She rubbed them but couldn't get rid of the sensation.

She started distinguishing words. Blown into her eardrums. A strange voice saying: 'Come – something – seven child'?

A shiver crawled down her scalp. She turned to leave, then froze.

There was someone behind her. Or rather, some*thing*. A frog-like creature the size of a man.

It lunged at her. She leaped out of its grasp just in time, and fell back on the cold, wet ground.

She screamed, but the crashing water and howling wind

swallowed the sound. The creature turned to her. It was a tall green-skinned man, with webbed feet, bulging orange eyes, and an eerie smile permanently traced on his face.

He bounded towards her, stretching out his long scraggly fingers so they looked like two enormous spiders. She rolled out of the way, jumped to her feet, and sprinted as fast as she could away from him when something wet and spongy hooked around her face.

She tried to pull whatever it was off, but it was drenched in a thick glue. She tried to run on, but the thing on her face held her back. Then, it started drawing her towards the frogman. She dug her heels in but they just dragged through the mud.

Viscous treacle covered her hands as she kept trying to wrench the blob off her face. It was so soft and flabby. Yet powerful enough to pull her in. Almost like...

Nausea clutched her throat. The blob around her face was the frog monster's tongue! Frogs caught flies with their tongues, and now, *she* was the fly.

Alessia jerked and thrashed, and tugged with all her might at the tongue. But it stayed stuck to her, and slowly reeled her in.

Then it dawned on her. If this was his tongue, that meant he could *feel* it.

She let the fork under her sleeve slip to her hand and stabbed it into the tongue. There was a pained squawk and the tongue was yanked off her face. Mr. McCrum was right about the fork being sharp after all.

Alessia didn't wait to see how long it would take the creature to recover. She ran and ran across the moor, trying to wipe the frog monster saliva off her face and hands.

"Yech!"

She only turned back when she'd finally reached the main building. He'd vanished.

Rain poured in thick sheets and she took shelter under the front door awning to catch her breath. This may have been a different area of Scotland than she was used to, but one thing was sure: that was *not* a normal moorland animal.

She went inside and called, "Mr. McCrum! Mr. McCrum!"

He was going up the staircase with a group of boys crowded around him. "Get out of my way," he grumbled at them. "I need to put these in the lab for the S3 Science class."

"Mr. McCrum!" Alessia shouted.

"What now?" he said, turning to her.

Alessia's blood ran cold. In his arms was a terrarium full of frogs.

She backed up against the wall to steady herself. Questions tumbled through her mind. Was it a coincidence? Did he set free the frog monster? Was *he* the frog monster?

"What is it, Alessia?" Mr. McCrum repeated, as about ten pairs of globular frog eyes blinked at her from the tank in his arms.

"Erm...Just... wanted to say hi," she said. He groaned and continued on his way up, and Alessia bolted back out the door.

Time to panic. None of the other teachers would be in before Monday. If Mr. McCrum couldn't be trusted, what was she supposed to do until then? Quietly wait for another attack?

The bell rang but she didn't move. She needed to think. The rain had slowed and the low trundle of a distant bus came within earshot. That was it! If she could only work up the courage to run to the bus stop, she could go to her mother's village. Surely she'd find a policeman there, or someone with a phone to call George.

She took a deep breath, steeled her nerves, and sprinted.

She spent the bus ride preparing her story for the police so it sounded believable, and then lapsed into daydreaming about her arrival at the village. She couldn't help it. Despite everything else going on, the excitement of going to her mother's hometown still simmered inside her. She'd been imagining the scene all her life. How she'd arrive and walk by a group of villagers and see the recognition of her mother strike their features the moment they laid eyes on her. 'You must be Cecilia's daughter! You're exactly like her!'

She'd tell the police her story, and while they went in search of the monster, she'd meet her mother's childhood best friend. She'd hear about all the adventures the friend and her mother had growing up, and find out whether her father had been from the same village, and how her parents had met and fallen in love. The friend might even have pictures of them!

George had known Alessia's mother for such a short time that Alessia had quickly reached the limit of his knowledge. He'd told her that her mother was charming, that she loved jacket potatoes and that she had a funny accent (though the latter, George said about everyone that wasn't from Inverness – which wasn't promising for how he'd fare in Germany.)

Mostly George had told her about her mother's passion for boats. Even after she went blind following Alessia's birth, Cecilia had continued to go out sailing with whoever would take her – and it was in a sailing accident that she'd eventually lost her life.

The bus pulled over with a hiss in the tiny hamlet. And 'tiny' was no exaggeration. The entire village was made up of two rows of white cottages with dark grey slate roofs, nestled between a rocky outcrop and the seashore. So much for finding police here.

But as Alessia walked down the empty street, she almost didn't care. To think she might be walking in the *exact* same spot where her mother walked when *she* was her age; that that house with the green door might have been her mother's childhood home! Her blood tingled in her veins. She'd go knocking on doors to find help about the monster in a bit. Right now, she wanted to explore.

She reached the end of the street, and a tinkling sound chimed. Up ahead, behind a small knoll of dark rocks and short grass, the top of a sailboat mast was rattling in the wind.

The docks! If her mother had been such a fan of boats, that *must* have been her favorite spot. Alessia ran past the last house of the village and over the knoll, stones crunching under her feet. A white ladder on the other side led her down to a narrow beach from which a weathered wooden pontoon stuck out into the sea. A sailboat and a few rowboats were tethered to it with mooring lines covered in seaweed and mold. Faded paint flaked off the boats so Alessia could barely make out their names, 'The Diving Belle', 'The Yellow Submarine'...

Alessia had never been on a boat, let alone one that might have been her mother's childhood play den. There were probably rules against climbing into a stranger's property, but the temptation was too strong. She walked down the pontoon, whipped her head around to check the coast was clear, and lowered herself into one of the rowboats (that seemed less intimidating than the sailboat).

The bottom rocked beneath her as she put down one foot, and then the other. She felt like a fizzy drink that had just been shaken. But before she even sat, a glimmer caught her eye and she froze. Something about the sea had her mesmerized. Glints of pink, gold and blue from the fluttering surface competed for her attention, like fireworks at the end of a display. It was too much for her eyes to take in, yet she couldn't detach her gaze from it. She couldn't even blink.

She forgot about her parents, and the frog monster, and school, and ambled to the front of the rowboat in a daze. The soft movement of the wavelets was hypnotic, continuing into infinity until the surface appeared flat.

Then, the murmuring started. Like what she'd heard on the cliff at school. Whispers. Hushed voices speaking over each other fast, tickling inside her ears. She tried to understand what they were saying, but it was useless, like trying to hold on to the fragments of a dream just before waking up.

It grew louder, more rushed, more unintelligible. A salty sea mist sprayed her face. The whispers sounded like hissing now. The hypnotic wavelets of a few moments ago had become ferocious waves, torn with great white slashes. Was it normal to have waves like this in a marina?

Without knowing exactly when it had started, Alessia realized she was now hearing distinct words through the hissing:

"Come to us, oh Selvan child, to waters calm, to waters wild. Hear today the Sirens' Song, in Nethuns deep do you belong."

It jolted her back to her senses like a cold shower. They were the same words she'd heard that morning.

"Come to us, oh Selvan child, to waters calm, to waters wild ..."

What did it mean?

"Hear today the Sirens' Song, in Nethuns deep do you belong."

The sight of the endless sea was suddenly overwhelming.

"Come to us, oh Selvan child..."

The chanting was clear – coming faster, and more forceful. The sea was even choppier.

"to waters calm, to waters wild..."

She had to get out of there.

"Hear today the Sirens' Song..."

She stepped back from the bow.

"in Nethuns deep do you belong!"

A flash of green caught her eye, appearing for just an instant as the sun vanished below the horizon. And then – without knowing if she'd tripped in her distraction, or been pushed, she tumbled overboard.

As she sank into the water, everything fell silent. The world slowed. Water enveloped her body. This was it. She didn't know how to swim. She was going to die.

She kicked her arms and legs ferociously, in all different directions. It was completely futile. For all her thrashing about, she stayed wrapped in the water's soft indifference.

The sinking slowed. For a moment she hovered. Then, like a gentle trampoline, the ocean released her back up.

Her face broke through the surface. The noise of her wheezing and the smashing waves crashed into her ears. Water slapped her face. Then, her head was back below. Everything was muted again. Her nose and mouth were full of salty water.

Kicking and beating her hands, she burst through the surface again. She moved frantically to stay above as the waves charged at her. She looked around for something to float on.

Suddenly, she was engulfed in darkness. The rowboat had flipped over her.

The chant sounded again, clearer this time, spoken

aloud in a woman's voice: "In Nethuns deep do you belong."

Suddenly, the overturned rowboat plunged underwater. It happened so fast that the upside-down boat remained full of trapped air, and she was thrown up into the bottom of it, facing straight down into the abyss.

She screamed, but it was useless. The boat was somehow powering on, as if it were being propelled across the ocean and down to its floor.

A shimmering cloud of fish dashed out of her path. A huge brown spotty sea trout further ahead stopped in its (swimming) tracks and gawked at her wide-eyed and open-mouthed. And she just kept plummeting through, completely helpless, tucked up into the boat's air pocket.

She passed schools and schools of every color and shape fish imaginable, for what felt like an hour, until she came face to face with the lifeless eyes of a woman's statue, staring at her in petrifaction. The statue belonged to the prow of a sunken ship on the sea floor: a giant voyager, no doubt once destined for greatness, now laying forgotten in the dark, seaweed fuzzing its shape.

Alessia seized up. If she was seeing this ghostly ship, it meant *she* was reaching the sea floor. She was about to crash into it. If *that* didn't kill her, drowning would – when water finally filled the pocket of air trapped in the rowboat around her.

And there was nothing she could do about it! The rowboat soared forward at full speed. She winced in anticipation of the impact. She was about to become a shipwreck herself.

4

The hard thud against the bottom sent a flurry of sand and salty water into her face. The boat ricocheted off the ocean floor and zoomed away, and the last of the trapped air bubbled out. Water wrapped her instantly. It was much colder here, and her eyes stung from the salt, and ears and nose throbbed from the pressure.

She kicked off the ground in panic. She had to get to the surface. She tried to pull down the water around her in some semblance of swimming. If she ever got out, she'd have a great "I told you so" story for George not letting her take lessons.

Luckily, her random water-pulling moves were kind of working. She was rising alongside a towering coral outcrop. She pulled and pulled. She didn't have much control over her movements underwater and kept bashing against the coral, scraping her legs and arms. But she gritted her teeth and kept going.

Her lungs started burning for air. She was surrounded by towers of coral like the one she was rising beside. In fact, it seemed like she was in a *tunnel* of corals, with no end in sight.

Her arms and legs grew weaker. The water seemed so light and silky between her fingers but was so deceptively heavy to kick. She noticed her legs stop. She couldn't command them to move anymore. This was it. She drifted. It was almost a relief to only feel despair.

The back of her head hit the top of the coral and her mouth was thrown open. Air rushed into it.

Air? Was she imagining it? Was it part of dying?

She looked down. The surface of the water was below her neck. She gasped. A violent coughing fit took hold and water spurted out of her mouth. It *was* air. It was really air. She grabbed onto the coral underneath her to stay above surface, and inhaled deeply. After the first few breaths contaminated with salt water, there was nothing but pure, delicious oxygen. She felt it filling her lungs. She felt it pumping through her veins in her blood. Each breath gave her a colossal burst of energy.

The coral felt harsh and rough against her hand and it was potentially covered in sea creatures, but she was beyond feeling squeamish. She threw her head back, looking up to see the sky she'd thought she'd never see again.

It was already very dark. And starless. Strange.

It was also strange that she'd been so quick to reach the surface, when the boat had hurtled down at such speed, for such a long time. A gentle drip-drop sound echoed around her.

It wasn't possible... it was foolish to even think it... but Alessia had the nagging feeling she was still under the water.

That's when Alessia noticed something even more perplexing. Or, to be precise, someone.

5

"Hello," the stranger said, with no surprise in his jolly voice.

His face was round and friendly like the face of the moon in a children's book, and the resemblance didn't even stop there: his skin and the little hair remaining on his head also had a luminous white glow.

"Do you understand what I am saying? My English is a little rusty I'm afraid," he continued. His voice was pleasant and gracious, and his accent unplaceable.

Alessia opened her mouth to explain her predicament, tell him how relieved she was to have met someone, and ask him about a thousand questions. But all that she managed was a confused, "Yes."

"Lovely bubbly! Ooh, I'm dreadfully sorry, I've forgotten to introduce myself! My name is Felthor and I work at the Imperial Poseidium – oh, sorry for the terminology: Poseidium is like what you call university I think. Anyway, delighted to meet you, my dear!" he continued with a large smile that creased his slit eyes. "Let's take it one by one. What's your name?"

"Alessia," she managed, at least.

"You're almost twelve years old, is that right?"

"Yes."

"Do you have any idea where you are?"

"No! I fell into the sea, and made my way back to the surface, but I don't recognize this place. I traveled pretty far when I was under the b-boat..." Alessia faltered as she heard her own unbelievable story.

"Right, the diving bell boat," Felthor said, matter-of-factly.

"The... yes! The Diving Belle. How did you know?" Alessia stopped focusing for a moment on the thoughts tumbling inside her head and looked at Felthor.

Had he mentioned why he was here? Also – how was he not struggling to remain above the surface of the water? He wasn't holding onto the rocks like her. His legs were making small moves, from side to side like an eel. Was that keeping him afloat? Was that *normal*?

And what was he wearing? A light blue wetsuit, with each leg covered with what could best be described as *aprons,* tied at the hip under a large belt, and again at the ankles, and gleaming like silver fish scales, as they rippled in the water. She was no expert on fashion, but even *she* could tell something was off. And that wasn't even to mention the form-fitting silver socks covering his feet.

As if he read her mind, and decided to give her *more* evidence of how weird he was, the next thing he chose to say was, "My dear, have you ever heard about the Lost City of Atlantis?"

Alessia would have been hard-pressed to find something more random for him to have asked her in that moment.

Yes, she *was* aware of the myth of a city that disappeared under the sea back in antiquity – but that wouldn't have been her conversation topic of choice if *she'd* just happened upon a shipwreck survivor.

"I can see you're a little puzzled," Felthor said. "Perhaps you will come with me? It should answer your questions."

Alessia didn't know what to do. She never *ever* went with strangers. It was so dangerous! But stuck here in the middle of the sea, what other option did she have?

"Okay..." she said. "I can't swim though."

"That's alright. Give me a moment." He drew a large sea-snail shell from his belt. He pressed its hole hard against his ear and closed his eyes in apparent concentration. Alessia wasn't sure where to look.

"Lovely bubbly! I called us a Marcaval," Felthor announced.

Before Alessia could ask, a line of purple spikes appeared ahead. They grew out of the water, until a knobby, purple surface emerged beneath them. Alessia pressed her back into the coral as she realized what it was.

Rising out of the water was the horned head of a giant, purple seahorse. The creature's eyes surfaced next: two purple globes the size of small cars, dotted with black, one facing Alessia and one facing Felthor. Shortly after, came its snout: a purple tube as long as a bus.

The monstrous head and neck towered above them. Felthor didn't seem surprised at all, and Alessia wondered if she should have fled when she had the chance after all. But before she could make a move, the giant, purple head turned to Alessia and sucked her up in its snout.

6

"Help! HELP! Let me out!" Alessia screamed. After she'd shot up the animal's snout, she found herself hovering in the air for a moment in what must have been the seahorse's head, or throat. But it was... empty. No tongue, no wet gums, no teeth, no saliva.

She was suspended in a vast, empty space, like she'd been in the water, but without being wet. And... the space wasn't dark, but basked in a bright purple light that danced magically around mosaics of glistening shells. But why were there mosaics *inside an animal?*

"Where am I?"

"Not to worry," came Felthor's voice from behind. "Just push your body down."

"So this monster can swallow me more easily?"

"It's not a monster, my dear. The Marcaval is a contraption *inspired* by nature. It shuttles between the territories of Selva and Nethuns. It's quite remarkable, actually. It's designed with the suction power of a seahorse, and its good, strong tail to hold a stable parking position – but altered for more traveling speed. You'd be astounded how slow real seahorses are! Now, tense your muscles and *think* of your weight going downwards."

He floated down past her. Alessia took a deep breath, and followed his instructions. She shot down, whizzing past him, then gasped and stopped.

"Hello Felthor, hello Alessia!" said a voice that trickled sweetly like caramel. It came from a woman, standing in a sumptuously-furnished room to Alessia's right – what must have been the seahorse's 'belly'. She had red, wavy hair that reached her feet, and clung to her long white dress like flames cling to the air. "I'm the nereid taking care of you on your travels today. Please make yourselves at home. I have delicious delicacies and symphonious symphonies for you."

"You're the... what?"

"Nereids are a species similar to humans, but with a gentler nature, and better grace and coordination. Here, they've specialized for many years in public service," Felthor explained floating down to Alessia's level, and then stepping into the belly-room. "She'll drive us where we want to go."

As soon as Alessia followed Felthor in, the nereid swept her into a plush, violet throne.

"My dear, we won't need a tour guide today. I have much to tell the girl," Felthor told the nereid as he took his seat in the adjacent throne.

"I'll make myself as discreet as a Moonjelly!" she replied, and pranced behind thick purple drapes across the room.

Alessia's throne had somehow instantly dried her soaking wet clothes and hair, and she sank into the soft cushions.

"So this is... magic?"

Felthor smiled. "You could say that. It's what happens

22

when you harness the wonders of nature. That's what Atlantis was built on," Felthor explained.

"But Atlantis isn't real, it's a myth," she said.

"My dear, I know this will be a lot to swallow... but Atlantis is real. It's one of many city-states spread across the planet's oceans that make up 'Nethuns', the undersea world. You're among the lucky few to have experienced both the overland world – what we call 'Selva' – and Nethuns."

He spoke to her like a grandfather would speak to a child, with a caring look on his moon-shaped face.

"But, how am I here? Did I go somewhere I shouldn't have at the dock?"

"Not at all! You came just where you needed to– to the coralway. Alessia, you were called here today because you're an Atlantide citizen."

"What? No, I'm not Atlantide! I'm Scottish, just like my parents," she explained, but as the words left her mouth, a thought struck her. She actually knew next to nothing about her father's side of the family.

7

"Many people are Atlantide descendants without knowing it," Felthor said, as the nereid danced in and out of this curtained section, tweaking a shell here, plumping a cushion there. "You see, like any nation, we've had ups and downs. Great, fair rulers, and tyrants. Under these tyrants' reign, people fled. Some fled to other Nethuns city-states. Some fled overland to Selva and left Nethuns behind altogether. Those then went on to have children with Selvans, and their children had children, and the descendants lost trace of their Nethuns origins."

It wouldn't even need to go back as far as *that* with Alessia. Her father himself was a mystery. George had met him only once, a couple of years before Alessia's birth. By the time Cecilia had returned to Inverness *with* baby Alessia to ask George for help, a terrible accident had left Cecilia blind, and killed Alessia's father. She touched the fork under her sleeve, with the tips of her fingers. Could it be from Atlantis?

"But, are you sure *everyone* that finds themselves in this

coralway place had ancestors from Nethuns?" asked Alessia.

"Quite! You can only get there after your 'calling' back to the water," Felthor explained. "The Siren's call. 'Come to us, oh Selvan child...'"

"I heard that! So a mermaid called me?"

"Not a mermaid – a siren. Merfolk have fish tails, sirens have swan wings and hawk claws. I know Selvans tend to mix them up, don't feel bad."

"Oh."

"A former king of Atlantis tasked sirens with calling landfarers back to Nethuns. That's our name for those like you, by the way: landfarers."

Questions were buzzing in Alessia's mind. The more she heard from Felthor, the more this new world intrigued her.

The Marcaval came to a stop. The nereid drifted out of her curtained quarters into the middle of main room and put her hands on her hips with a satisfied smile.

"Here we are!" she cheered.

8

Alessia and Felthor stepped out of the belly room, and floated back up to the seahorse's head. As soon as they'd reached the top, they were blown right out of its snout onto a milky green floor of seaweed-embedded glass.

They'd arrived at a station, with a green crystalline ceiling through which early-evening light from outside glimmered.

On either side of her, as far as the eye could see, different-colored Marcavals were popping up from the water to line up against the quay. People were hustling along, chattering, laughing, and calling out to friends as they shot out of Marcavals' seahorse snouts, or were sucked up into them.

"Welcome to your new home, my dear," said Felthor, his friendly moon face beaming.

"My new home?" Alessia blurted out. "What? I-I can't stay here. I'm meant to be at boarding school! And George – my stepfather – he'll be looking for me if I don't show up."

"Not to worry! There's a special squad of nereids that's permitted to go to Selva, to activate 'Goldfish Memory' operations. They'll erase every trace of you from your new school's files, and from this George's memory thanks to Slumber Smoke."

"What?"

"I'm dreadfully sorry! Slumber Smoke is a smoke that lets you talk directly to someone's subconscious – like hypnotism. Landfarers use it when they come to Nethuns, to erase themselves from the memories of people in Selva, or to go back and visit them when they miss them, without being remembered as anything more than a dream. It's made from burning seaweed macerated with Sea Lion Milk–"

"No Felthor, that's not what I meant. I don't want to leave George forever!"

"Oh. Of course! Then, we'll only erase you from the memories of the school staff and students. George never needs to find out you're not in boarding school. You can stay in touch with him through letters. The nereid squad can deliver them and intercept his letters back to you. And you can go back to visit him from time to time," Felthor paused, checking himself for getting too carried away. "This assumes you *want* to stay. You don't have to. Most landfarers are *excited* to discover where they belong. But if you'd rather go back, we can just hop back into this Marcaval, and..."

Felthor continued, but Alessia was lost in thought. The fork resting against her wrist under her sleeve seemed to be radiating warmth straight into her veins, reminding her that she was possibly in her father's homeland. She *wanted* to explore this new land. And her being here or at boarding school would make little difference to George.

"So I can go back whenever I want? To visit, or... for good?"

"Of course! The only rule you must respect, now that you know about Nethuns, is not to tell Selvans about it. It is very important for the fine balance of peace we have, that Selva and Nethuns worlds remain separated."

Alessia knew she was making the most important decision of her life. Her stomach turned. It was like getting onto a rollercoaster, momentarily considering jumping off before it starts, but knowing deep inside that you won't.

"I'll stay for now," she answered.

"Splendid!" Felthor said, clasping his hands together.

Now that the decision was made, excitement bubbled inside her.

"Let's get you to your new home, and I'll arrange the 'Goldfish Memory' operation, before your teachers get worried," said Felthor, tapping a stubby finger on his temple.

He took a sand-colored coin with what looked like the picture of a flower engraved on it from a hidden pocket in his belt. He pressed it against a similar coin in the nereid's hand and a circle of bright white light appeared around the two coins, growing and then fading into the air like a ring of smoke.

"Whoa!" exclaimed Alessia. "What was that?"

"Just my sand dollar. It's how we pay here, my dear."

"Oh." Alessia would have to get used to having the level of knowledge of a toddler here.

They walked down the platform and she took in every nook and cranny of her new world. Despite having different-colored hair or skin, the people here all had the same strange glow about them as Felthor; as though all the colors were backlit by a fluorescent light.

"The people..." Alessia started hesitantly, afraid to offend him. "They seem very... 'luminous'."

Felthor smiled. "Ah, yes. I sometimes forget these differences with Selvans. You see, Atlantide humans have spent their lives away from natural sunlight for generations. So our skin and hair colors have adapted over time. We're also shorter than Selvans, because of the higher pressure down here. The only exception would be landfarers whose ancestors spent a good deal of time above the surface."

Suddenly, years of feeling different made sense! Her whole life Alessia had been 'short for her age'. And even for a Scot, she was unnaturally pale. (One of her many charming nicknames at school had been 'pally wally'.) Was her height actually regular Atlantide height, and her strange complexion actually just the 'Atlantide glow'?

"Merfolk and sirens aren't the same, mind you," Felthor continued, "because they can spend so much time on the surface. Then of course there's the Minchans, otherwise known as the blue people of Minch..."

"Blue people? In the Minch, in Scotland? I've been there on a school trip!"

"Fancy that! You wouldn't have seen them, though. Awfully discreet. We don't even see much of them in Nethuns. But then that's because of the whole 'outcast' thing."

Talking with Felthor was like opening a toy box. Before you'd finished marveling at one of the treasures it contained, you were already getting distracted by the next.

"So are we under the sea right now? Why isn't there water everywhere?" Alessia asked.

"Look at me! Such a scatterbrain! I didn't even explain the basics!" Felthor chuckled. "We are indeed underwater, but not *submerged*. You see, when Atlantis sank, the Atlantide people were in the middle of building a 'city in the sky' where they had planned to migrate, to be safe from natural disasters.

"When the earthquake and tsunami hit, engulfing Atlantis, the City in the Sky wasn't ready for them to escape to, but it saved them in a different way! It collapsed onto Atlantis, creating a huge underwater cave with trapped air, where they – we – could continue to live."

"Wow!" Alessia straightened her stance. These ingenious people were *her* people. If only her classmates back home knew how cool her origins were.

They walked on, past a line of station shops and restaurants, and Felthor kept rambling on, explaining how they'd recreated artificial sunlight on the underside of the City in the Sky for light and heat. But Alessia couldn't bring herself to listen as she let the world around her soak in.

The shop names were written in a curly foreign alphabet, with symbols of bubbles and waves apparently acting as punctuation.

Alessia passed a mother crouching in front of a little boy, untwisting the fish scale aprons hanging over his wetsuit, and scolding him in 'Atlantide language'. The language *sounded* as curly and fluid as it looked. One word oozed into the next, and the sentences flowed with the gentle lull of a rivulet.

What Alessia hadn't expected, was that she understood everything.

She stopped dead in her tracks and a young man ran into her.

"Palladiú, Authentor," she said instinctively – to say 'pardon, sir'.

So she not only *understood* the language, she could also *speak* it. The language of a civilization she hadn't known *existed* until fifteen minutes ago. Were there any other secrets her *own brain* was keeping from her?

Alessia stumbled back, head spinning, and crashed into a few more innocent bystanders before Felthor, who'd still been chatting distractedly, finally noticed he was alone, and hurried back to join her.

"Is everything alright, dear?"

She tried it again: "Ceram Atlantú hiulsa, Felthor Authentor, seda nothiam ousautú." In English her words translated to, 'I speak the Atlantide language, Felthor Sir, but I don't know how.' (She was even spontaneously observing the local etiquette of adding 'Authentor' or 'Authenta' after someone's first name, to say 'Sir' or 'Madam').

Felthor gave a small giggle.

"Marvelous! You've already made yourself at home!" He answered in Atlantide. "Of course, there's nothing unusual there. Landfarers often have an innate knowledge of the language," he continued, as they approached the end of the dock.

"But I can't *read* anything."

"That's quite normal, my dear! As far as I know, landfarers remember how to speak and understand the language because they hear it without realizing, every time they're by a body of water in Selva. But you can't learn to *read* that way! I'll teach you that."

"Thanks," she said, trying to sound relieved. Felthor was certainly optimistic about how easily she could learn to read in a whole new alphabet.

They went through two enormous wavy-edged doors into a large milky-blue hall. Giant tadpole-like eggs with long tails were arranged in concentric circles. People were clambering into them through openings in the front of the eggs. In the largest tadpoles, five or six people sat side by side.

A red tadpole dashed past her, floating in mid-air with its tail rippling behind it. It came so close she almost lost her balance. The tadpole stopped in its tracks, swiveled around so the driver could wave an apology, then continued on its way out of a hole at the back of the station. The thing was – the driver was a *child*. No older than seven.

"These are ovehics. We'll take them home to Junonia building – that's our address. You get this one," Felthor said, beckoning her into a yellow one-person tadpole.

Alessia climbed in as he pressed the coin from his belt pocket against a small mast nearby.

"I can't drive though. Maybe we can take a bigger one together? Or if there's a bus that can come and collect me–"

The ovehic rose off the ground, and with a sudden jolt, darted forward.

"Alessia!" shouted Felthor. "Come back!"

"Stop! Stop!" she screamed at the ovehic, but it was no good. It shot straight out of the station into the chaos of the Atlantis street traffic. A green ovehic hurtled towards her. At the last second, it dove and passed below her. A blue ovehic came at her from the right. She ducked into the corner of her ovehic, clasped her eyes shut and braced herself for a 'death by tadpole crash', but her ovehic swerved out of the way just in time.

Suddenly, she was pushed back into her seat as her ovehic ascended sharply. Then, she came to a stop.

She was at the entrance of a dark alley. The scent of rot from its seaweed-covered walls clung thick to the air. A twinge of fear gripped her stomach.

She craned her neck around the side of the ovehic, and immediately wished she hadn't.

At the end of the alley stood a man and woman, both one and a half times as tall as normal humans, with short black hair, red tartan togas, and *royal-blue skin*. Minchans.

"To find the truth you seek today, it is, I fear, the only way," the Minchan woman murmured in a deep, rich voice. She was talking to a third person, shrouded in shadows.

None of them appeared to have seen Alessia yet – and she was keen to keep it that way.

9

"**D**rive us away," Alessia whispered to the Ovehic, but it didn't budge. Alessia groaned inside. First, a hungry frog monster, now, a stubborn tadpole car – Amphibians were officially her least favorite animal class.

"Everyone I know who tried got stuck there," a voice croaked to the Minchans from the dark. "I'm not doing it if you can't give me some sort of guarantee."

"Be not hasty, be not brisk.

Everything worthwhile has risk," the Minchan man answered firmly in a voice just as noble as the woman's had been.

"Frogwash! And stop with the poems already," said the hoarse voice. "I see your youth. They don't speak in rhymes. Maybe you old-timers could try adapting a bit too?"

"Our culture–"

"Let's not waste time on a history lesson about your culture," the voice interrupted the Minchan man. "I'm taking enough risk as it is. If the Emperor finds out I'm dealing with you people–"

"The Emperor pays little attention to the Minchans, or

to tales of the intuition the Whirlpool of Firnor brings," the Minchan woman cut in with her sumptuous voice.

"Look," the croaky voice continued. "The 'truth I'm seeking' is just as interesting to you as it is to me. If it really *was* the Instigator that gave old Jimmy Greenteeth that mission-- Wait, who's that there?"

The Minchan couple turned towards Alessia.

"Uh, hi," she stammered.

"This is not a discussion for humans," the Minchan man said with calm menace.

"I got lost," Alessia started. "I didn't mean to–"

The man who'd spoken from the shadows came into the light and Alessia froze. It was another frog monster. Just like the one who'd attacked her, but with brown spots on his green skin.

"Rude to eavesdrop," he cawed walking towards her.

Alessia remembered too well how far his tongue could reach.

"Drive!" she screamed at the ovehic, without success. She needed one of those coins like Felthor had to get it going again.

"Ooh, is that a Selvan accent?" said the frogman. "That takes me back. The good old days when us grindylows could snatch up little Selvans, drag'em into the deep."

Alessia jumped off the ovehic and bolted from the alleyway. As soon as she turned the corner, she found herself on a street lined with four-story, narrow apartment buildings, made from the same cloudy green material as the station floor, standing uniformly like a patch of newly planted grass. The station was nowhere to be seen.

Suddenly Felthor came dashing down the street in an ovehic.

"Felthor!" she called out.

35

His ovehic swung around.

"Thank Neptune!" he said, drawing to a halt beside her. "I thought I'd lost you. Hop in!"

He didn't need to ask twice.

"So sorry, by the way," Felthor added. "This neighborhood is sometimes nicknamed the–" he hesitated and lowered his voice slightly, "–the Collect. So when you said 'a bus to *collect* me', the ovehic misunderstood."

The ovehic gave them a little jolt as if it had been offended by the accusation against its kind. Then, it sped on to a red building as tall as a skyscraper, shaped like an olive seashell – long and oval with a small spiral pointing out at the top. The ovehic shot upwards and came to a stop in front of one of the top floors of the building. There, from an open doorway, a stranger's face beamed at her with the largest open mouth grin she'd seen in her life.

10

"Get yourselves in here already!" the new stranger cheered.

"Wimmi, this is Alessia" said Felthor.

"Hello, nymphlet," the man apparently called Wimmi said. He bowed and kissed her hand and she caught a waft of his nutmeg scent. "Welcome home."

He was a bald, stocky man with a glowing peachy face, bushy carrot-colored beard, and broad features which reminded Alessia of root vegetables. He fit in perfectly with their apartment and its walls of swirling red, orange and yellow waves.

"I'm... um... repentant of my... decayed Selvan English," he articulated slowly in English.

"Actually, I speak your language," Alessia answered, in Atlantide.

"Thank Poseidon!" Wimmi exclaimed, throwing his arms up in the air. "Also - Selvans above! That's fantastically fast to learn a language! You're some sort of a prodigy!"

Alessia laughed, "No, I just immediately recognized it."

Even though he was hulky, his smile was warm and goofy and Alessia immediately sensed she could trust him.

Felthor stepped towards him and in a calming gesture, put his hands on Wimmi's shoulders, "I've explained to her about Nethuns, the language, the landfarers, but there's still plenty we'll need to teach her. Now, why don't you introduce yourself?"

"My name is Wimmidor Mennador Badisol," Wimmi declared, contorting his hands into elaborate poses. He paused for effect, then caught Alessia's eye and cracked up in laughter, slapping his knee with his thick, heavy arm. "A bit of a mouthful, I know. Just call me Wimmi."

"Wimmi's my partner," Felthor explained, trying to hug Wimmi a little closer but struggling to get his arm around his broad shoulders. "You can ask him anything too."

"Actually, I wanted to ask about those creepy frogmen," Alessia said. "If they're dangerous, or just, well, 'normal' monsters for Nethuns."

Wimmi and Felthor looked at each other in confusion.

"Frogmen?" Wimmi asked.

"Yeah. One of them tried to grab me in Scotland, I thought it might be my teacher Mr. McCrum at first, but I guess it was part of the Siren's call. And then I saw another one now in the Collect place. I think he said they were 'grendeloos', or something?"

"In the WHAT place?" blurted Wimmi.

"She took an accidental trip to Seagrass-City, when she said 'Collect' in the Ovehic," Felthor explained to him.

Wimmi's eyes widened. "*Good Tirnanog!* That's a bit of a rough start. So wait, you said 'grendeloo'? I don't suppose you mean grindylows?"

"Yeah, that's it! Grindylows."

"They're not dangerous," Wimmi started. "Just another

Nethunsian speci- Wait. Did you say one of them *tried to grab* you? In *Scotland?* Scotland, *Selva?*"

"Yeah, at the seashore."

Wimmi and Felthor exchanged a grave look.

"What is it?" Alessia asked.

"That shouldn't be happening," Wimmi said, stroking his orange beard, dead serious. "It's been *over a century* grindylows haven't been charged with getting Landfarers. Too much accidental eating. Summoning Landfarers is strictly siren work now. If a grindylow tried to take you in Selva, that wasn't part of your call back to Nethuns. That was an attempted abduction."

Attempted abduction? Now she wished it *had* just been some stray, hungry mutant frog from Mr. McCrum's terrarium. Felthor looked anxiously between Wimmi and Alessia.

"Alright, alright, it's been a long day already. No need to scare the girl. Whatever happened, she's safe now," he said to Wimmi, before turning back to Alessia. "We should let you sleep, you must be exhausted."

Her room was large and blue, with a wavy door and a balcony. Alessia rested her hands on its curly railings, and took in the Atlantis skyline.

In the center stood a mountain that had been carved into an enormous palace. Its façade was dotted with lit rooms, some adorned with balconies, others just framed with Greek-style pillars.

Two moats surrounded the mountain, and between them lay the older part of town – a hodgepodge of temples, arenas, and large beautiful villas with open courtyards and fountains like the ones in books she'd read about Ancient Rome.

Beyond the second moat was much more modern. The

buildings were giant shells of all shapes and colors – like the building she was in now. They were all lit from within so they glowed with soft multicolored hues, like a garland of Christmas lights seen from a distance.

The part of town she'd accidentally visited – what Felthor called Seagrass-City—lay on the far right of this new town. With its straight, translucent green, seaweed-covered buildings, it looked like a small meadow on the edge of the cliff that lead down to the scallop-shell-shaped, green, crystal building where she'd first arrived – the Port of Atlantis. Below the Port, was the start of the sea, and the end of the Atlantis air pocket.

Somewhere out there lay the answers about her origins. The thought was so powerful, she found herself clutching her father's fork.

Eventually the city lights stretched out as her eyes grew bleary. Alessia turned to her bed: a huge clamshell open ajar, filled with colorful pillows and duvets. She dove in headfirst and sank deep into the mattress.

She was so excited she was sure she'd stay up all night. But buried in the comfort of the clamshell, with the light noise of the city in the background, she drifted off in moments.

As reality began to dissolve into dreams, and her thoughts scattered like fish swimming off in every direction, wisps of Wimmi's voice from the next room slipped into her mind.

"*...grindylow going to Selva... should follow the Siren's call if she chooses... someone trying to lead her here... You don't think she's in danger do you?*"

11

Alessia woke the next morning to a warm, comforting smell like bread baking. She hadn't slept so deeply in as long as she could remember. It took her a while to recognize the world she'd seen the night before, now that the mountain and old town were draped in their true ochre color. From the new town around her, the symphony of the city rang out: voices bubbling up through the clatter. She squealed. Her voice was part of it too.

She secured her father's fork under her wrist with her hair tie, so its three prongs curled around the base of her thumb, then covered it with her sleeve. She needed to keep the fork close to her wherever she went, to help her find him – but it was best to keep it concealed in case another Mr. McCrum-type tried to take it.

When she saw Wimmi, a thought tugged at her memory. Words she'd heard as she fell asleep, that she couldn't quite grasp right now.

"Nymphlet!" he said. "What a day we have ahead of us! Shame Felthor can't join because of his urgent meeting. His loss! I've concocted a delicious traditional Atlantide breakfast:

Whale butter biscotti with kelp jelly, and a manatee white cheese pastry." He made a chef's kiss gesture and pulled out a giant turtle shell for her to sit in like a rocking chair.

"Thanks... Um, Wimmi, did you say I was in danger last night?"

"What? Me?" Wimmi took a dramatic step back to show his shock. "Not at all, nymphlet! Nothing for you to worry about!" he added in a voice that was a little too high-pitched, his ginger beard quivering.

He was a bad liar. But there was no point pressing the matter. Even if she *was* in danger, she wasn't about to give up on her chance to find out about her father just because she was scared. She'd be careful. And steer clear of grindylows.

After breakfast, they set off for town. Or they were *about* to. But as Alessia walked out of the wavy front door, she screamed and jumped back in.

They'd just walked out – from what was probably the thirtieth floor – into the void. Wimmi stood there, floating outside in the nothingness, like a cartoon character that's walked off a cliff but hasn't realized it yet.

"How are you doing that?" she screeched.

"Come out and give it a try!"

"No... I can't fly," Alessia answered, backing away further so he wouldn't pull her out.

"I'm not flying! There's Fluita in the front porch of the buildings."

Alessia looked at him blankly.

"Ah... right. So Fluita is like... not solid, but also not liquid..."

Wimmi wasn't the best teacher.

"It's liquid crystals, like you find in fish scales. You can float in it, but you don't get wet. Trust me, it's one of our oldest inventions."

Alessia lifted a trembling leg to step out into thin air. Her leg was held in place. The sensation was familiar. This was the same material she'd gone down in the Marcaval. She stepped out with her other leg as well, and gasped a laugh. She knew what to do. She tensed her body and shot down.

"Nymphlet! You're an expert!" Wimmi laughed. His aprons puffed out below his hips as he floated down to join her. "Race you back up!"

With a deep breath in, Alessia soared up. Wimmi could say what he wanted – this was *basically* flying. And it *knocked the socks off* taking the stairs like in Selva – even if you included sliding down the banister.

"Dolphin roll!" Wimmi exclaimed next. Then, he roly-polyed right up into a stern-faced neighbor, and that ended the Fluita games for the day.

When they were done untangling Wimmi's foot from the neighbor's leg aprons, they went into town. Overhead, different colored ovehics zoomed around at various altitudes, maneuvering up and down, front and back, and side to side in the air.

"So first stop is to get you your proper Atlantide-human attire. It's important to stick to the dress code here – and you'll need an outfit like this if you're keen on *breathing* in your underwater excursions," Wimmi said.

"Yeah, I'd say I'm quite keen on breathing!" Alessia answered.

"Great! Come. I know the place with the best outfits! We'll make you the rage of the Octopus's Garden!"

"Of the what?" Alessia asked.

"The Octopus's Garden! The OG! Octo. Ockies. The Garden."

She looked at him blankly.

"Don't you have that in Selva? It's where you go to get cultivated by octopuses," he explained.

"Cultivat-- you mean taught? Like school? And my teachers are going to be octopuses?" Alessia felt the blood drain from her face.

"Nah, it's a figure of speech. 'Octopus' is what we call humans with particularly big brains -- like Felthor! You go to Octopus's Garden until you're old enough for the Tentacles."

"I'm going to grow tentacles?" Alessia needed to sit down.

"No, Ten *Tackles*. They're challenges – a contest, if you will. To decide what job you'd be most useful doing for the Empire. But don't worry, that's not for this year."

It was a good thing too. Those Tackles sounded suspiciously like tests, and Alessia wasn't exactly in a position to be tested, considering she couldn't even *read*.

Wimmi led her into a purple limpet-shell building. What had looked from the outside like a cute, little plum-colored teepee was, in fact, an enormous department store. They were standing in thin air – or rather, Fluita – and below them, shop floors extended down further than Alessia could see. A beautiful plump, red-haired nereid tapped on Wimmi's shoulder from behind. Before even turning around, Wimmi exclaimed, "If I turn around and that wasn't my beloved Ballina, I'll *never* get over the disappointment."

The nereid giggled, "I've missed you, Wimmi! We need a catch-up around a good cockle of hot whelkee!"

"I know! Sorry I haven't been around much. From the

moment Felthor announced we'd be guardians for a landfarer, I couldn't think of anything else. You should've seen me yesterday. I was this close to jumping on her, wasn't I?" he turned to Alessia.

"He was," Alessia nodded to Ballina.

Ballina laughed as she floated down one floor and opened a concealed side-door. They followed her into a room decorated like the Marcaval, with bejeweled benches, and fairy lights in seashells sprinkled around the room.

They were interrupted by a wail: "Get away from me!"

Outside their room, in the Fluita, a young man was hurriedly floating away from a stooped old lady.

"Tell me where you're hiding my Cariesa!" the old lady shouted after him. The thick green and purple scarves she had draped around her wetsuit billowed in the Fluita like a dark cloud around her.

"I have no idea what you're talking about! I just came to buy new breeches!" The man protested, tugging on his leg aprons (or apparently 'breeches').

"Not again," Ballina said. She rushed out, grabbed the old lady, and gently directed her to a lower floor.

"Who was that?" asked Alessia.

Wimmi sighed. "It's Dolia. She lives on the top floor of our apartment building, and she's the owner of this place. Ballina helps her manage it because... well, Dolia's a few shells short of a beach these days. And I can't blame her, poor woman. After everything she's been through..."

"What did she go through?"

"Her daughter disappeared. Years ago. It happened shortly after the Emperor surprised everyone by naming Dolia the owner of Iceberg – this big chain of department stores – out of nowhere. It was all very strange."

45

Ballina floated back into the room with three large cockle shells on a silver tray.

"Your hot whelkees!"

She carefully handed one to Alessia and one to Wimmi. Inside was a frothy, beige liquid. Wimmi tipped it between his thick lips, and Alessia followed suit. It tasted like a smooth, liquid cookie dough – and filled her mouth and stomach with a delicious warmth.

"So it's not getting better," Wimmi said to Ballina.

"These days, when she's not accusing clients of being spies, she's chewing their ears off about her 'family curse' and how her daughter should've known better," Ballina answered shaking her head with sorrow. She looked at Alessia and straightened up.

"Anyway, you came to get some outfits, I presume?" Ballina asked with forced lightness. "Let me bring you a few pieces. You enjoy your whelkee."

~

When they left the store, Alessia couldn't have been more delighted. As Ballina had explained to her, their clothes were made from threads glossed in liquid crystalline droplets from crab shells, so they adapted their color to the wearer's character. On top of that, you could constantly adjust the shape of an outfit, like molding clay. On putting on the grey, shapeless wetsuit, Alessia had watched with fascination as green patterns crawled over it, twisting and turning like vines climbing up a column until white blossoms bloomed from them to fill in the last gaps of grey. She'd then reshaped her clothes to fit her form, leaving only her sleeves loose, ballooning out by her wrists to hide the fork, and the neck of the suit curling outwards like the top of a vase. Wimmi had tied her white shiny trouser 'breeches' around her hips, and they'd flapped out before clasping themselves tightly around her ankles, growing around her bare feet to form a white shiny sock, soft as silk. She looked like a cosmic princess from a comic book.

"Now let's show you the Octopus's Garden," Wimmi said, plodding down the street, "so you can mentally prepare for when cultivating starts in three days. And before I forget: Here you go, prawncake!" He handed her a beige, porcelain-textured coin that she recognized as being a sand-dollar, like Wimmi and Felthor had used to pay.

He tapped his own sand dollar onto one of the hundreds of bright blue masts lining the road. After the usual rings of white light, a one-person ovehic shot in behind them and hovered on the spot.

"You do the same with your sand dollar. Short tap for a single-user ovehic, long one for a multi-user one."

"Thanks!" she said, tapping her sand dollar onto the next mast.

Her ovehic arrived, they shouted, "Octopus's Garden!" and both ovehics shot off. But when her ovehic drew to a stop outside a great fence of wavy white bars, Wimmi was nowhere to be seen.

12

The cloaked man paced slowly, trying to contain his impatience, listening carefully for any other sound than the hollow echo of his footsteps against the damp, stone floor.

A huge splash of water shattered the silence as a figure covered from head to toe in a dark purple wetsuit emerged abruptly from the depths of the water.

The cloaked man was overcome by sudden emotion. After all these years. His friend. His leader. The Instigator.

He hesitated to run out to the water from the cave in the cliff where he'd been waiting, but his friend's raised hand told him to stay back and wait. The Port of Atlantis wasn't far. This may have been a clandestine entrance into the state, but it wasn't a well-concealed one, and staying discreet was essential.

The familiar purple figure waded slowly through the water and stepped into the cave.

Falling to his knee in reverence, the hooded man tried to steady his quivering lip, but his voice cracked as he began. "Instigator..."

Gulping back the tremor, he continued: "His power has evolved; I watched him. I'll go in three days at dawn, with another Soldier of the New Current. I've been observing his schedule and we won't be disturbed if we attack then. We can get them both at once.

"With Alessia in Atlantis now, the time has come. We can finally begin again."

And under the mask of the purple wetsuit, the Instigator smiled.

❧ 13 ❧

Alessia stepped out of the ovehic, and it hurtled away into the distance.

"No, no, wait!" she shouted after it in vain. Clearly, she and these tadpole cars weren't on the same wavelength.

She looked around. Was that the school? Behind a fence of wavy white bars, on top of a hill sat a three-story Roman Villa with a red terracotta tile roof and Tuscan yellow walls punctuated by a large archway, that led to an inner courtyard.

"Wimmi?" she called. Perhaps she'd arrived before him. She made her way down the street to find him, letting her hand glide along the bars of the fence until she reached a gate.

A clatter tore through the air. Alessia jumped back and whipped her head around to see stones tumbling down the hillside. On the ground in front of the Villa's archway lay the broken remains of a large stone slab. The middle of the slab had apparently exploded, revealing beneath it a mosaic of green gemstones spiraling like the sky of an impressionist painting. In the center of the mosaic, a blue symbol glowed.

Alessia pressed her face against the bars of the gate. Could it be? The distorted symbol seemed to stare back at Alessia in defiance. Her hand grasped the fork against her wrist.

From her vantage point she couldn't be completely sure. The symbol was far from her, and with the perspective, looked squashed. And yet...

She could have sworn it was the symbol of a sun with eight rays coming out from it, and a bubble at the end of each ray. A symbol she was so familiar with, that seeing it out of context sent chills down her spine. The symbol engraved on her father's fork.

✤ 14 ✤

"Is somebody there?" she called out. The street was deserted. Nobody around to ask about the symbol. She looked for a doorbell but couldn't find one.

"Hello?" she tried again. She started biting her nails. The excitement was too much to bear. If that *was* the fork symbol, it confirmed her father's connection to Atlantis! But was her mind playing tricks on her? Was it just perspective? It seemed like the stone covering the mosaic had shattered when she'd passed in front of the gate. As if the mosaic had been 'activated'.

She needed to know for sure. She needed to get closer. She glanced around and tried the gate handle. It was locked.

The fence towered at least one and a half meters above her. Sports had never been Alessia's strong suit. And among all the sports, her *worst* was climbing the rope in gymnastics class. It was always the same ordeal: She'd try to hoist herself up, away from the circle of her gawking classmates, her arms shaking with effort, but she'd never leave the ground.

Still, she had to try. She found a part of the fence which had a hedge on the other side of it, to soften her landing. (And crossed her fingers that the fluorescent blue, wavy-edged 'oak-like' leaves of that hedge weren't poisonous).

She grabbed two of the fence bars, wrapped her legs around them, and pulled herself up. After about five seconds, wincing with effort, she let out a moan and came back down. She'd barely lifted herself at all. She looked around for something to stand on. Nothing.

So she turned to the fence, mustered all her strength, ran up, and jumped as high as she could. She was midway up.

She couldn't lose her momentum. She forced one arm up and pulled herself, then the second arm. Before she knew it, she'd reached the top. With one final push she swung her right leg over the fence and sat up on it. She erupted into delirious laughter. She'd made it!

She looked down at the hedge on the other side. The blue bush seemed sturdy enough. She lowered herself onto it carefully, then scampered down.

There still was no sign of anyone around. She launched into a mad sprint towards the mysterious symbol. With every step closer, it revealed itself more clearly.

She was right. It *was* the symbol from the fork! Her father's family – or her father himself – was from Atlantis!

If she hadn't yet fully decided to stay in Atlantis until this point, this sealed the deal. Whatever it took, she would stay and find out who her father was.

In all her excitement, she noticed with a few seconds delay the movement in front of her, and it took another few seconds for her to grind to a horrified halt.

Ten giant soot-black crabs had scuttled in from either side of the building ahead.

15

A lessia's heart skipped a beat. Each crab was as tall as an adult, and as wide as ten. They held up their enormous pincers perfectly still, and stared at her through tiny eyes. Small clicking noises sounded as they shifted their weight between their six pointy legs. It was a sight to make you miss a grindylow.

Alessia took a very slow step back and the clicking accelerated. The crabs had become agitated. She shot a furtive glance at the street behind the fence. Would she be able to run and climb up the hedge fast enough? Were crabs good climbers?

She took another step back. All at once, a nightmarish black wave of crabs poured down the hill towards her.

Alessia sprinted towards the hedge. She no longer heard the scuttling of the crabs, or white noise of the city. Only the thumping of her feet on the ground and the beating of her heart.

The crabs were faster than she was and gaining on her. Without even questioning if the hedge could hold her up this time, she threw herself at it and scrambled up. One crab was almost at the bottom of the hedge and extended his deadly pincer. Its tip grazed her back and her whole body shuddered. She climbed faster.

The branches slashed at her wetsuit and tore her skin. The crabs had all reached the bottom of the hedge now. SNAP. SNAP. Their pincers opened and clasped shut, opened and clasped shut just below her feet.

She grabbed the top of the fence, pulled herself up, wrapped her legs around two of the bars, and slid down the other side, wincing as the friction scorched her hands. As she landed, she let out a sigh of relief. The crabs had stayed behind the hedge on the other side of the fence. She'd made it.

A chilling clang rang out. The gate swung open. One of the crabs had his foot up on the gate frame. He'd unlocked it. It wasn't enough they'd chased her out. They were going to catch her.

Alessia ran for her life. Crabs swarmed through the gate like a troop of soldiers, flooding the street with darkness. At the first intersection, she took a right to lose them. For a few hopeful strides she thought she'd succeeded, but within seconds, they came rattling behind her.

She took a left. A crowd of people! She couldn't believe her luck. At the end of the street was the entrance to a market, and it was bustling.

"Help, they're chasing me!" she screamed.

The crowd looked at her sympathetically.

"Who? Come, guppy, you're safe with us!" one woman said.

Then something shifted in the people's faces. As soon as they caught sight of the crabs, they became indifferent, even disdainful, and to her horror, they spread away from her.

Alessia grabbed a man's sleeve in desperation.

"Help! They're going to hurt me!"

The man pulled back his arm.

"Go away, we don't want trouble!"

The crabs were catching up. She didn't have time to compel people to help. She darted through the crowd.

How was she going to get away? She'd never outrun the crabs, let alone overpower them if they caught her. Her eyes welled up, blurring her view. She slapped her tears off but couldn't stop the sound of panicked sobs mingling with her panting breath.

Her muscles were screaming and her mouth tasted of blood. Her legs were giving way. She couldn't keep running much longer. She needed to think of another way to beat them. What was she good at?

An idea sparked in her mind. With no time to think, she ran straight into the market. It was enormous, and the paths between the lines of stalls were narrow and crowded. Perfect. That would slow down the crabs. She pushed through the current of people, scouring each stall to find what she needed. Finally – there it was. A nereid clothes stall.

"I'll take a tunic." Alessia said to the stall owner, holding out her sand dollar. "With a hood. Floor length."

"But dearie, these are for nereids. You don't want to wear that," the nereid explained gently.

Clicking noises. Two crabs appeared about a dozen stalls down.

"Please, I need it," Alessia begged.

"Um... very well, then." The nereid looked flustered.

"Can I pay now?" Alessia rushed her. Two more crabs had emerged on the other side of her.

"Sure! That'll be eighty Plutus. Just pop that there," she answered, indicating her sand dollar. Before she finished her sentence Alessia had already pressed her own sand dollar against it.

Alessia grabbed the tunic, and threw it over her head.

She tied the sash and pulled up the hood. Now, it was time for the years of getting into other peoples' skin and overreacting on their behalf to pay back. She took a deep breath. She needed to channel Wimmi's nereid friend, Ballina. Nereids were taller than she was. They were the very image of grace. They had a constant flow of lively movements that were fascinating to watch.

She stood as straight as she could, rose up onto the bulbs of her feet, and launched into a balletic stroll down the street. The clicking behind her got closer.

She needed to get into character. To be believable, she needed to believe it herself. She tried to imagine she was Ballina, in the market, looking to pick delicious delicacies to bring back for poor, old Dolia. She perused the stalls offering pastries, drumming her fingers on them lightly in a nereid-like manner.

"Ooh, doesn't this look exquisite! That's sure to get her out of her low spirits," she said to herself in a soft, graceful voice. The crabs that had been at the other end of the line of stalls advanced in her direction. She further lowered her hood and moved on to the next pastry stall. She shouldn't rush. She had to pay the crabs no attention, like the others around her. She got back into Ballina's character.

She wandered along focusing on the stands, when a crab bumped into her and grabbed her arm in his pincer. She froze.

"Please pardon me," she mumbled, staying in character. The three other crabs from the pathway approached.

She had to ignore it. Apparently the crabs *weren't* unusual here. Her nereid character wouldn't expect this accidental encounter with the crab to be an issue. She'd expect him to let her go.

Alessia raised her free hand in a graceful, apologetic gesture, without looking up, and turned to walk away, as though concentrating on a purchase. The crab held up his other pincer, and let go of her hand. He was apologizing. He'd just grabbed her out of instinct. Phew.

She continued to meander between the stalls. She didn't dare look back yet. She needed to keep the aura of a nereid. She waited to hear the clicking follow her. It didn't. She stopped at one stall which seemed to sell decorative objects. She picked up a metallic bowl, as if to inspect it. The reflection showed the four crabs were still huddled together in the middle of the path. They were trying to decide where to go. They had no idea where she was.

She continued to wander, allowing herself to pick up the pace a little as she got out of their line of sight. She got to the market entrance, but to her dismay, one large crab was waiting there, carefully watching each person as they exited.

She took a deep breath and strolled towards him as nonchalantly as she could. Even from under her hood she could feel the intensity of the crab's glare.

"Hi!" She pretended to wave at someone outside. She walked confidently past the crab and out of the market to her fictional friend.

The street was lined with ovehics. She ran up to the first one, sank into its seat and exhaled for what felt like the first time in ages.

That's when it caught her eye. Someone was watching her. Across the street from her ovehic, a boy in a blood-red wetsuit stared. His hair was jet black with an almost purplish glow, his skin, bone-white and his eyes dark.

Something about him made her uneasy. Why was he staring? Had he witnessed her deception?

Suddenly someone jumped into the ovehic beside her.

"Hey! What are you do–" She stopped. Her face went cold. Beside her was a girl, two meters tall, with short black hair and royal-blue-colored skin.

"I'm sorry," said the girl, rolling the r's. She had a deep voice, like the Minchan couple Alessia had seen, though she seemed younger - like a teenager. "I have to get away from the crabs and I don't have a sand dollar to take an ovehic myself."

"You're running away from the crabs too?"

"Yeah, this place is crawling with them. They're *never* in nereid markets normally – that's why I thought it'd be safe to come here. If they catch me outside of Seagrass-City–"

The desperation in the girl's eyes seized at Alessia's heart like an icy hand. A clicking sound came into earshot again. Alessia glanced around. A crab was approaching, its feet sharp and quick like a chef's knife.

"Okay, we go there, then?" Alessia asked quickly.

"Yes! Seagrass-City. Thank you!" The Minchan girl smiled with relief. Two other crabs appeared ahead and stormed towards them.

"Seagrass-City!" Alessia ordered. The ovehic took off and then stopped with a jolt. The Minchan girl screamed. The crab from behind had caught the hem of her tartan toga in his pincer and was holding them back.

Alessia reached over to help her pull the toga from the crab's grasp but he held on firmly. He started pulling the girl out of the ovehic. She breathed in panicked fits, trying to kick him while clinging onto the seat.

The two crabs in front had almost reached them too.

Alessia had to slow them down. She looked around for something to throw. Nothing. She reached under her nereid tunic, untied the breeches from her wetsuit, made them into a ball and launched the ball at the two crabs in front. It streamed through the air, unravelling as it went and landed right on top of their heads, covering their eyes. They stopped and thrashed around to get it off.

The Minchan girl kicked the other crab between the eyes, and there was a great tearing sound as he fell back holding just a small piece of tartan in his pincers. The girls' ovehic shot off.

"Oh, thank Shony," the Minchan girl exclaimed, dropping her head back with relief. She turned to Alessia, "and thank *you!*" She looked Alessia up and down with curiosity. Now that she wasn't so preoccupied with surviving a crab attack, she was probably wondering what this clueless landfarer was doing wearing a nereid's cloak.

"I'm Alessia, what's your name?"

"Ebrie," she said. "You're a Landfarer so you probably don't realize, but you just saved my life. We're not allowed out here, us Minchans. Well, almost all non-human species, to be honest. If the crabs had caught me... well, let's just say they'd have made an example of me."

Alessia shuddered.

"That's terrible! Why?"

Ebrie looked at her with great sorrow, and Alessia's empathy kicked in. Her heart was flooded with Ebrie's hurt pride, and the pain of years of being treated as a barbarian, while knowing her peoples' superior power of insight and rich culture. Alessia choked back a sob and looked away to avoid creating a scene. They arrived at the street of putrid seaweed-covered buildings where Alessia had seen the blue people and grindylow.

"If I can ever help you with anything, you know where to find me," Ebrie said, as she got down.

Alessia waved her goodbye, hoping it meant the same in Nethuns.

A group of grindylows turned onto the street.

"Uh oh."

No need to stick around and find out if the one who'd tried to abduct her was part of that group. She tapped her sand dollar on the nearest mast in the street, and ordered "Octopus's Garden!".

The ovehic whisked her off, only to pull to a halt in front of a scarily familiar fence..

16

N ot again! Alessia was about to ask the ovehic to take her home when Wimmi's voice rang out.

He stood at the gate talking to someone on the other side.

"Carcinor, *please*. You've got to help me find her! She's this tall," Wimmi said, waving a hand down by his hips. "She's wearing a green and white top. Has a weird accent. Lost-looking. Isn't it kind of your job to protect the guppies?"

"Wimmi!" Alessia shouted, jumping off the ovehic.

Wimmi spun around.

"Alessia! Thank Poseidon, I was so–" he stopped short. He ran to her and grabbed at her nereid robe urgently. "What's this?"

"Oh... nothing... I accidentally tore the outfit you got me, and lost the breeches. Sorry. I ran into the market to buy this."

Wimmi looked as though he'd seen a ghost. "Alessia, these are nereid robes," he said. "You can't wear these. It's very important to keep the differences visible."

Wimmi twisted his orange beard between his fingers and looked around nervously to see if anyone had seen them.

"Are you wearing your ripped wetsuit underneath?"

"Yes..."

He pulled the robe off her and threw it into her empty ovehic before it whizzed off.

Alessia was about to ask him why the 'differences' were so important, when she noticed the man Wimmi had been talking to through the gate. Though 'man' wasn't quite the word.

He was only 'human' down to the hips. His legs were giant crab legs. And he was flanked by two giant crabs like the ones she'd been running from. She stumbled and hid behind Wimmi.

"Well, will you look at that? I've found her!" Wimmi said in an overly pleasant voice to the crab man. "As you were, Carcinor."

Carcinor folded his arms across his bare chest, and his thick, straight brow dropped a notch.

"Don't disturb us again," he said in a flat voice. "I've already got ten crabs busy looking for an intruder who committed a serious act of vandalism. We're security, not lost and found."

Carcinor and the crabs scuttled off.

"I think the ovehic dropped me on the wrong side of this building," Alessia explained.

"Ah... probably at the old entrance. For the love of lanternfish. It's been more than ten years! They shouldn't be making that mistake anymore!" Wimmi tutted.

"The old entrance?"

"Yeah, students used to come in that way. There was a mosaic doormat on the floor that would light up with the

Octopus's Garden emblem and let through people carrying their class trident, while tripping up anyone else."

Alessia's eyes widened.

"I know – a bit much," said Wimmi. "But it was just after the Emperor had decided to separate the species' roles and education, like forty years ago, and he wanted to make sure people obeyed. Anyway, that entrance is no longer in use, now that the tridents are gone."

"The tridents were like... little forks?"

"Yeah, little forks the students had, engraved with the Octopus's Garden Emblem. But the Emperor later outlawed the emblem because a group of former students started using it as a rallying symbol for an insurgency against him. He had all the tridents destroyed and the mosaic doormat plastered over."

Alessia's heart raced. Her father's fork was the Octopus's Garden trident! And if those tridents had only existed for forty years, it couldn't have belonged to an ancestor: it had to have been his. Her father *himself* had been Nethunsian. And not just Nethunsian: he was a graduate of *her future school!*

"What a day, Fel!" Wimmi exclaimed as they erupted into their apartment's cozy, tangerine light.

Felthor folded away the book he'd been peacefully reading, rocking back and forth in a giant turtle shell, and gave them a gentle smile. But upon seeing Alessia, his moon-shaped face dropped, and she remembered she was still wearing her ripped clothes.

"I'll just go change," she said, and headed to her room to the sound of Wimmi energetically recounting the day's events. ("Oh, and Carcinor, Fel, Carcinor! You should've seen him! *Unsavory* as ever.")

When she came back, Felthor and Wimmi were speaking in hushed tones.

"Right," Wimmi said when he saw her, slapping his large peachy hands on his laps. "Wish I could stay with you guys, but I have to go warm up for the concert."

"You're a musician!" Alessia said.

"I am! You'll hear me tonight. Get ready, you'll be impressed," Wimmi said cheekily, crossing his arms.

"Are you famous?" asked Alessia.

Wimmi laughed but answered in a strangely serious tone, "Unfortunately."

"What, don't musicians *want* to be famous?"

Wimmi and Felthor exchanged a glance but didn't answer.

"Go practice, Wimmi. Alessia and I will talk through some basics to prepare her for her first day at the Octopus's Garden."

"Good, I'll only miss the boring stuff." Wimmi winked and left.

Felthor slid a platter of unfamiliar objects, which Alessia assumed were food, towards her.

"Here, my dear," he said sweetly, steepling his fingers under his chin. "Help yourself."

Alessia grimaced at this new challenge.

"I'm not sure how..."

"Of course!" He smiled knowingly. "You only had breakfast, right? Please," he said, offering her his palms. "Allow me."

Alessia shifted the platter to him, and with his usual calm demeanor, he proceeded to crack what looked like an egg over a handful of white beans, and flick in a pinch of pink salt. A mint green foam escaped from the egg and as soon as it came into contact with the beans, they merged and blossomed into a soufflé.

"Meals in Nethuns aim to entertain *all* the senses. Only breakfast, and very traditional meals like Etruscan crockpot are still served in the rustic Selvan way."

He carefully poured a golden syrup onto the soufflé, and it let off a hiss of steam that smelled like warm prunes and waffles.

Then, he pushed the platter to her, a proud smile splitting his round face. The cake was ice cold while the syrup was piping hot, and its taste was as delightful and unique as the sensation it gave. She gobbled it up ravenously.

"I see you've taken to Atlantide cuisine!" Felthor beamed.

"Yeah, it's really good!"

"And that's not the *only* new experience you'll have had here today," he continued. His hand gestures were deliberately compassionate, as though he were giving a well-rehearsed speech. Alessia raised her eyebrows in agreement, and continued munching.

"The ovehic, the Octopus's Garden, the Fluita, even the clothes!" Felthor continued, with a chuckle of false surprise. "It must have been quite a whirlwind of emotions. Tell me about it, dear. Tell me how you feel – what were your... sensations?"

"Well... I guess I feel a little nervous," she answered, trying to be honest without drawing more of his pity.

"Right," continued Felthor, narrowing his eyes in slightly exaggerated concern. "That's completely understandable!"

He didn't move his gaze from her.

"You should know I'm here to help you..." he added, "with anything. Any concerns or... unknown sensations you may have here. Remember that."

He reached into his pocket and drew out a pink conch shell, the size of the palm of her hand. "This is what we call a 'shell'."

Alessia looked at him blankly. So he thought she was an idiot, then.

"In Nethuns, we transmit our thoughts to whomever we're thinking about, through shells," Felthor explained. "It's not unlike this telephoning you do in Selva, but less complicated. None of these codes to type in, no need to talk out loud and risk other people eavesdropping. Once you've tapped shells with someone once, you can transmit your thoughts to them through this at any time simply by pressing it to your ear. Anyway, I got this one for you and already tapped your shell with Wimmi's and mine, so you can truly reach me *whenever* you need help."

"Thanks, Felthor!" Alessia squealed as she took the device. She'd never been trusted with a phone before and was thrilled she'd start her new school equipped like a grown-up. She looked up at Felthor's eager face with the biggest smile in her arsenal, so he'd stop feeling this obligation to reassure her. "Wimmi mentioned you'll give me lessons this week. That'll be great. I'll feel much more confident."

"Please, it's normal!" He said, blushing happily. "So, what other sensations did you have my dear?"

Alessia looked at him quizzically. Felthor pressed on.

"I mean..." he was a little fidgety and awkward, as though he couldn't find the right words. "Did you have any other... perceptions? Anything strange?"

She hesitated. How would Felthor react if she showed him her father's trident with the outlawed symbol? She could get into *big* trouble. Then again, he might also be able to *help* her find out about her father.

"Well..." she began.

His slit eyes glittered with curiosity and he leaned in. "Yes?"

"I... I think my father may have gone to my school- I mean, Octopus's Garden," she said flinching in anticipation. Felthor didn't immediately react. She decided to take the plunge and slowly rolled back her sleeve to reveal the trident tied to her wrist.

Felthor's eyebrows shot up. Alessia untied the bracelet and placed the trident down on the table in front of him. Felthor's gaze lowered to the object. He didn't feel the need to pick it up immediately – it was clearly already familiar to him.

"An Octopus's Garden Class Trident," he muttered, finally picking it up and rolling it between his fingers.

"My stepfather George gave it to me. It was all my mother had from my father apparently. George hardly knew anything about my father. He couldn't even remember his name. Just that he was in his early thirties the time George met him, and very much in love with my mother. That's why when I got here I wondered if my 'Atlantide ancestor' could be my dad. Then when I saw the Octopus's Garden emblem..."

"You saw the Octopus's Garden emblem?"

"From behind the fence," Alessia lied. "It's still on the mosaic doormat on the floor by the side door."

"What, they haven't plastered over that?"

"Guess not," Alessia answered in a voice weaker than she'd have liked. Now wasn't the time to mention she'd already unwittingly vandalized her new school when her trident had caused the mosaic's cover to explode.

Felthor was quiet. He pursed his lips and gently nodded, stirring his hot whelkee with a crocodile tooth, deep in thought. After two dings of the crocodile tooth on his cockle shell, he placed it delicately to the side and cleared his throat.

"My dear," he said. She looked at him apprehensively, unable to read his reaction. "This is nothing short of a miracle."

She relaxed into a smile. "I know!"

"I mean, what are the odds of you having this trident,

and happening upon the emblem at the Octopus's Garden! This is the most wonderful coincidence!"

"Exactly!" Alessia laughed in relief.

"And how exciting for you to have found these answers about yourself after only a day? It seems your decision to stay has already paid off!"

"Yes! I'll find out who my father is in no time and–"

"Now, that's the tricky part," Felthor interrupted. A dark veil fell over his face. "As wonderful as this is, you should understand the risks..."

"Risks?"

"First of all, that trident should have been destroyed. It's fortunate you have it, but it's most important you keep its existence a secret."

"Sure, I understand. When I ask about him, I don't need to mention the trident–"

"I'm afraid you can't ask about him."

"What?"

18

"I know how frustrating this must be," Felthor said, lowering his gaze compassionately. "But understand: our Emperor has made a point of making certain people *disappear*... and investigating the past, or searching for people – for *anyone* – is now against the law. It qualifies as treasonous behavior."

Alessia shifted in her seat. This Emperor sounded a bit extreme.

"The Emperor eliminated public records in Nethuns – even Octopus's Garden yearbooks – and outlawed private investigators," Felthor continued. "He also encourages the public to step forward if somebody is behaving suspiciously, particularly if someone is trying to find information about missing individuals."

Alessia was crushed.

"But... but there must be a way. I can't–"

"I'm afraid there isn't. And you mustn't talk about this, with *anyone*. For Wimmi and my sake, and for your own. It's too risky... I'd never forgive myself if I let harm come your way," Felthor said.

Alessia must have looked unconvinced because he added, "Alright, I wasn't planning to show you this yet, but it's important you understand how things work around here."

He left the room and returned holding a large, purplish pearl. He dropped it on the ground and a tube of bright light appeared in the middle of the room, reaching up to the ceiling.

"Follow me," he said, stepping into the light. As soon as Alessia did the same, her surroundings completely changed. They were in a large town square, that gave onto a road bridging over the moat to the Palace of Atlantis.

"How did we get here?" she asked.

"We're still in the living room, dear. This is a Drift."

"A what?"

"Something that seems to be there but isn't really..."

"You mean like a film projection?"

"Hmm... I suppose that's what you Selvans have that comes closest," Felthor answered. "When a scene comes to you by Drift, you can see, feel, hear, and smell it."

There was indeed a faint scent of wet sand in the air, that there hadn't been in the apartment. And all around, people were chattering as they went about their day, apparently oblivious to Alessia ogling them.

Felthor looked straight ahead at a young man with long dark hair who was making his way through the square towards the palace with determination.

"This Drift was captured about fifty years ago – and the teenage boy you see there is Oscor," Felthor explained. The road leading to the palace was lined with Mother of Pearl statues of the Greek sea-god Poseidon. In front of the palace gates stood a row of guards wearing silver wetsuits, and helmets with hounskull pointed visors from which fangs jutted out, so they looked like barracuda fish.

The young man made his way across the bridge straight towards them. When one of the guards approached him, he turned slowly to look at him.

Without blinking, he raised his thin, muscular arm swiftly and to the guards' – and Alessia's – surprise, the stone tridents of the Poseidon statues levitated behind him. Alessia gasped and looked at Felthor for answers but he simply nodded towards the scene unfolding before them.

A smirk crept upon the boy's face and he swished his arm towards the guards. The tridents shot forward and pinned the guards against the palace walls.

Alessia grabbed Felthor in horror, and he put a kind hand on her shoulder. Cries and screams filled the air. More guards came out from the palace, not knowing the danger. As they emerged, the boy bowled both his arms forward, and with each of his movements, a civilian from the square was lifted into the air and thrown onto one of the guards. A young man flew right past Alessia and landed on a guard with such speed that both were knocked unconscious. Alessia shrieked and ran away instinctively. As soon as she'd run a few steps back, she found herself back in the living room, feeling more than a bit silly for running away from a hologram. She took a deep breath and got back into the tube of light.

The young man walked to the palace doorway and turned back. He had dead, dark eyes, like those of a shark, and gazed without expression at the remains of his macabre spectacle on the bridge.

Around Alessia, the square filled with an army: ten lines of fifty male and female soldiers, like a fearsome battery of barracuda fish brandishing a variety of weapons from water cannons, to ice spears. The soldier next to her raised his trident and electric sparks danced from its tips.

They charged towards the palace door crowding into the bridge of disarmed Neptune statues. Once they were all on the bridge, paces away from the gate and the boy, a grumbling started. The soldiers slowed to a halt. Alessia threw a furtive glance at Felthor, tempted to jump out from the scene again. When she looked back, she could swear Oscor's eyes were boring right into hers. He gave a spine-chilling smile and waved.

With his wave, the front façade of the palace – a whole *layer* of the mountain – crumbled down onto the road. Alessia gasped. The soldiers tried to run back, tried to shield their heads from the falling rocks. The air became thick with the metallic tang of blood.

The whole scene collapsed away. Alessia was back in the living room, basking in its warm, orangey light, and smelling the scent of hot whelkees again.

"Oscor continued with his murderous quest inside," Felthor said, returning to his seat. "The Drift recording stops when he arrives in the throne room. No one witnessed exactly what happened. However, the king, Gurthor Rexol, his brother and his daughter, who had a young son herself, died an atrocious death.

"When the remainder of the army finally burst into the room hours later, Oscor was on the throne. After disarming the soldiers with a flick of his hand, Oscor ordered them to call the people of Atlantis to the square for an announcement. The army obeyed to avoid more bloodshed, and gathered a large crowd.

"Oscor appeared at the palace balcony and made a speech about how the Rexol Dynasty had dragged the country into mediocrity, how the country was in deep moral and economic decay because all species were living together as equals. He said that's why Atlantides were squandering their rightful transcendence over 'backward' Nethuns states. And finally, he explained that since he'd been endowed with the superhuman powers they'd witnessed that day, it was his responsibility to bring about this 'transcendence'. So he named himself Emperor."

Alessia stayed silent.

"It's a lot to take in, I know," Felthor said. His eyes glinted with a deep sadness. "But it's law that every household should have this Drift, and every Nethunsian should watch it... And it's critical for you to understand this, to stay safe."

"So, he's the Emperor? He stayed in power this whole time?"

"Yes. After Atlantis, he invaded the other eight states that make up Nethuns. He eliminated all other royal families, like the Lin Mo family, who'd been ruling the state of Penglini for centuries. Some states, like Azlanu, he practically wiped off the map. Many died from those wars, so very few dare to challenge him now. And none have succeeded to date."

Alessia's skin crawled.

"And he really has those magical powers?" She tried to stop picturing him tossing people across the square with his mind.

"We call them 'Sensate Powers'. In his case: the ability to make objects move."

Alessia slumped back into her turtle shell seat.

"How can you live with that maniac as your ruler?"

Felthor threw a cautious glance around.

"Well, it's difficult," he answered, keeping his voice down. "Today, we're not free to say or do as we please. But quality of life is good in Nethuns – for humans at least. If you ask people whether they'd sacrifice the stability they have today for the chaos of a coup, just to regain the freedoms they've lost... I'm not sure many would take the leap, without a little push."

Alessia's eyes glazed over and she stared at a crumb on the floor.

"Anyway, the point is, you need to be careful," Felthor concluded.

"Okay, I won't ask about my father," she mumbled.

But even as she said it, she knew it was a lie. She'd been trying to find out more about her real parents her whole life, and she was so close now. She was terrified of the Emperor, but that didn't mean she had to stop her search. She'd just be careful.

"I know it's a sacrifice. We've all made them. The reason Wimmi wanted to stay away from fame was to stay away from the Emperor," Felthor explained. "Sadly, he's so talented, he became famous anyway, and now we have to go to his concert in the palace."

"The concert's in the palace?"

A lump formed in Alessia's chest. Now she wasn't looking forward to Wimmi's concert at all.

19

The venue was an amphitheater nestled between the back of the mountain palace and the first moat. To Alessia's relief, the Emperor was tied up with "urgent state business" and didn't attend the concert in the end.

Wimmi played with another performer, a tall, thin man with long, grey, sparkling hair, and pale grey skin – who somehow hovered above the ground! He spent most of the time at the back of the stage, fully absorbed by the wistful sound of his strange instrument: a hand-held harp that consisted of strings of dried seaweed tethered to a miniature ship anchor.

Wimmi, on the contrary, was a natural-born entertainer. He played with the audience, threw himself to the ground, sang standing, sang lying down, and even once sang hanging upside down off a monkey swing, his shaggy ginger beard fluttering wildly all the while. With each song, he picked up a new weird and wonderful instrument. From a monstrous contraption of winding tubes tied together like a head of medusa, to a weird device made up of two long, thin spyglasses placed in each corner of his mouth and blown into like flutes.

Alessia sat up straight and grinned. The duo's sound was manic and gripping. Their spectators roared with laughter when they weren't silenced with fascination. And this man they were all watching in awe was *her* Wimmi.

As the crowd filed out at the end of the concert, Wimmi stayed behind and talked to fans, while his ghostly bandmate joined his partner – a similar floating young woman with long, silver hair – and Felthor.

Alessia's mind wandered. The magical setting and interesting characters gave her a sudden itch for make-believe. It was a lame habit to have kept at eleven years old, but every now and then, she couldn't help herself and played pretend.

She discreetly made her way to the Palace Gardens they'd walked through to the amphitheater. They were an intricate labyrinth of paved paths, lined with pillars and surrounded by exotic fauna like she'd seen in the Octopus's Garden.

When she was sure she was alone, she gave into the urge. She broke two twigs off a fluorescent blue bush, picked some pink floppy tube-like leaves from another plant, and fastened them together so they looked roughly like an anchor-and-seaweed-harp.

"You've been called 'the best artist of all time' by the Atlantis Times. Why not enjoy your fame and fans more?" she asked herself in a deep commentator voice.

She sunk into the character of Wimmi's bandmate with a deep sigh, and looked at the strange 'instrument' in her hands mournfully.

"There's a cost to fame you don't see. Just because I'm talented, doesn't mean I want to be famous," she lamented.

"Oh, I wish I could get out of these handcuffs of expectation."

"Do you?"

A boy in a blood-colored wetsuit was leaning nonchalantly against an ancient-looking fountain in the gardens. She froze. It was the boy who'd watched her escape from the crabs in the market.

"Oh, ha ha! No, I'm just... reciting from a play." She hoped she'd sounded more believable to him than she'd sounded to herself. "Anyway, I should be off..."

"Where are you going?"

Behind her was a fork in the path. She couldn't for the life of her remember which way she'd come from.

"That way," she pretended to know.

"So... you're not trying to go back where you came from?" the boy asked.

"No, no," she said, her cheeks burning like they were being engulfed by a swarm of fire ants. "Though actually, I just realized I lost my, um, necklace there," she lied, turning onto the other path. "So I *will* go that way first."

His deep, dark eyes pierced through her. She couldn't hold up his gaze and focused on the path ahead.

"What does it look like?"

"What?"

"Your necklace. If I'm supposed to look out for it, you should tell me what it's like."

"Uh... Green. Gemstones and stuff."

She walked hurriedly down the path – exaggeratedly swinging her head to check the floor for the made-up necklace.

"You're new here, aren't you?"

The boy was walking with her on the lime green grass

beyond the path's pillars. Stress gripped her insides again. Why was he following her?

"Yeah, I got here a couple of days ago."

"Where were you before?"

"Overland – in Selva."

He rolled his eyes. "Yeah, I got *that*. I meant *where* in Selva."

Without ever saying anything really insulting, he had the skill of making her feel stupid.

"Scotland. I was visiting the village my mother was from, when I came here."

"*Was* from? So she's not *still* from there?" he said. Smart-aleck.

"Well, she's dead," answered Alessia. He stopped for a moment. As awful as it was to profit from her life's tragedy, she savored the small victory.

"I see," he finally answered, then he continued walking with her without speaking.

Eventually, the silence weighed on Alessia, and she found herself trying to make conversation.

"So, what are you doing here? Did you watch the concert?"

"Why?" he answered.

Just as the strangeness of his response sank in, Felthor appeared at the end of the arcade.

"Alessia!" he shouted. He ran up to her, the lines of tension vanishing from his round face. "Thank Poseidon, we were worried sick!"

He glanced at the boy and, after a double-take, turned to him.

"Why hello, young man! Thank you for helping our Alessia back. I don't believe we've been introduced." Felthor grinned, his eyes shining with curiosity. Alessia cringed. Felthor's obvious parental interest at her meeting a boy was mortifying.

"We haven't," answered the boy.

Felthor chuckled good-heartedly.

"He's certainly a no-nonsense fellow! Good for you, finboy. Then, may I know your name?"

For a moment, the boy stared back at Felthor with dark expressionless eyes, then after glancing at Alessia, he finally replied.

"Vulcor, Authentor."

"Pleased to meet you, Vulcor." Felthor's forced manner barely concealed his excitement.

"She's lost her necklace – but we weren't able to find it," Vulcor said. Then he added quietly: "Perhaps it's in the nereid market."

He knew. He *had* recognized her. Alessia quickly turned away. She couldn't bear to see the look he must be throwing her.

"Why don't you exchange shell channels with Alessia in case you find it?" Felthor suggested. Vulcor hesitated.

"I can find her," he answered.

Alessia couldn't take any more. "We should go now. Wimmi'll be waiting. Bye!"

"Yes, yes... we'll be on our way..." Felthor was scrutinizing the boy's face with an enigmatic smile, obviously wondering if she liked this boy. Thankfully, he was courteous enough not to ask about it, or bring it up in front of Wimmi, who would *never* have let it go.

20

A lessia let the sight of the huge, gated Roman estate sink in: her new school.

"Remember Alessia, if you feel anything unusual or frightening, take an ovehic straight home and we'll fix whatever needs fixing, okay?"

"I know, Felthor," Alessia smiled. "Thank you."

Felthor had spent the last three days teaching her the necessities, from reading their alphabet, to the basics of all her school subjects.

Apparently, the Emperor had reformed schools to teach what he believed had made Atlantis great in the past: how to come up with ingenious inventions inspired by nature, how to be victorious in sea battles, how to convince other species to work towards Atlantide goals, and how to harness the power needed to live underwater. So Biomimetics, Jousting, Rhetoric and Power would be her new Math, Physical Education, English and Science. They also had to take 'Selvan Studies' – which came as a relief to Alessia (finally something she wouldn't be completely clueless at!) – until she discovered the objective of the class was "better knowing the Selvan enemy".

"You flick the fish scales off that Octopus's Garden, nymphlet!" Wimmi said, punching the air.

With a final wave, Alessia went through the gates. Children piled in either side of her. She tried to meet eyes with another student, but no one seemed to notice as they rushed around greeting each other, and chatting about their break. Alessia rubbed her arms, tightened her grip on her satchel and pushed past.

To her relief, a boy was walking by himself ahead of her, with his head hung low. Finding someone shy always had the effect of making her feel more confident.

"Hi, I'm Alessia. I'm looking for the First Year Class. Do you know where it is?" she asked him.

The serenity of his face with its thin crescent moon eyes appeased her. That is – until she noticed the winged baby crocodile perched on his shoulder.

She shrieked, "Don't move! There's a dragon-type thing on your shoulder!"

"Don't worry about him. He's a crocogull I found. He has an eye infection, so every hour I have to give him these eye drops my grandpa and I concocted." He spoke each word softly, as if to minimize the disturbance they caused on the aura of quiet surrounding him. "He should be fit to go back into the wild tomorrow. You can come with me, if you want?"

"Err..." How to tell this boy that there was possibly nothing in the world she wanted to do *less* than go 'into the wild' with his weird mutant crocodile-seagull thing.

"Come with me *to class,* I mean. I'm in first year too," he said.

"Oh! Sure then!"

"I'm Larthuzor. It's nice to meet you," he continued in his well-mannered way, a perfect blue sheen reflecting off his straight, black bangs. "If you don't mind me asking, are you from Selva?"

"I am! Is it that obvious?" grinned Alessia.

"Oh, I didn't mean to offend you. It's actually remarkable you learned our language so well."

"No, don't worry! I'm not offended. Just wondering what gave it away."

Larthuzor stopped and watched her as he pondered. "Hmm... I think Selvans are more... jolty than the people here. Maybe it's the difference in pressure."

"Jolty?" Alessia laughed in surprise.

"But perhaps it's me who's 'under-jolty'," he added, and Alessia laughed again at his extreme politeness.

Only a handful of students were in the classroom already. Four concentric circles of tables surrounded a large round platform where two professors stood. Just as Alessia sat, someone shouted: "LARTHU!"

A boy jumped to give Larthuzor a big, hearty hug – complete with a loud pat on the back, which shook the whole of Larthuzor's skinny body, but otherwise left him unsurprised. It gave the crocogull a start though.

"Gently, boys, gently!" snapped one of the professors: a narrow, older woman who had that quiet air about her of someone not to be messed with.

Larthuzor's friend turned to Alessia, his bright amber eyes sparkling playfully. "I'm Herior. Who are you?"

"Alessia."

"No way!" he belted out. "Like this girl at home!"

So Alessia was an Atlantide name. She'd always wondered why her two supposedly Scottish parents had given her such a non-Scottish name.

"She makes us call her 'Aless' though," Herior continued. "Says it's poetic. She's always getting poetic."

Herior had tousled, brown hair and healthy bronze-colored skin with the standard Atlantide otherworldly glow.

"Herior! Quiet! And sit down!" the elderly professor growled, giving them all a foreboding look.

"Oops." Herior gave a large dimpled smile in apology. "Sorry Sterna Authenta!" He slid onto the bench behind Alessia together with Larthuzor.

"Her actual poems are rubbish though," he continued in a loud whisper. "Aless' poems, I mean. The other day she rhymed 'trout' with 'splat'. I mean, I don't want to judge, but that's not getting past even the most generous Minchan.

"Don't tell Aless' I said that though! She'll kill me. Or make me polish her aquamarine gemstone collection or something. I can't do that stuff anymore! It's killing my credibility. Now everyone at home's asking me to polish stuff! I'm not a Cleaner Wrass!"

They giggled at Herior's outburst, not realizing the skeletal professor Sterna had glided behind them until she grabbed both boys' shoulders with firm claw-like hands.

"Boys!" she exclaimed in a shrill voice. Herior's golden eyes rounded like those of a cat awoken by a loud noise. "I believe I told you to be quiet. I cannot imagine what is so important that you needed to disobey your Octopus's Garden Head Authenta on the very first day..."

So Sterna was the School Principal! *She'd* be a good place to start the investigation into Alessia's father. Alessia would pay her a visit at the next break.

The last of the twenty-four children from their class arrived, almost all shouting "Herior!" as they walked in, and dashing straight to him like magnets.

Despite being on probation, he couldn't resist chatting

with them: "Titor! How's it going? Tamaya! Sivaria! Poseidon almighty, I've got the best thing to show you. Naror! What weird story are you telling these days?"

When he was done greeting everyone, he prodded Alessia and picked up the conversation again.

"You know, me and Larthu are brothers. I mean, not really *brothers* – but we've known each other since we were three – can you believe it? Like when we met, I couldn't pronounce 'Larthuzor' properly."

"You still don't! You call me Larthu!" Larthuzor laughed.

Sterna cleared her throat and the room fell silent. The other professor who had been busily rummaging through a large shiny purple chest in the middle of the room, finally emerged, his wisps of yellow hair fluttering back into place.

"Guppies, before we begin, you know the drill," Sterna chirped, motioning them to stand with a swift hand gesture. In perfect unison, the whole class stood with their hands behind their backs and chests puffed out. Alessia scrambled to her feet, looking left and right to mimic her classmates. But she was lost again seconds later, when they recited:

"I recognize the Emperor's Shield and bow to its ruling.

I accept the Truth of the 5 Sensate Powers; that 5 beings were blessed with exceptional abilities in the 5 senses. It is my honor, as much as my duty, to render loyalty to the two surviving beings, the Oculate, our nation's grand advisor, and the Manibate, our Emperor."

Alessia mumbled gibberish in time with the rest of them, blushing whenever she accidentally spoke during a pause.

Then, they all sat as though nothing had happened.

❧ 21 ❧

Sterna gave the typical headteacher speech about how the Octopus's Garden was the 'pride of Nethuns' and they should work hard, then she glided out.

An expectant pause came over the class before their professor – the short, luminous-pink-skinned man – realized that his cue had come.

"Oh right, erm..." he spluttered, looking around as though he had lost something. "I'm... erm... Rascor Authentor. Professor of Power."

Alessia eyed the room quickly to see if anybody would chuckle at the fact this mousy man called himself 'Professor of Power'.

"So... Who knows why we study power? You there, front row. And your name please."

"Quina," answered a girl with an intricately plaited crown of golden hair, sitting in the front row. "Historically, our mastery in finding and exploiting the powers hidden in our world has been our competitive edge against rival civilizations, and the key enabler for our survival." She pursed her lips. But before she could get the praise she was clearly fishing for, the professor was distracted by a kerfuffle at the back of the class.

Two boys were arguing in 'whispers' that could probably have been heard from across the courtyard.

One of them was a brawny boy with an alabaster-white face and pale lemon-colored hair. The other was tall, with a mop of black hair and deep brown skin.

"I'm telling you!" he answered his lemon-haired neighbor. "The Emperor's Shield is fake. The *Chaco's* shield is the original text about Sensate powers. *That's* the one that tells the whole truth. You just don't know it because it's secret."

Rascor shrieked and dropped a box of pearls he'd been carrying, sending about ten Drift light beams streaming across the classroom, projecting different holographic scenes.

"Stop that!" Rascor yelped at the boy. "Stop that at once! What do you think you're doing?"

"Don't worry, Authentor. It's just Naror. He's always making things up," explained the boy's neighbor, as Rascor scrambled to gather the pearls he'd dropped.

"I am not!" Naror protested, scrunching up his freckled nose. "Chaco's Shield is real! I heard it and it has tons of information about the five Sensate powers–"

"STOP!" Rascor was livid. "Sensate powers are out of scope, Naror. Utterly out of scope! This class is about harnessing *natural* powers. No talking about Sensate powers. Okay?" He flinched, realizing something. "I mean, of course we can talk about what *the Emperor's Shield* says about Sensate Powers. We *have to*--I mean, we *want to*. We recite it. Each morning. With delight. Like we're meant to. Nothing more, nothing less."

"But – doesn't the Emperor's Shield *itself* mention that

there were five Sensate powers?" asked plait-crowned Quina.

"No! I mean yes," spluttered Rascor. "But we don't talk about those. There were five. Now there are two. And those are the two we're allowed to talk about, as per the Emperor's Shield. There's Manibancy, the power to move objects with the mind – the power held by Emperor Oscor. And there's Oculancy, the power to see through others' eyes – his advisor, Espior's power."

"But there *were* other powers," Naror pressed. "There was an Aurate who could hear what anyone was saying at any time, and was poisoned with a mix of water hemlock and Green Pung. And Chaco was the Nasate, with powers of extraordinary scent, and he was murdered—"

"Enough!" Rascor screeched. "Extinct Sensate Powers, Chaco ideology, or indeed *any* ideology other than the Emperor's, are all OFF LIMITS. You're lucky there's not a member of the Emperor's Guard in this room. And you better hope your classmates don't go and tell people what you've been asking! It's forbidden. Very, very forbidden."

The classroom fell silent.

"That Oculate guy though," Herior sighed behind Alessia. All twenty-four heads in the room whipped around to look at him. Herior's dimples twitched into existence at the corners of his mouth. "He can see through our eyes! So embarrassing! I hope he's not looking at what I'm doing. I'm keeping my eyes closed from now on."

Laughter fluttered across the room and Rascor relaxed a little.

"Back to safer topics," he said. "What is the main natural power we harness? You, there. The boy next to the loud one."

"Hey! I'm not loud!" protested Herior, loudly.

Larthuzor answered, "We use the power from the heat of the Earth's core, which we can easily access because of the thinness of the crust under the ocean."

"Right," Rascor said. "Now... You! How is that power transferred from the Earth's core to us?"

Naror's lemon-haired neighbor blinked mutely. Quina gave a loud 'I know the answer' sigh, and twirled a loose strand from her plait crown.

"For transfer of any kind of power," Rascor explained, "you need a source of power, a destination you want it to be transferred to, a conductive material linking the two, and something to trigger the transfer – an imbalance." Quina mouthed along with his words as if it were her favorite song.

"So what would those be in the case of transferring the Earth's core heat to power Nethuns?" Quina asked, hand up and waving around.

"Well, I was just about to expl–"

"I know!" Quina's hand shot up again. "The source of power is the heat of the Earth's core. The place we want to get it to is Nethuns. There's an imbalance because deep in the ocean is very cold, and the Earth's core is very hot. And the conductive material through which the power can circulate is the Atlantide-discovered liquid crystal, Orichalca."

"Y-Yes, thank you Quina for answering, well, *your* question," stammered Rascor. "Now let's take a look at one of the mines, so you can see the Orichalca conduction for yourselves."

He dropped a pearl and a tube of bright light appeared in the middle of the round room, stretching up to the ceiling. Alessia was glad she knew about these holographic experiences so she could act as unphased as the others when they walked into the Drift.

By the time the class ended, they'd 'Drift-ed' both to an Orichalca mine and to the Centre of the Earth. (A little too 'fiery-pit-of-hell'-ish for Alessia's taste, but interesting nonetheless).

Alessia rushed out and went from door to door to find the Headteacher's office before her next class. Luckily, when she finally found it, Sterna was there. Brushing away the little voice in her head that said she was endangering Felthor and Wimmi by doing this, Alessia walked in.

"E-excuse me?"

"What can I do for you?" Sterna asked courteously, but without moving from her seat. "I must warn you, I'm expecting company and don't have much time. We can schedule an appointment."

"That's alright, I won't take long," Alessia said. "I was wondering if... if maybe you knew my father. He went here, to the Octopus's Garden..." She considered pulling out the trident but decided against it. The less she revealed, the less she was putting them all at risk.

Sterna stared at Alessia with an indecipherable face.

"Who's your father?"

"That's the thing. I don't know," Alessia answered, bowing her head slightly. Sterna cocked an eyebrow.

"He was in his early thirties when I was born," Alessia explained. "So he'd have been at the Octopus's Garden around twenty-five to thirty years ago."

"That isn't something we should be discussing! You're clearly a landfarer, but I'd urge you to familiarize yourself with our laws here, fast."

Alessia's shoulders fell. "I understand."

She turned to leave, her mind racing to find ways she could still get it out of Sterna.

"You might ask Iktor Authentor, or Gizma Authenta,"

came Sterna's voice just as Alessia was stepping out of the door. "*Discreetly*. Around thirty years ago Iktor Authentor and Gizma Authenta were Imperial Poseidium students, coaching our Octopus's Garden pupils."

A smile burst onto Alessia's face.

"Thank you, Authenta. Thank you so much!"

As Alessia left, a young man passed her to enter the office. He wore a red wetsuit emblazoned with a golden crest she recognized from the palace. He didn't appear to take any notice of her but shut the door so violently it made Alessia jump.

Curious, she lingered a little.

"Look, the palace needs them..." a high-pitched male voice was saying rather snobbishly.

"All of them?" retorted Sterna's biting voice. "On top of the Emperor's guard, the palace needs Carcinor and *all of his crabs* there full-time? The crabs are here for the security of our students!"

The crabs were leaving the Octopus's Garden? Alessia couldn't believe her luck. No risk of them recognizing her as the intruder they'd chased.

"Those are the Emperor's orders," the man answered. "There's a highly delicate situation in the palace, and the Emperor needs to be sure he protects–"

"If it's so dangerous, does the Emperor not think some protection is worth sparing for the Octopus's Garden?"

"Authenta, if you have words for the Emperor I'll let you be the messenger of those yourself."

"It seems I have to, since he's clearly not been adequately briefed on the consequences of his choices. Not to mention the new power targets the Octopus's Garden has been given. Really, what are we meant to do with those?

Just stop heating the place? Stop lighting it? Hope our students turn into lanternfish?"

"The power question is beside the point. The Orichalca-conduction mine linked to the Octopus's Garden hasn't been functioning correctly. Our kappa team is on it. It has nothing to do with the Emperor."

"Of course it doesn't."

"Since we're talking about things not being as they should, I might bring up, Authenta, that it was highly unusual to see an uncovered mosaic doormat with an illicit symbol at your side entrance."

Alessia stumbled back, then quickly leaned in again to hear Sterna's answer.

"Yes, we've left it uncovered while we investigate the act of vandalism that led to its cover's destruction. That's neither here nor there. What I understand is that you're capable of giving us neither the crabs, nor the power we need. Very well. We'll no doubt be raising the most capable generation of students yet: working without light or heat, defending *themselves*... If they survive, they'll be remarkable indeed!"

✢ 22 ✢

"Settle in! Settle in!" shouted a petite woman with owl eyes and glowing coppery skin, standing in the middle of the room. The concentric circles of desks were elevated like in a lecture hall, so her small figure was even further diminished, but that didn't seem to dampen her verve.

"Your Biomimetics professor was sadly the victim of a burglary and has had to stay home to deal with that. I'm Moxia Authenta, I'll be filling in for him today," she articulated, her wide eyes unblinking, as though she were in shock at her own introduction.

"To start the year, he wanted to assess your knowledge and ingenuity with a field assignment. You'll go out to the ocean and take inspiration from something existing in nature to invent an escape mechanism. You need to capture the creature and be ready to present a proposal on how we humans could replicate the mechanism to escape from captivity."

Alessia glanced at her classmates. They didn't seem surprised. This was really happening. She didn't even know how to swim! How on earth would she catch a sea creature, let alone one that was a master of evasion?

They each grabbed a large pearl-encrusted jar from under their desks, and headed towards the back of the room, following Moxia.

"Hi! Naror Gavrol, nice to meet you!" The boy who'd scandalized their professor of Power with his talk of 'Sensate Powers' was walking beside Alessia, his cloud of black hair bobbing with each step. "Are you the landfarer staying with Felthor now?"

"Yeah! Do you know Felthor and Wimmi?"

"Felthor's friends with my parents—"

"Would you look at that? Naror found the *one person* who might believe his lies – the new landfarer who doesn't know any better," a girl muttered maliciously with a flick of her brown plait as she walked by. The black freckles on Naror's nose bunched together as he scowled.

"Don't believe anything this one says, landfarer," the girl told Alessia. "We were all in Roe-Nest together – that's the school before Octopus's Garden – all he did was lie."

"That's not true! Cut it out, Sivaria!" spat Naror.

"What was it you told us again?" Sivaria's triangular eyebrows sunk a notch, twisting her self-satisfied air into something more wicked. "That the Emperor awarded you the cup for 'Biomimetics Invention of the year'? Making you the only guppy *ever in history* to get it?"

"That was... a joke," Naror replied, a slight quiver in his voice.

"And didn't you say your mother wasn't an 'ordinary Selvan', she was a 'Selvan sorceress who taught you magic'? And that your father was the world jousting champion?"

"Those were like four years ago!" Naror protested.

"Can you give me a break? I haven't told a single lie since then."

His head slumped between his shoulders. A spike of fury at Sivaria electrified Alessia's skin, leaving it feeling raw. She felt for Naror. If there was anything she understood, it was wanting to make a fresh start. But before Alessia could try to defend him, professor Moxia's cracked voice rang out.

"Anyone for the Baltic Sea?"

Moxia stood behind the last row of desks. Beside her were four giant soap bubbles, with rainbow colors slowly sliding along their thick, shiny membranes. Moxia brushed the surface of the first bubble with her forearm, and an opening appeared.

Four students tugged on their wetsuit collars so they covered their noses, and walked in through the created gap. One girl gently stroked the inside of the bubble to seal the opening, and just like that, they vanished.

Alessia swallowed the wrong way and went into a coughing fit.

When she'd finally finished choking, the professor had opened the second bubble and said: "Sulu Sea?"

Larthuzor left his crocogull on a desk with a gentle pat on its head and walked into the bubble. He was the person Alessia was closest to 'knowing'. She couldn't lose him.

"Me!" she yelped, rushing in behind him at the same time as Herior, his amber eyes sparkling with eagerness for their adventurous first assignment.

Sivaria the mean girl, pushed past Naror, her plait almost smacking him in the face. She grabbed another girl by the arm and urged them to join the Sulu Sea bubble too. Her friend was a dainty girl with Atlantis-glowing sepia brown skin, long raven hair and doe eyes. She looked unimpressed, but on Sivaria's insistence, trudged into the bubble.

As soon as the girls entered, Herior chirped excitedly: "Come on, Tamaya! Better put up your gills!"

He grabbed the reluctant girl's turtleneck and pulled it up over her eyes.

"Herior, you're such a seaweedbag!" Tamaya shrieked. She peeled the wetsuit off her face to delicately place it back over her small nose. Then, she proceeded to swat him on the shoulder, her slick black hair shaking with each strike.

Herior cowered, a mischievous grin dimpling his cheeks. "I just wanted to make sure you could breathe when we're under water!"

That's what the turtlenecks were for. Alessia tugged hers over her nose. The others then bumped their shells together, so Alessia quickly took hers out and did the same.

"Come on, let's go now," Sivaria moaned, sealing the bubble.

With a boom of thunderous noise, everything went dark and quiet. A sensation of effervescence grew from the pit of Alessia's stomach, and the blackness around gradually dissolved into specks, before disappearing altogether.

Alessia's eyes prickled. Her vision was blurred. The light around was dim and blue – different from the light in the classroom. And she felt something cold and creamy on her skin, like how the water had felt when she'd been submerged after the Diving Belle incident. The picture sharpened through the bubble and she understood. They were underwater, on the sea floor.

Their shells shot up to each of their ears.

"Wow, when Sivaria means action, she means action! I barely had my gills up! You could've drowned me!" Herior's voice came into Alessia's mind. So this was how shells worked! They didn't even need to speak!

Little flaps on the sides of their turtlenecks opened and closed. The wetsuits must have been extracting oxygen from the water like fish gills – that's how they were able to breathe.

Larthuzor swiped the bubble open and drifted out.

"So, we meet back here in forty-five minutes," Larthuzor's voice said through the shell.

"Sure!" Alessia smiled uselessly under her wetsuit. Tamaya and Sivaria plodded off in one direction, while Larthuzor and Herior went in another. Their outfit's socks were pulling their weightless bodies down to the sand.

Alessia pressed her eyes to get rid of the saltwater sting, then looked around. There wasn't much in terms of life around here: a little seaweed dotted about the sand and rocks, a few shrimp drifting, a large crab strolling, a beige flatfish gliding just above the seafloor towards the critters.

None of these were sparking any ideas. Suddenly, the flatfish decomposed itself before her eyes. Two large tentacles broke away from the sides of its body, and in the blink of an eye, the body itself was no more. In its place stood a nightmarish creature: an octopus almost half Alessia's size, painted with ominous dark brown stripes. It looked like an eerie puppet with its eight large tentacles undulating independently from each other under its extra-terrestrial elongated head. It pounced on the crab below, enveloping it without much struggle.

Alessia froze. Did octopuses eat humans? She cautiously took a step back towards the bubble. The octopus froze. It had seen her. Alessia looked around. She couldn't outrun it under water. She wasn't sure how to scream for help through the shell. Her best bet was to try to scare it.

She lifted the heavy jar over her head, and puffed out her chest to make herself look as large and menacing as possible. The octopus dropped the mangled remains of the crab and floated down to the ground.

Was he posturing himself to better pounce on her? She gulped and held her position.

All at once, five of the octopus' tentacles sank into the sand. Alessia's breath quickened. The octopus was burrowing into the ground. Would it tunnel its way to her concealed by the sand and grab her by the ankles?

She needed a better escape strategy. And to think, if she'd made it to the end of this assignment, she'd have learned a bunch of them from her classmates. Ironic.

Now, the octopus' head had vanished. Only two tentacles remained above ground and their color had changed from stripy white and brown to a noxious-looking black and yellow. Slithering on the sand like that, they almost looked like a venomous sea serpent.

Then it hit her.

The octopus was *pretending* to be a snake. She smiled. If she'd learned anything from the whole debacle with the nereid's disguise, it was that imitation was a *great* escape strategy. The octopus was scared and trying to escape from *her*.

She crept towards the fake snake, still holding the jar above her head. The 'snake' wriggled around on the spot in a frenzy. Had she not known its secret, she'd have been petrified.

All of a sudden, the octopus flew out of the ground, revealing its whole massive body, now deadly black, only to crash into the jar she'd thrown onto it. It thrashed around inside the upside-down jar, but she held it firmly in place.

She couldn't believe what she'd just done. She tried not

to panic. This was just like collecting spiders at home – she needed to get closer, and slide the lid of the jar under it... Only, this octopus knew how to burrow into the sand. And she didn't know how venomous it was. Perhaps one touch of its skin would kill her on the spot! It was no use thinking about that now. She'd come to the point of no-return. If she released the octopus now, it would jump out and attack her.

She got a little closer. In the spot where the octopus had sprung from the ground, an unusual-looking cream-colored, pointy rock poked up from under the sand. She leaned in. Strange runes were carved on it. It wasn't like the Atlantide alphabet, or any others she'd seen. She gave it a small kick. When it rolled out of the sand, she shrieked.

It was a skull. The skull of an animal with a long, beak-like mouth. And it was etched with mysterious letters.

Just then, something touched her shoulder. With a scream she whacked it off and spun around.

Behind her, nursing his smacked hand was a confused-looking Larthuzor.

"I'm so sorry! You scared me, I..."

"Did you trap a mimic octopus?" Larthuzor asked.

"Yeah!" Alessia said proudly.

"Why?" Above the neck of his wetsuit, Larthuzor's eyes looked horrified.

Alessia stared at him blankly. "For the a-assignment?"

Larthuzor's eyebrows rode up his forehead in sudden understanding.

"Of course. No one explained. When we say 'capture' in Biomimetics, we mean to capture Drifts. We don't touch the animals! We have a harmonious relationship with them. We never disturb them."

"But the jar?"

Larthuzor held up his jar. Inside it a sperm whale was

swimming around. It *looked* real enough... but it was the size of a hand. Larthuzor had 'captured' a Drift of it.

"You turn the pearl on the jar and it captures the full likeness of the creature: Sound, smell, look and all. I got the sperm whale because of the debilitating sound it makes to escape from orcas."

Suddenly, she knew where she'd seen the shape of the skull on the ground before. *Whales and dolphins* had skulls like that. She'd seen them on a school trip at the National Museum of Scotland. But what would anyone write on a dolphin's skull?

"Well, let's release your octopus and capture its Drift then," Larthuzor suggested.

Alessia looked back at the angry octopus. Warily, she stepped forward, tipped the jar, and jumped back. The octopus grouped its tentacles so it looked like the flatfish again, and shot out of the jar. Thankfully, it seemed keener to escape than to seek retribution.

"The pearl!" Larthuzor exclaimed.

Alessia quickly turned it and a green flash of light was emitted from the bottom of the jar, rippling out into the sea, and vanishing into its depths.

Alessia put the lid back on the jar. Inside it, the replica of the poor creature she'd tormented was dashing away into the ocean, on loop.

"Cool!" Larthuzor said. "Let's go back."

In the bubble with her four classmates, Alessia blinked Larthuzor a 'thank you', and he blinked back a 'you're welcome'. A moment later they were back in their classroom, with their Drifts captured in their jars. And the mysterious inscribed skull burned into Alessia's memory.

✣ 23 ✣

The variety of presentations was astonishing. The professor was happy with Alessia's proposal to make a wetsuit with the mimic octopus' color-changing properties as an escape disguise, and only disappointed that she hadn't captured the color changing scene in her jar. High praise was given to Larthuzor and Tamaya.

Tamaya wasn't only beautiful, but apparently successful at school. She showed a squid launching itself with ink, then brought out a makeshift backpack she'd quickly put together, and explained how if you were in danger you could pull its strap and a powerful inkjet would come out of it and propel you to safety. Her presentation was met with applause from the class, and cheers from a particularly enthusiastic Herior.

Then, a girl Alessia hadn't noticed before walked on stage and introduced herself as Kella.

"So... my idea's kinda weird," Kella warbled in a deep, sardonic voice which didn't fit at all with her appearance. Her skin and hair were both seafoam-white and her features were small and far between, giving her the delicate look of a

Japanese ink painting with only few traits drawn. The exception to this was a distinctive long and bulbous nose.

"It's basically about changing someone's *body* to help them escape from captivity... like sea cucumbers do," she continued, showing the big leathery slug in her jar. "I know, kinda stupid..."

There wasn't a noise in the class except for the awkward creaking of benches. Alessia started picking at her nails, then dropped her hand. She was feeling Kella's discomfort.

"Anyway," Kella continued, wearing an exaggeratedly disinterested look on her face. "These sea cucumber things can liquefy their body and then make it firm again. That way they can squeeze into hiding places. It's kind of gross, but also, helpful, I guess... So, I thought if we could put the same stuff that liquefies into human muscles, then people could... well liquefy their flesh to get in and out of places."

The twenty-four pairs of eyes in the class were watching Kella blankly. Alessia's stomach churned.

"Anyway, like Tamaya, I tried to do a little experiment myself..." Kella said. "I used a syringe to extract some of the cartilage type of material from the sea cucumber's spine and inject it into my hand... But, it's kinda strange, the stuff's just staying in this weird, hard lump under my skin."

As if on cue, a viscous, yellow liquid started pouring out from the pores of her skin. Her hand looked like a water balloon that had been pierced all over.

Moxia's already round eyes widened further: "Wait, you... injected yourself with fluid from a sea cucumber?"

There was a murmur of excitement. Alessia squirmed in her seat. She started seeing black spots as if she were about to faint. She was being oversensitive again. She had to stop.

"Sea cucumbers produce a toxin in their skin!" Moxia exclaimed. "It's extremely irritant to..."

"Oh, Triton," Kella murmured. "I've gone blind."

Moxia rushed Kella out of the room. The class giggled and whispered about the dramatic turn of events. Alessia swallowed back her nausea and regathered herself.

"Iktor!" came the panicked echo of Moxia's voice from the corridor. "*Good Tirnanog*, I'm glad to see you! I need you to finish your class, we have a bit of an emergency!"

Alessia sat up. Her Biomimetics professor was Iktor Authentor! The man Sterna said potentially knew her father! She craned her neck towards the front door.

"Settle down! Is this how a class of Nethuns' finest students behaves?" an impatient bark came from behind her.

A bald man had come in from the back of the class, and was gliding to its center. His night-blue wetsuit was tight against a small but muscled frame and its neckline crawled up right below his jawline.

"We've given your classmate an antidote and they're cutting the catch collagen out of her hand," he said coldly. "She'll survive. Let this be a reminder not to experiment without expert supervision. Class dismissed."

His pointy face had a devilish quality. He had a v-shaped jaw that jutted forwards and rippled up his face to the V of his eyebrows. He seemed preoccupied, probably because he'd been dealing with a burglary that morning.

Alessia blew out a breath. She probably shouldn't bother him with her questions at a time like this. She might end up crying with him over the precious photo album he lost in the robbery or something (assuming they had photo albums here). She'd better wait to catch him on a better day.

She joined the students walking out. Mean girl Sivaria

walked up to Herior, tossed back her coffee-colored plait and proudly told the joke she'd clearly been cooking from the moment Kella's presentation had gone south:

"Well, with all that stuff spraying all over her, she *has* managed *something* like a cucumber. Don't they say in Selvan English 'As cool as a cucumber'?"

A strange, almost electric thrill hit Alessia. Herior grimaced and batted Sivaria's comment away, unimpressed, and suddenly Alessia's thrill subsided and a gnawing insecurity gripped at her insides. What? Was she empathizing with bullies like *Sivaria* now?

Tamaya twirled a shiny, black hair strand between her fingers and muttered under her breath as an afterthought, "It's Kella-za-cucumber."

Somehow *this* got picked up. The class erupted into laughter, and "Kella-za-Cucumber" echoed down the hall.

Alessia looked around. As she dreaded, Kella stood there, against the wall, within earshot, her blobby nose reddening.

"Did you hear what she said?" Under her plait-crown Quina was grinning at Alessia.

Alessia repeated in her head, 'Don't cause a scene. Don't shout at them. Don't cry. Don't cause a scene. Don't cry.'

"Yeah, so funny," she answered Quina, failing to smile.

She looked back at Tamaya, standing in the middle of the crowd with her smug, beautiful face, and Sivaria giggling maliciously beside her. Alessia rolled her eyes at herself. Why was it so hard for her to watch something like this happen when these girls didn't feel an ounce of guilt?

She needed to pull herself together. She was stopping herself from asking Iktor the very thing she came to Atlantis to find out, because she was scared of getting all oversensitive about his burglary! That wasn't normal! Kids should be able to go and ask their teachers things without worrying that they might start *crying* over their teachers' problems!

She turned back and marched down to Iktor.

"Professor, I wanted to ask you about my father."

He spun around sharply. When he laid eyes on her, he looked petrified for a moment.

"I think you know him from when you were at the Imperial Poseidium, and he was at the Octopus's Garden," Alessia pressed on. "I want to find out anything you know."

Iktor stepped closer to her. His nose was thin and hooked like the beak of a vulture – and Alessia got the strange feeling that she was prey.

"Do you know about the faint-banded sea snake?" he asked.

"Um... No, Authentor."

"No?" he repeated softly, his eyes ablaze. "You'd barely notice its bite, but its venom would paralyze each muscle in your body until you could no longer breathe. You'd suffocate in plain air. Did you know that?"

A lump formed in Alessia's throat. "No, I didn't," she tried to say, but only a hushed croak came out.

"Capabilities exist in nature that can bestow on those that harness them, a power much greater than any inherited power. Only the humble see these, because only *they* really look. That's why I'm not interested in those who believe themselves all powerful – those who know nothing, yet feel entitled or special. And it appears to me, you are one of them. Am I wrong?"

What? Maybe she'd interrupted him at the wrong time with her request... but 'believe themselves powerful'? What made him think that?

"I believe I asked you a question. Am I beneath getting your answer?" he snarled.

"Yes," Alessia breathed quickly.

"Yes, I'm beneath getting your answer? Or yes I'm wrong?" There was a tinge of amusement in his voice, but his eyes were stone-cold.

"No... Yes, I mean... I don't think I'm better than everybody." A hot flush rose on Alessia's face and prickled her eyes, teasing them for tears.

"Get out," he muttered through gritted teeth.

"B-but—"

"Get out! GET OUT!"

Alessia stumbled backwards, and ran to the door. Just as she passed the threshold, Iktor hissed: "Why the Styx would I talk to the likes of *you* about your father?"

She shut the door behind her, and burst into tears. This was a disaster. She'd garnered the hate of one of two professors who might have information about her father.

But it was so strange. What had she done for him to react so violently without knowing her?

There was a short sniff. Kella, the 'sea cucumber' girl, was standing in the same spot as before, looking dejected.

The sight landed on Alessia like a punch in the heart.

"Hi," she said, wiping the remnants of tears off her own cheeks.

Kella looked up at her. "Oh, hi." She waited a beat. "Yes, it's me. The girl who injects herself with poison, apparently."

"Are you okay now?" Alessia asked, ignoring her self-mockery.

Kella's face softened slightly. "Yeah, it's okay. My pride was hurt more than anything else, as my mom would say," she sighed. "I was so stupid to think I could do that."

"Well, for what it's worth, I thought it was a brilliant *idea*," Alessia replied.

"So brilliant it didn't work. Of course, *Tamaya*'s experiment was flawless. *Perfect Princess Authenta* strikes again."

"You mean her idea of ink coming out of peoples' backside and propelling them like a squid?"

Kella let out a laugh. "I didn't think of it that way."

"I don't think PP Authenta did better than you. It was just simpler. It's easy to laugh at people who try something different, when you play it safe."

"PP Authenta?" Kella burst out laughing. "Okay, that's her code name from now on!"

Alessia grinned.

"You're from Selva aren't you?" Kella asked.

"Yeah."

"Oh Triton, you're so lucky!" Kella's eyes gleamed with awe. "I wish I were from Selva."

"Really? Why?"

"You've got this whole experience none of us have! You lived in like this old world with really weird antiquated traditions. And it's so cute how landfarers discover all of these things we already know, and are all amazed by them."

"Well, I definitely feel clueless."

They both giggled.

"What's your name?"

"Alessia."

"Can we sit together?"

"Sure," smiled Alessia. And just as they entered the courtyard to go to lunch, Kella quietly said, "Thanks."

24

By the time they arrived for lunch, the break was almost over. Hundreds of sandy-colored platters glided around the Octopus's Garden courtyard, their edges rippling gently like the fins of a sole fish. Kella showed Alessia how to grab food off them and the girls settled down in some giant turtle-shell chairs, when a red-haired woman appeared out of thin air in the middle of the courtyard.

Alessia jumped and shrieked, and the other students and teachers started charging in every direction. But not because they were running away in fear. They were scrambling for the best place around the newly materialized woman.

"Kella, who's–"

"Shh! Haven't you ever seen a Tiding before?" growled an older student next to them as he leaned in closer to hear what the apparition had to say.

"No, seaweedbag. As a matter of fact, she's a landfarer and she hasn't. You want to nag her about it?" Kella retorted. When she was outraged, her round nose turned scarlet apparently. She gave a gusty sigh, shook her head in disbelief, and turned to Alessia.

"We call big news a Tiding. It comes on everywhere across the land."

"And that woman has special powers?" Alessia whispered back.

"Not really," Kella murmured, leaning towards her as the courtyard quietened in anticipation. "She's a nereid journalist. She's not really here – it's a Drift."

The woman spoke through a neutral newscaster smile. "Good afternoon Nethunsians. We come to you with a special Tiding. The Emperor's own personal advisor Espior – commonly known as the Oculate – was abducted earlier today. Let's catch the Drift."

She disappeared and the whole middle section of the courtyard morphed into a completely different room, plunged in the creamy light of dawn. Its walls and floors were made from Mother of Pearl and delicately reflected rainbow colors. An old man in a matted gold wetsuit, with a long cream-colored beard and long cream-colored hair to match stood there. His large, almost colorless eyes were fixed on a point in mid-air, as though he were listening to someone. But he was alone.

He held heavy-looking books with beautiful gem-encrusted covers, and the familiar musty scent of ancient books permeated the air, mingling with the soft, floral fragrance of the room. The gentle pitter patter of footsteps from other rooms around echoed against the Mother of Pearl walls.

A shadow emerged slowly behind the old man. He didn't notice it. The Octopus's Garden spectators gasped and shifted around to see the shadow's owner. Naror, the alleged class liar, got so excited, he ran right into the Drift, his black curls bouncing as his head moved this way and that, to get the best angle.

The intruder quietly crept in behind his shadow. Alessia's chest tightened.

He wore a dark hooded cloak. Everyone in the courtyard instinctively bent down to look up from under the cloak, but shadows pooled on his face like ink, concealing his features. When he was close enough, he threw a pile of seaweed over the old man's head. Before the old man could even start to struggle, the seaweed spread and tightened around his shape. The man grappled at it clumsily, with weak fingers, his papery skin stretching tightly across his knuckles, and whitening.

The attacker kicked him behind the knees and the old man crumbled to the ground. His cries were muffled by the tight seaweed netting. The hooded figure looked around for something. But when the sound of a voice drifted in from a nearby room, he gave a start. Not without difficulty, he picked up his seaweed-wrapped victim and slung him over his back, before leaving the way he'd come.

Then, the room morphed again.

A huge throne made from red coral appeared, its branches intertwined like bloody veins. On it sat a man with jet black hair streaked with white and slicked back in the style of an old mobster. His nose was crooked, as though it had been broken a couple of times. And his eyes were cold – like the eyes of a shark. It was the Emperor.

Very slowly he raised a hand to his shoulder and with two sharp gestures, brushed a piece of lint off his wetsuit. He was dressed almost entirely in the darkest olive-green color, breeches and all. Only a band of brown stretching from his shoulder to his hip stood out on his wetsuit, like an ammo bandolier.

The room was deathly quiet. Alessia couldn't help but take a step back, to avoid his gaze finding her, even if he was just a projection.

He opened his huge twisted mouth just a crack.

"People of Nethuns," he muttered slowly. "Today a small band of you took my loyal advisor, the Oculate Espior. This is an act of treachery, against our regime of peace. I don't need to remind you our great nation hasn't always been blessed with such stability. Such an attempt to trigger unrest is..." he paused, cocked his head and finished, "regrettable."

His speech was unhurried. He savored the pause between each sentence, dragging them on to make his audience uneasy.

"I also consider this act to be a direct affront to me, your loving ruler – and, needless to remind you – one of the last two holders of a Sensate Power." He raised his hand to stroke his jaw. "Anyone withholding information," he continued, "will suffer the consequences of being an enemy of the Empire."

The Emperor disappeared. A chilling silence hung in the air. The students and teachers eyed each other nervously.

"Triton, that means trouble," muttered Kella.

❧ 25 ❧

Teachers ushered the students into their classes, and Kella and Alessia quickly finished eating and made their way to the gated archway at the far end of the courtyard for their next class.

A giant woman (by Nethuns standards), with an orangey complexion, caramel hair and a vibrant red wetsuit pushed her way to the front of the group.

"Zimana Authenta," she introduced herself in a thundering voice that quieted all the nervous gossiping from the class. "You can talk about the Tiding later. For now, I want you down on the four boats on the other side of this door faster than I can say grindylows. Six in each boat. Oars are on the benches. DON'T start before I tell you to. What did I say, Herior Authentor?"

The class turned to Herior. He was making sword-fighting movements with a large, wooden stick with paddles at each end. It was obviously a homemade contraption. All sorts of random objects had been stuck along the length of the stick, from bubble hoops, to sparking antennae. Through the power of habit, Larthuzor seemed not to notice his friend's antics beside him – though the crocogull on his shoulder squawked complaints whenever Herior's jousting paddle got too close.

Zimana stared, arms crossed, and fingers strumming on her bicep, until Herior finally noticed the noise of her talking had stopped, and looked up.

"You know my name! I'm flattered Authenta," said Herior, his broad, dimpled grin lighting his face. "Did you hear about my notorious jousting skills?"

A smirk drew up the corner of Zimana's lip. "I heard about your notorious cheekiness! Now drop that and focus."

"But Authenta, we're about to witness a historic moment: The HeriOAR's first joust!"

"The what?" Sivaria asked.

"My super-oar, enhanced with secret Herior technologies. Can't say more. If I told you, I'd have to kill you."

"I bet it'll break in the first joust, like all other Herior upgrades," groaned 'PP Authenta' Tamaya.

"Aw Tams, I'm hurt! How can you say that?" Herior feigned offense, his honey eyes twinkling. Kella rolled her eyes at Alessia.

"Give *one* example of a Herior upgrade that worked," Tamaya said.

"The HeriMOBILE – machine of fury," Herior said.

"The flying fish board you rigged to go faster, that ended up going *slower*?"

"...And I painted green shark-fins of fury on it. You forgot the green shark-fins of fury!"

"Only bad jousters spend so much time on their oars. I could offload you from your rowboat with a *broken* oar," boasted the beefy, lemon-haired boy that had been arguing with Naror 'the liar' in power class.

"You didn't last time, Gulusor." Herior grinned.

"You were lucky. The rematch is on!" shouted Gulusor.

"Oi!" shouted Zimana. The class fell quiet. "Time to see if your bite is as big as your bark."

She opened the gates and the students rushed through. They were at the top level of a gigantic Ancient-Greek style amphitheater that was filled with water except for the uppermost six rows of stone benches. Four rowboats and a raft rested on the water, tied to hooks on the front row.

The class hurried down the benches towards them. It took Alessia back to her dreaded sports classes, and her throat tightened. Meanwhile, Herior had already jumped into a boat and was standing with his homemade oar held up at shoulder-level, and chest pumped out like a proud warrior.

"Reminder: we don't kill people at the Octopus's Garden," Zimana began monotonously. Alessia choked a cough. "Your objective is to unvessel them. Still, jousting is a *noble* sport. Do it justice by fighting to the end. You wouldn't give up your life easily in real combat. Treat this the same. Winner's the last one standing."

Zimana stamped her foot on an oar lying on the ground. It sprang up and she caught it one-handed. Then, she jumped onto the raft, landing heavily on both feet.

"Demonstration."

Alessia tried to make herself small. She *dreaded* being picked to demonstrate in front of the class. If it hadn't been given to her by her dead parents, she'd have hated the name Alessia simply because of all the times she was chosen to go first because of the unjust but unchallengeable system that was the alphabetical order.

Thankfully, Zimana turned to face Herior. She plunged

her oar into the water and with just three powerful strokes, her raft was within oar's reach of him.

"Ready, Herior?"

"Abso-Triton-lutely!" Herior was bouncing around on the balls of his feet, like a caged animal waiting to be released. "You don't even need to ask, Authenta."

Zimana blew into a large shell. A whale's cry resounded.

"Am I *ready*? Of course I'm ready!" Herior chortled.

Zimana raised her oar to shoulder-level, pulling her right arm back at the elbow, like an archer about to shoot.

Herior looked back at his classmates, "I was *born—*"

Before he could finish the sentence Zimana hit his left shoulder and he toppled overboard with a splash.

The class burst into laughter. Herior re-emerged, his wet hair awkwardly tossed to one side.

"Authenta! That was so mean! You didn't give me a chance to—"

"I gave you a lesson you'll remember! When I blow the conch-horn, the game starts. And when the game starts, don't expect any favors."

Herior's hands splatted heavily on his wooden boat. He hauled himself up, flopped onto the deck, then clambered to his feet, and shook his whole body ferociously like a wet dog, splashing all those around and earning a 'hey!' from Perfect Princess Tamaya herself.

"Maybe you should practice with *humans* instead of your lesser-species *Collect friends* next time!" Gulusor shouted, his face red from laughing, under his lemon-colored hair. "Or better yet, just stay in the Collect where you belong!"

Herior scoffed and gave a dimple-less smile.

A weight dropped in Alessia's chest. She couldn't really

understand Gulusor's comment, but something about it made her queasy. Then, before she knew it, she heard herself say, "Weren't you challenging him just now, because you lost against him last time, Gulusor? Maybe *you* should learn from those friends he's been practicing with."

Her classmates joined together in a group gasp. Even Zimana seemed gobsmacked. Their stares hit Alessia like a heat wave, burning her cheeks. She'd overreacted *again!* How could she keep making the same mistake?

"Sh-Shut up, landfarer!" Gulusor spat, flustered.

"Oh, pipe down," said Zimana, pulling herself to shore. "You're only angry because she has a point. Now, back to it!"

The students each picked up an oar and divided themselves into the four boats. Alessia and Kella got into the same boat, and were joined there by Naror 'the liar', and two girls and a boy Alessia didn't know.

In the next boat stood Gulusor, backed by five boys and girls built like wardrobes. The boat facing theirs held the Herior-Larthuzor-Sivaria-Tamaya gang, and two other boys, with Herior standing at the front, leading with an eagerness undampened by his soggy state. (To Alessia's surprise, Tamaya loitered at the back not looking terribly keen. It seemed Alessia and the 'perfect princess' had something in common after all.)

Plait-crowned Quina led the last boat, nervously shifting her grip on her oar in imitation of Herior.

"At the sound of the horn... Joust!" Zimana shouted.

The students raised their oars as Zimana and Herior had. There was no escaping. Alessia would have to joust. She'd either win, or be violently knocked into the water with an oar. Prospects weren't bright.

💥 26 💥

The deafening lament of a whale echoed around the amphitheater. Before the sound had even stopped, Alessia's boat rocked violently. Gulusor's boat had shot across the water and rammed Alessia's against the front stall. With one sweep of his oar, Gulusor brushed Naror off.

"So, I need to learn jousting, do I?" Gulusor shouted at Alessia, pushing past his crew members to face her directly.

There was no way she could take him on. She braced herself for a watery crash and said, "You just need to learn respect."

Gulusor jabbed his oar at her but she stepped aside just in time. He swung it across and she ducked.

"Hey! Ready for the rematch?" Herior shouted. His boat had just come in behind Gulusor's.

Gulusor turned away from Alessia and thrashed at Herior. But Herior was ready. He struck back, again and again. With every swoosh of his weird contraption of an oar, a fresh flock of bubbles filled the air.

Then, there was a fast smack. Tamaya fell lightly onto the water in a bed of her own long black hair.

Herior couldn't help but look and Gulusor lunged, hitting Herior straight in the chest. Herior dropped his oar and fell back into his boat, winded.

A choking pain took hold of Alessia. She looked down at her chest, but she hadn't been hit. The pain throbbed and she groaned, wrapping her arms around herself only to hear her groan echoed by Herior who was now holding the sides of *his* chest.

That was weird. It was one thing to empathize with Herior's *feelings*, but was she now also experiencing his *physical pain?*

"What are you doing? Joust!" came Zimana's voice from behind them.

"We can't! They blocked us, Authenta!" defended another girl from Alessia's boat.

Alessia's pain vanished, and was replaced by indignation. She was *furious*. As though she'd just suffered a deep injustice. But why?

She started panting. She needed to get a grip. She looked at her trapped boat.

"Wait... They're all on the far side of their boat. It's off balance. The front of our boat being on top of theirs is the only thing holding them in place."

Kella immediately got it. She planted her oar between their boat and Gulusor's wedged underneath, and pried them apart. The side of Gulusor's boat which had previously been held down, lifted into the air, and Gulusor's whole team toppled into the water. Gulusor pushed down on his teammates as they sank, and managed to keep himself on board.

Suddenly, Alessia couldn't breathe. It was like she was drowning in plain air. She flailed about desperately and Kella spun towards her.

"Are you alri–"

An oar swung swiftly across the front of their boat toppling Kella into the water head first before she could finish her sentence. Quina's boat had arrived.

The fighting intensified. All around, children were whacking each other into the water with cries of pain. It felt more like war training than sports class.

And then out of nowhere, Alessia was thrown into the air. She barely had time to make sense of the new angle from which she was seeing the amphitheater, when she came crashing back down on the boat.

An enormous thunderstorm tore through the water. Alessia's boat was almost vertical, tossed up against a huge wave.

"Come on! You're not going to let a little bad weather simulation kill your game. Keep jousting!" blared Zimana.

Screams filled the air as colossal waves tossed most of the remaining children into the water. Alessia dug what was left of her bitten nails into the floorboards of her boat.

Sivaria grabbed the back of Herior's wetsuit to regain her balance, after a wave hit their boat, and accidentally pulled him out of his entranced fight with Gulusor... and out of the boat. Gulusor, who'd thrown his full body weight forward onto Herior, followed him into the hellish waters.

Their splash was barely audible over the crashing of the waves, but Alessia felt it. She felt the cold water slapping Gulusor's skin. She felt the pang of disappointment in Herior's stomach.

Her over-empathizing problem had reached a whole new level. She was now imagining *all their sensations* as her own – and it was completely out of control.

Suddenly, everything went still. Alessia looked up. The storm simulation had ceased as abruptly as it had begun.

Water trickled softly behind her. She whipped her head around. Sivaria was now standing an oar's reach away, eyes fierce, hair strands straying wildly from her long, dark plait and a single, clean scratch marking her cheek like war paint.

A rush of fury came over Alessia. Hers or Sivaria's – she couldn't tell anymore. The next thing she knew, there was a thundering splash.

The water embraced Sivaria and dragged her deep below for a moment before hurling her to the surface again panting.

Alessia stood on her boat stunned, watching Sivaria's angry face bobbing up and down in the water. She'd had the peculiar intuition that Sivaria would twist her oar at the last second and swipe at her ankles. She'd jumped out of the way just in time, and as she'd done so, her oar had swung up into Sivaria's jaw, sending her flying out of her boat. A roar of cheers came from the crowd.

"Born a girl in Sel-va, Became our Starfish Jous-ta! A-le-ssi-a! A-le-ssi-a! ALE-SSI-A!" Herior belted out, as if it were a football chant.

It immediately caught on, and soon a whole group of students was shouting it joyously at the top of their lungs.

In any other circumstance, Alessia would have been thrilled. But with the cheers from the crowd, a cacophony of emotions was unleashed. Sivaria's anger, Kella's elation, Gulusor's frustration, someone else's bitterness all wailed in her mind. She threw her hands to her ears but it was no good. It was deafening, and it was coming from inside her head.

Zimana climbed onto Alessia's boat and gave her a heavy-handed slap on the back. "You've got a strong survival instinct in you. That's an asset. Keep it up."

Alessia barely heard her above the noise in her own

head. Joy, worry, guilt, relief, jealousy, disappointment. The stadium spun. She was in crippling pain: a stomach ache, nausea, a headache and dozens of other ailments plagued her. She couldn't take it anymore. With a wild cry, she leaped from the boat and bolted up the amphitheater stairs and through the Octopus's Garden courtyard.

Kella ran behind her, pushing past the crowd of students leaving their classes.

"Alessia! Stop! Wait!"

Alessia kept running, tears streaming down her face. But running wasn't helping. She wished her brain would stop – it was excruciating. She trod on somebody's foot and *his* pain seared through her own foot. What was happening to her?

Her chest felt full to the point of bursting. Suddenly, she slammed into something.

Vulcor, the boy from the palace gardens.

"Alessia, what's wrong?" His deep black eyes were marred with concern.

Alessia couldn't believe it. Quiet. Emptiness. Peace.

All the overwhelming feelings had dissipated and in their place was a wonderful nothingness.

"What? Are you memorizing my face as a suspect in your necklace theft?" Vulcor said, his lips twitching to smile.

Alessia burst into an almost manic laugh of relief.

"No, no," she said. "It's... hard to explain."

"Okay... Try."

"I'm happy to see you," Alessia let out finally.

His smile widened, completely changing his face.

"Alessia!" Kella shouted. She'd caught up and she wasn't the only one. A crowd of students swarmed out of the Octopus's Garden, and their random emotions washed over her again.

"Who are you?" Kella asked Vulcor skeptically. "We don't need your help."

"Who are *you*?" Vulcor replied.

Alessia didn't hear the rest of their discussion. All she knew was that Kella felt indignant, because the feeling hit her own chest like a thunderbolt, and she collapsed.

"Move!" Kella ordered the crowd of people flocking around her. Alessia curled up into a ball on the floor, contorting her body, but nothing helped with the pain. Kella put her arm under Alessia's shoulder and half-dragged her out of the Octopus's Garden gates.

"Wimmi..." Alessia mumbled, seeing his face in the crowd of parents.

"Alessia!" he shouted, and ran to the girls.

He grabbed Alessia's face between his hands. She was soaking with sweat and must have looked as bad as she felt, because a feeling of shock and helplessness sprung from Wimmi and reverberated in her head.

"I don't know what happened," Kella told him. "We were just jousting... She *won*! I don't know why–"

"Thanks, nymphlet. You're a good friend."

Wimmi scooped Alessia up into his arms, his nutmeg scent enveloping her, then climbed into an ovehic and zoomed home.

～

"Felthor!" he cried, pushing open the door to their home. There was no response. "Great. Brilliant timing to be out, Fel."

He put Alessia into bed and she sat there hugging her

knees with both fists pressed hard against her head, trying to crush the pain in it.

"Oh nymphlet, my poor nymphlet. What happened to you?"

Through clenched teeth, she cried: "Make it stop. Please. Please, make it stop".

"Alessia!" Felthor barged in the door and turned to Wimmi. "Get some sea lion cheese."

"Ok," Wimmi said, almost tripping as he ran out. He returned with what looked like a white mousse in a clamshell. Felthor pushed a spoon of it into Alessia's mouth as she cried. She slowly swallowed it. Then, everything went black.

✣ 27 ✣

Alessia woke the next morning, still wearing yesterday's clothes and feeling groggy. Light had rolled into her room and a hum of activity came from the city below. She got to her feet dizzily and made her way to the corridor. Felthor was in the kitchen munching on something crispy.

"Alessia, you're awake!" he said, rushing to her. "How are you feeling?"

"Err...ok. A little confused..." she squinted at the light. "What *was* that?"

"It happens to some landfarers, unfortunately. Your mind is so busy figuring out your new environment, that it latches onto understanding what people around you are thinking and feeling... And you get overwhelmed by that."

It was reassuring that this was a common condition, and not just her usual oversensitivity growing out of control. But being delusional because she was a landfarer didn't sound great either.

"To manage it, you need to do two things," Felthor explained, as he helped her into her turtle shell seat. "First, try to reconnect with what *you* were feeling before your mind got invaded by what you think *others* are feeling. Then, while holding that feeling, focus on the person whose sensations you imagined."

"Isn't that contradictory?"

"It's hard to explain but you need to try. If it doesn't work, come straight home. You can eat some sea lion cheese– it's a sleeping remedy."

"Okay," Alessia said, hoping she'd remember all these instructions in that frenzied state. "How do you know all this, when you're not a landfarer?"

"A friend had it, I learnt all of this from her," Felthor replied.

Wimmi barged in.

"Fel! You didn't tell me she was up!" he complained. He knelt by Alessia's side, and spoke incongruently gently for his burly build. "How are you feeling? Maybe you should lie down, nymphlet."

Alessia smiled. "Don't worry about me. I'll just get ready for Octopus's Garden."

Wimmi and Felthor looked at each other.

"What?" Alessia asked.

"Well, it's early afternoon now – you've missed most of the day. Maybe it's better you rest and go in fresh tomorrow?"

"Early afternoon?" She had no idea she'd slept so long. If she hurried she could still make it to Gizma's class – the other teacher Sterna had said might know her dad. "It's okay, I'll go now! Bye!"

It took some insisting, but she finally convinced them she was fit to go, and headed off. On every street corner on the way to the Octopus's Garden, the Drift of the Oculate's abduction followed by the Emperor's threat was playing on loop.

When Alessia arrived, her classmates were lining up for Gizma's class.

"Alessia, where were you?" exclaimed a low-pitched voice Alessia immediately recognized.

"Kella!"

"Are you okay? What–"

"I'm fine! I was just still sick this morning. All better now."

"Sure? Because–"

"Yes! It's nothing."

"Ok. Well, I don't care if you're on your deathbed you are not leaving me alone in rhetoric class again," Kella moaned.

"I'll try." Alessia laughed. "Trust me, if I'd wanted to skip a class, it wouldn't have been rhetoric. I'd have dodged the next Biomimetics class with Iktor."

"Why? Your presentation wasn't so bad."

"It's not about the presentation. I asked him something after class and he flew off the handle for no reason," Alessia explained.

"Pfff, I know the feeling," Kella sighed. "These professors are meant to be all wise and objective and stuff, but all it takes is for you to remind them of someone they don't like, and they take it out on you. Same thing happened with my swimming teacher two years ago. No way to get her to like me."

Alessia froze. Of course! Iktor *did* know her father. He just didn't *like* him. She must look like her father, and Iktor had recognized him in her. That's why Iktor seemed so shocked when he saw her. And whatever vendetta he had against her father, he was taking out on her. That's why he was so mean. It all made sense. If Iktor didn't know her father, he would just have told her so. But he specifically said he *wouldn't tell* her about it.

"Did you see that guy yesterday?" Kella asked, oblivious to Alessia's epiphany.

"What guy?"

"The angry boy."

Kella meant Vulcor.

"I'm there being all friendly," Kella continued, "and did you hear how he answered me!"

Alessia suppressed a smile at Kella describing herself as being 'all friendly'. She may not have been on top form the evening before, but Alessia remembered enough to see a slight mismatch between Kella's version of events and reality.

"I've never seen him at the Octopus's Garden, why was he lurking around? Who *is* he?" Kella asked.

Alessia opened her mouth and shut it again. It occurred to her that she had no idea.

When they got into the classroom, the teacher that must have been Gizma was standing perfectly still by the door. She was a sight to see with her curly black and red hair, eyes looking in opposite directions, and wetsuit of black and purple swirls constantly shifting shape. Alessia wanted to ask her then and there about her father, but she needed some privacy.

"What do we do in Performance Arts class again?" Alessia asked Kella, as they took their seats together. The classroom looked like a dungeon, with windows painted black and walls covered in dark grey bricks. The only light came from a creepy purple jellyfish-shaped chandelier.

"Music, drama, poetry, athletics..." answered Kella. "All

the things that make up our 'cultural dominance', according to the Emperor."

Gizma ambled into the middle of the room, and picked up a pearl from a desk strewn with dried algae, squid ink pots and fish skulls. She dropped it and a Drift appeared. Silver young men and women with dead stares floated in a strange, circular ballet, like ghosts, their long hair falling lank down their narrow backs. They resembled Wimmi's melancholy bandmate and his partner.

"Who are they?"

"Rusalka," a gravelly voice murmured in the girls' ears. They turned to see their professor's face between their heads, a smile creeping across it, then she slowly walked to the middle of the ghostly circle.

"Today," Gizma announced. "We prepare for the most important time of the year: Inundanza – the Celebration of the Forthcoming Water. It's our duty to make sure that this precious *one surviving tradition* rings with the splendor of the scores of other festivals that have been outlawed.

"Our inspiration this year will be rusalka, grindylows, kappas, Minchans... The indigenous populations of Nethuns that have been relegated to the status of second-class citizens."

There was an uncomfortable shifting in the class – as though she'd said something quite scandalous. Alessia looked at Kella expectantly for a translation, but Kella hadn't been listening. She was watching Herior pick a strand of Perfect Princess Tamaya's hair and dip it into the small pot of squid ink on his desk, while Tamaya sat, oblivious, in front of him.

"Kella, what's she talking about?"

"Inundanza. It's just this ancient festival," Kella said, bored. "In the old days, they weren't sure how healthy it was to live in this closed system under the sea. So for three days each year, they'd flood the place, and then drain out the water, hoping that would remove anything toxic. They don't do that anymore. They realized it's useless. But it became kind of an event, and people still stay in their homes for the three days like they did back then. There's the 'pre-festival' for about a week, with performance arts contests in the Palace Amphitheatre and charitable food-sharing feasts. Then there's a big procession at the start of the three days. Everyone from the city walks down the streets together and Octopus's Garden classes perform dances and stuff as they march, and when you pass your house, you leave the procession to go home for the three days."

When they went back to listening, Gizma had gone off-track and was complaining about how misunderstood rusalka were. "...it was the Selvans *own* fault if they drowned in the arms of rusalka. Rusalka are *water spirits.* When you get into a frenzy in a rusalka's hold, it's just like getting into a frenzy in water: you only lose your breath and exhaust yourself."

Alessia turned back to Kella: "So what do you do at home for the three days?"

"Nothing. Eat Inundanza food -- which is mostly different types of seaweed made into cakes, teas and crisps -- and think of the good ol' days," Kella said mockingly, swinging her arm. They both giggled.

"So let the inspiration come to you, beautiful souls of Nethuns. Collect your ideas and we'll discuss them at the end of class," Gizma concluded. Then she left the classroom, and sat cross-legged on the floor in the courtyard, gently swaying from side to side, in a trance-like state, while the students chatted.

"So what are we meant to be doing now?" Alessia asked.

"Preparing the procession, I guess. Don't know, don't care," Kella answered.

Suddenly there was a scream. Running her fingers through her hair, Tamaya had discovered Herior's masterpiece. Kella turned to watch the scene unravel.

This was Alessia's chance. She mumbled a quiet excuse that Kella paid no attention to, and slipped out the door to join their professor.

"Authenta," she began. Gizma didn't appear to react. Alessia was just about to interrupt her professor's meditation more forcefully, when a husky voice spoke.

"You have a question for me," Gizma said without opening her eyes.

"Yes, I was wondering if you knew my father. I don't know his name, but he'd have been in the Octopus's–"

"I do not," Gizma answered simply.

"Oh... perhaps, though, you remember if there was someone who looked like me–"

"There was not."

"But maybe–"

"I cannot help you," she answered cryptically.

"You can't help me, or you won't?"

It was infuriating! Gizma wasn't even trying, or not even lucid, perhaps. And now she was back to rocking on the spot, quietly humming. Alessia let out an exasperated sigh.

She'd need to get it out of Iktor, one way or another.

⚜ 28 ⚜

At the end of the day Kella went to the infirmary to check on her sea cucumber injury, so Alessia headed out of school alone (well, except for the moment Naror accidentally pushed past her in his excitement to watch the Oculate's abduction play for the thousandth time on the Drift platform outside the fence).

Alessia had almost reached the gate when she saw an unexpectedly familiar face. Once again, standing in a far corner of the Octopus's Garden grounds, was Vulcor. Alessia's heart jumped in her chest. Before she could avert her gaze, his coal-black eyes had locked on her.

Why did he keep coming? Was he going to turn her in to the crabs? And what had she said to him yesterday while she was in her weird daze?

She waved, more nervously than she would have liked.

"Are you better?" he asked.

"Yes, no need to worry. Just... something I ate." She smiled brightly, trying hard to look comfortable. "What are you doing here?"

"All the crabs have left this place."

Was that meant to be a threat? Reminding her he'd seen her escaping from crabs in the nereid market. Alessia chose to play dumb. "Yes... they did leave. I heard Sterna Authenta talking about it. They moved to the palace."

Vulcor exhaled loudly through his nose, his eyes still expressionless.

"How are you getting home?" he said eventually.

"By ovehic."

"Stay with me a while first."

It wasn't clear if he meant it as a suggestion or an order.

"Sure, I can," she answered, clarifying that it was her *choice* to stay.

He glanced around, as if to check no one was within earshot. For a boy about her age, he already had a very manly neck. The Octopus's Garden yard was mostly empty now, but he still led them away from the front gate.

"So, do you like this place?" he asked. She wished he wouldn't look at her unwaveringly like that. It was so uncomfortable.

"Yeah. It's cool! I've got this friend Kella, who really looks out for me. You saw her yesterday. And there's these guys Larthuzor and Herior..."

Vulcor let out another unidentifiable sigh. His mouth was a grim line.

Alessia tried to ignore the reaction. "In my previous school, uh, I mean Octopus's Garden, guys like Herior only talked to the 'cool people'. But *he's* friendly with *everybody*. He sat just behind me before even knowing me..."

"Alright, alright, I got it," Vulcor interjected abruptly.

What had she said *now*!

"Basically, it's good to have friends," she finished quietly. "I didn't have many in Selva."

For a moment they didn't talk, and just kept walking to

the back of the Octopus's Garden grounds, out of sight. He seemed calmer as soon as they were alone. He leaned back against a statue of an octopus patting children's' heads with its tentacles.

"I don't really understand the point of having friends," he said eventually.

"What?"

"I mean you always hear the same stories. People trust their friends and get betrayed. Or rely on their friends too much and get disappointed."

"Well, not *always*. Why would they disappoint you?"

"Because most people are stupid or weak. I rarely meet someone I find as smart as myself, for example."

He spoke so naturally, it took a moment for Alessia to register the full extent of the arrogance in his comment.

"Well, people are smart in different ways," she said trying to temper his point for him.

"Not really."

"Come on, you can't say people are all stupid!" she scoffed. "It's a bit pretentious."

"No. If it's true, it's not pretentious – just observant. Let me put it this way. I've always gotten by well enough on my own, and until now, I haven't met anyone I've thought can add value to my life beyond what I can just do myself. So I made it my rule: Don't depend on anyone and don't let anyone depend on you."

Alessia was just about to excuse herself and turn back, when he added, "And I didn't say *all* people were stupid. I said *most*."

Even though she knew what he was saying was completely outrageous, Alessia couldn't help but wonder if his talking to her meant he deemed *her* 'worthy'.

"So why didn't you have friends in Selva?" Vulcor asked.

"Well... I have some weird sides," she said, deciding to be honest.

"Weird how?"

"I'm sort of... *abnormally* sensitive. And I end up having pretty embarrassing outbursts."

He looked at her expectantly. So she told him about the incident with Mr. McCrum's introduction activity.

"Everyone laughed," Alessia finished. "So I waited till breaktime and ran out to the seashore."

"The seashore?"

"Yeah, that school was near the sea. I was just looking for somewhere where I could be alone, without having to worry about others watching me. I used to have a place like that near the river, back in Inverness, that I'd go to sometimes. A 'safe haven'. Anyway, that's what I'm trying to change about myself: to stop being weird. I'm trying *not* to get involved in other people's business and create drama anymore. Just focus on myself like a normal person."

Vulcor just stared, like he was trying to peer into her mind. She averted her gaze and broke the silence: "Well? I shared something with you, it's your turn now."

"My turn for what?"

"To tell me a secret!"

In a matter of seconds, Vulcor's face went from shocked, to angry, to pensive. Finally, he said: "How about I *show* you one."

He walked to the hedge behind the statue.

"A few years ago, I was thinking about how kings have always been petrified of plots to overthrow them. That's why they employed the Aurate, the Oculate and the like, to warn them about what people were saying or doing," he said. "If you were scared someone might try to kill you, you'd plan an emergency escape route, right?"

"I guess."

"So I tried to imagine what passageways *I*'d create if *I* were king. Obviously, one from the Octopus's Garden – which all the previous kings' children attended – and, of course, another from the palace. And they'd have to lead to safehouses and eventually to the Port of Atlantis, in case you really need to escape."

He pushed apart two bushes of blue oak-like leaves. Between them, was a small cave opening.

"Follow me," he said, smiling.

They crouched to walk into the tunnel. It was dark and smelled of wet sand. They turned a corner and came to a passageway lit blue by a huge aquarium of lanternfish.

"This is incredible!" exclaimed Alessia, excitement coursing through her veins. "So, it's totally abandoned? No one else knows about it?"

"As far as I can tell. And the tunnels are all interconnected, so I can also get from here to the port, or to the palace."

"Wait, they go *into* the palace? That's a huge security breach! I mean, maybe that's how that guy was abducted?"

They reached the end of the passageway and found themselves at the bottom of a flight of stairs.

"Watch out for the steps here, they're a bit uneven and steep," Vulcor warned.

He pulled himself up the first step, which was almost a meter high. He turned to offer her his hand, but she'd already pulled herself up beside him.

They made their way up the irregular dirt steps until they reached a smooth, sandstone wall at the top, next to which was the entrance to another corridor. Vulcor leaned against one side of the wall with his full body weight, and slowly it swiveled to reveal a cave behind it.

The cave could have been an antique shop. The ground was strewn with brightly-colored Persian rugs. From the stone ceiling, old, torn tapestries and broken, dark wood beams hung down. Vulcor expertly ducked and dodged them and made his way to the back of the cave. A thick seaweed curtain hung there, letting in only a sprinkle of dappled light.

Alessia was awestruck. "This place is..."

"Kind of a mess, I know," Vulcor completed, "but it has its perks..."

He drew back the curtain to reveal a gaping space opening onto a magnificent view of the palace and below it, rolling out to them like a patchwork carpet, the old town.

"It's breath-taking," Alessia murmured.

She sat on a pile of cushions on the floor and Vulcor sat opposite her.

"So, this is one of the safehouses you mentioned."

"That's what I gathered. I think initially it must have been a storage place for possessions confiscated from landfarers. Then one of the kings must have decided it would make a good safehouse, given the nice view on the Palace on one side, and proximity to the Port of Atlantis on the other side. We're so high up, it's pretty impenetrable – apart from by the tunnel. I come when I need to get away from it all, and hide out for a bit." He hesitated, then added: "It's *my* 'safe haven'."

For a moment their eyes met, then they both looked away.

"So, what are *you* hiding from?" she asked.

"Sometimes at home, people can get a little... overbearing." His face darkened.

"Hmm... Overprotective parents?"

He hesitated for a moment. "Something like that," he answered, unconsciously running the back of his fingernails along his jaw. "There's a role everyone's impatient for me to play. It's kind of like what you said when you were talking to yourself in the palace gardens, this 'handcuffs of expectations' thing."

Alessia would have been mortified that he brought it up, if she hadn't been so happy he liked it.

"I constantly feel *pushed*," he continued. "Even in my sleep! My recurring dream is that I'm driving an ovehic and it's barreling at full speed into a crowd of people, and I can't control it. Anyway, that's stupid but it's just to prove the point."

"It's not stupid. I always wonder about my recurring dream too," Alessia reassured him.

"What is it?"

"Well, I've had it ever since I can remember, although – come to think of it – I haven't had it yet in Nethuns," she said. "It's the strangest thing. It's just me lying in my bed in pitch black darkness, and this soothing voice talking to me continuously. It's dark, so I can't see who the voice belongs to, and I know they can't see me either. And that person seems perfectly content with a monologue. They don't expect me to make conversation, or look or act a certain way, since I'm hidden in darkness. And it's just..."

"A relief," he finished for her.

They both started fidgeting uncomfortably, and Alessia rushed to change the subject.

"Hey, you know what this place would be perfect for?" she said.

"What?"

"Hide and seek"

"What's that?"

"Hide and seek! You must have it here?"

He looked at her blankly.

"One person hides and the other has to find them?" she explained. "With all these tunnels and safehouses, it would take ages! And it's so silent, you'd have to be extra careful not to make any noise and give yourself away..."

A sly smile curled his lips, "Okay, let's give it a try."

"You have to count to one hundred," Alessia instructed, getting up.

"Let the games begin," he whispered with a defiant smirk. He closed his eyes and started tapping count on the side of his thigh.

Alessia turned, and tripped on one of the rugs in her enthusiasm. She grabbed onto a copper pot to regain her balance, and it hurtled to the ground with a dramatic clatter. She whipped her burning face around. His eyes were still closed but he was grinning now. She turned back and quietly tiptoed out, squeezing past the sandstone door that was still ajar.

She decided not to go back down the stairs, and rather to take the passageway to the right, lit by Drifts of different species of glowing fish swimming on the spot like little ghosts. Wooden beams lay parallel to each other about half a meter under the curved ceiling, crossing over one large beam that stretched down the whole length of the tunnel. She considered her options. Tapestries hung from the walls and she could hide behind one of those, but it was a little obvious. There were also random little nooks in the walls she could squeeze into. But again, anyone looking would find her quickly. She took a right at a fork in the passageway. Here, the tunnel was lined with old rowboats, fishing nets and broken oars.

Alessia crouched behind one of the rowboats. Just as she was wondering how much longer he had with his counting, footsteps echoed nearby.

She held her breath. The uncontrollable grin on her face was pressing against her cheeks so hard, she felt they might burst. The footsteps stopped right in front of her. Then she heard one more. And another. He was turning back and forth, hesitating. She could barely resist the urge to jump out and scare him. But she decided it was better to let him struggle for a bit. Another step clacked, then another, followed by a grunt of impatience. She covered her mouth to stifle a laugh. The footsteps went back towards the safe house. She pushed back the rowboat she was hiding behind, ever so slightly, to watch him.

Her heart stopped. A chill ran down the back of her neck. It wasn't Vulcor. An adult wearing a cloak stepped softly down the echoey corridor. She'd seen that cloak before – in the Tiding, on the Oculate's abductor.

❧ 29 ❧

Alessia fell back against the wall, staring straight into the bottom of the rowboat. For a while she sat there, conscious only of her chest moving up and down with her quickening breath. She couldn't bring herself to look again. She pictured herself peering out from behind the boat only to come face to face with the hooded criminal.

Time passed and she couldn't hear Vulcor. What if he'd crossed paths with the trespasser?

She shook the thought. She needed to focus on her own situation first. If the cloaked man caught her behind the boat, she'd be trapped. She needed to get to another hideout: a safer one, where she could watch him without being seen.

She pushed the edge of the boat up ever so gently with the tips of her fingers to peer out. The hallway seemed empty. After another deep breath she slid out.

She tested the sturdiness of an oar on the wall with her hands, shot another nervous look around, and stepped on the oar, letting her weight onto it gradually. It held. Without losing time, she scampered up the two oars laying above it.

Now the ceiling beams were level with her shoulders. She reached out to the closest one and hoisted herself onto it. She sighed with relief and lay still on the beam for a moment, watching the corridor below.

Then, she crawled along. The splinters on the beam tore at her wetsuit. Another outfit destroyed in her first week. She was on a roll.

When she reached the beginning of the boat corridor, she continued along the beam of the tapestry corridor, towards the safehouse. Below her, was the top of Vulcor's head. He crept soundlessly down the corridor, gently lifting each of the tapestries, before silently placing them back against the wall.

"Psst."

His eyes shot up to where she lay. A smile crept upon his face and he opened his mouth to say something. Alessia quickly pressed a finger to her lips, hoping Nethunsians shared the same signal to be quiet. His face dropped. She motioned her head to the tapestries on the wall. He understood. He stepped back and ran up one of the tapestries, gathering it into a climbable bunch, then swung himself onto the beam in front of her. It seemed her dreaded climb-the-rope gym class exercise had practical applications, after all.

"There's someone here," she whispered more quietly than she'd ever whispered.

His eyes briefly filled with alarm, before settling back to their stony expression.

"The cloaked man who took the Oculate. He went this way," she indicated.

Only a short exhale betrayed an emotion from Vulcor's side – but whether that emotion was frustration, disappointment or relief was impossible to tell.

"Come," he muttered. He turned towards the safehouse, and crawled along the beam.

When they finally reached the safe house, they nodded at each other and jumped off the beam, trying to land as quietly as possible. Without saying a word, they crept down the dirt steps.

They were at the final stretch: the lanternfish aquarium corridor that led to the tunnel to the Octopus's Garden. With another nod, they started sprinting forward, and finally burst out of the tunnel.

They ran and ran across the Octopus's Garden yard, past the building, up to the gate. Alessia grabbed its white, iron bars and bent over, panting. Vulcor looked back in the direction of his secret tunnel, wiping sweat off his brow.

"I don't know how he found it! I've never seen anybody there!"

"Well, at least we can say we've officially found the best hide and seek hideout." Alessia tried to smile, to alleviate the tension.

"Yeah, that hiding place was a good call. I'll remember it if I need it again," Vulcor said. Then he added with a wry smile, "You're good at getting yourself out of tricky situations it seems. Running away, wearing disguises, hiding..."

She ignored the comment to avoid going into the whole crab chase story. "Actually, my hiding place wasn't originally on the beam. I was behind one of the boats."

"Now that's rubbish," Vulcor said, before they both relaxed into a laugh. "I'd have found you immediately, the guy can't be very smart."

Alessia's laughter weakened, then died swiftly as she was thrown back into what had just happened.

"We have to find the Emperor's Guard, to tell them

about him," she began. Vulcor's face fell serious again. "Now we know how he got to the Oculate..."

"No, we don't," Vulcor snapped.

"Wh-What? Yes, we do!" Alessia insisted. "We have to tell them. The abductor could still be there! They'll send men into the tunnels and find him."

"There's not a *chance* he's still in there. What, you think he's just hanging out there for the fun of it?" he snarled.

"No. I think he was obviously looking for somebody, scouring the place like that, and he could still be looking! Anyway, what does it cost to tell them?"

Vulcor scoffed. "What does it cost? It means the Emperor will know about the tunnels!"

"So what? Were you seriously planning to use them again? You'd feel okay to keep 'chilling' in this criminal's lair?"

"It's not his lair! Don't you think I'd have seen him in there by now if it were? I'm there all the time!"

"Well, you didn't see him today!"

"So much for you *not* creating drama around other peoples' business anymore," he cut in. "And then you're surprised when I say people disappoint you."

There it was. The cold gust of his judgment had finally blown in. Alessia was obliterated.

"So what are you saying?" she stammered. "That I'm one of those 'weak, not smart' people you've categorized in your little world? You don't know anything about me! You barely know me at all. I'm here trying to be nice, and you... d-do you *hear* yourself?"

She wasn't good at arguing. There was no structure or sequence to her thoughts and she was flustered. He, on the other hand, had a wild flame dancing in his eyes. He was enjoying this.

"Did I say you were weak, or stupid? No, I said you're not focusing on yourself, like you said you wanted to. I'm trying to be honest with you. Would you rather I lie and only say pleasant things?"

"What? No, I—"

"*You're* the one calling yourself weird, and *I* get told I'm insulting you? *I'd* never say something like that about you."

"You just did!"

"I definitely did *not*. I don't even *think* it, why would I say it?"

"Well, you obviously *do* think it."

"And why would I? The first time I saw you, you were duping crabs, for Neptune's sake! And now you tell me this story about how you stood up for a guy everyone was teasing. Why would I think that's weak? To be honest, I can't believe *you* thought that was bad. On the contrary, it shows you're *not* like those other stupid people I was talking about."

Alessia was confused. He was angry and condescending... but somehow he was defending *her* now. She had to get back to the subject at hand. She made her voice quiet and cold.

"You *can't* go back there."

"It's my place Alessia. It's my call. We're not telling anyone," he growled at her icily.

She looked at him in disbelief. His face was stern. He was downright foolish in his stubbornness.

He was right. She shouldn't be bothering about him. She turned to walk away. He tried to reach for her arm but she brushed his hand off and swung open the gate.

He watched her darkly, but didn't follow her. The disappointment stung. She fumbled at her belt pocket to find her sand dollar.

"Junonia building," she snapped, and shot off in an ovehic.

Her cheeks burned, and it made her even angrier to think her emotions were displayed so conspicuously. She sat back and let her gaze rest blankly on the buildings rushing by, while fiddling with the sand dollar in her belt pocket to keep herself from biting her nails.

A sudden sharp pain seared in her finger. A cut. From a scrap of paper tucked into her belt. She pulled it out and read.

'You have to leave. You're in danger. They're going to sacrifice you because you're the daughter of someone important. I can't say more (sorry). Don't tell anyone about this note or I'll be in danger too.'

The ovehic came to a halt, jerking her forward.

She read and re-read and re-re-read the note, as if it would make a difference. The words swam in her head.

She was in danger. Just like she'd heard Wimmi say on her very first night. And she was in danger because of whoever her father was. And someone *knew* who her father was.

Who could have left that note on her? Was it someone at school? Gizma hadn't gotten close enough. Was it Kella? Vulcor? It couldn't be! Why wouldn't they tell her directly? Was it the hooded man?

She felt sick. She needed to get off this hovering Ovehic before she threw up.

As soon as she stepped down, a strange intuition that she was being watched slithered into her mind. She was right. An old lady was staring at her, mouth ajar, her puffy eyes strikingly pale blue; as though a more vivid blue had been washed out of them, by too many tears.

Alessia was hit with the distinct sensation that she

recognized this woman. Not only that, but also that this was a woman she'd been looking for, for a long time.

Alessia's mind raced to piece together who it was. Then, she remembered. It was Dolia, from the department store where she'd bought her clothes. Dolia notoriously saw her missing daughter everywhere. Alessia must have seen that delusional recognition in Dolia's eyes, and now her own mind was fixating on it.

A cry from behind interrupted them.

"Alessia! Oh, thank Poseidon," came Felthor's voice. "I came to pick you up at the Octopus's Garden, in case you still felt poorly, but I was late and couldn't find you there." He hurried out of his ovehic, glancing at the old lady warily before politely smiling at her.

"Dolia Authenta, how do you do?" he asked sweetly.

An intense discomfort stabbed at Alessia's stomach. That was Felthor's. This was growing out of control. She was having another episode.

She had to stop herself before it got worse. She tried to remember what Felthor had taught her. She needed to focus on what *she* was feeling. What *was* she feeling? The crippling fear of having another public outburst.

She ran.

"Alessia!" Felthor called, running after her. "Alessia, are you okay, dear?"

"Yeah, I just felt a little..."

Felthor nodded knowingly. "Another attack."

"I guess..."

They turned back to where it had happened, but Dolia was no longer there. She was halfway down the street, hurrying away from them, apparently spooked by what had just happened.

"It's okay, dear, it'll happen," Felthor patted Alessia on

the shoulder, distracted by the sight of the elderly woman limping away.

"My, what happened to you?" he exclaimed when he noticed her ripped Nethuns suit. Alessia shrugged and gave an apologetic smile. She was going to have to start preparing answers to that question it seemed.

❦ 30 ❦

Preparations for Inundanza soon became peoples' main focus. Nereids were at every corner, covering the streets with a dark green foamy material, traditionally believed to cleanse the air, though now understood to be purely decorative. Covered in that thick, rich moss-like carpet, the whole place looked like a fairy habitat in a magical forest, and children rolled around in it enjoying its fluffy feel.

Female nereids had now left their tunics to don the typical Inundanza costume: an emerald-green dress fit for a medieval princess with a front laced bodice, long tulle skirt and flowing sleeves.

They stood in groups and sung upbeat jig-like songs that had passers-by visibly itching to dance.

"What you can't wash with a jug'a mead,
Trust Inundanza rains to take heed,
I came a-following, the Siren's Call
Jolly Inundanza to all!
Jolly Inundanza to all..."

In the Octopus's Garden as well, a contagious

excitement filled the air, and the students' focus in class had all but vanished. Of course, 'Inundanza Spirit' was the least of Alessia's distractions. She was in danger. It hadn't just been Wimmi overreacting to the grindylow attack.

And what her infuriatingly cryptic note-giver didn't know is that she *couldn't* just 'leave', like he'd suggested. The grindylow had come *all the way to Scotland* to kidnap her. Even if she were to go back, they'd just find her again.

So as Alessia sat in her Selvan Studies class going over her options (and reminding herself to keep blinking so the eager professor wouldn't realize her eyes had glazed over), she was forced to conclude that her best chance of survival was her fledgling investigation. She had to figure out *who* her father was, to find which of his enemies wanted to 'sacrifice' her.

The background noise had stopped. The Selvan Studies teacher Moxia – the passionate woman, who'd substituted for their first Biomimetics class – was staring at her, large eyes bulging from her bony face.

"Uh... Can you repeat the question?" Alessia asked weakly.

"Of course!" Moxia answered, completely impervious to her students' lack of attention by now. "I was asking you as someone who *lived* in Selva to tell the rest of the class how Selvans perceive the Cold War."

Alessia drew a blank.

"Well," Moxia picked up again, unbothered, "it's quite fascinating. Selvans are convinced that the Cold War was a conflict between two great Selvan Powers – the USA and the USSR – and that the Cold War is over!

"Apart from those very high up in Selvan governments, Selvans aren't even *aware* that Nethuns exists, let alone that it's another key player in the Cold War. So, to answer your question, Quina, indeed the Cold War still goes on to this day between Nethuns and Selva, but since the Emperor's Order of spies was dismantled, there have been fewer interactions between the two worlds."

The sound of a wave crashing resounded, marking the end of the day's classes, and the beginning of Alessia's first time hanging out with Kella after school.

"So annoying. We need to go to this Inundanza offering thing tonight. Vera's being totally unreasonable," Kella rolled her eyes.

"Vera?"

"My mother. It's really no big deal. I don't understand why she can't just go without us!"

"What is it?"

"Just an old tradition. In the past, some people couldn't buy enough food to last the time they'd be locked in during the rains, so everyone had a duty to bring one needy family one day's worth of food. And that's what we'll do now. Ugh. Anyway, on the bright side, I told her we were rehearsing for Inundanza Processions after class so we have some time beforehand to buy costumes," Kella said conspiratorially. "My mom wants me to wear the child costume *again* this year. What's she thinking? Sivaria and PP Authenta have been wearing the adult one for two years already! I'm buying the adult one, I don't care. She'll be furious, but whatever. She's *always* furious at me for something or other. I may as well give her a reason to be."

They boarded their ovehic giggling, and Kella directed it to a bazaar for humans. But when they arrived, its archway entrance was barred by fifty guards.

"Move away, move away, order of the Emperor," one of the guards shouted dispassionately.

"What's happening? We need to go to the bazaar," Kella asked the guard.

"Not today, Nymphlet."

"No! This is my only chance! We *need* to get in today!"

The guard gave her a formidable look, "Did you hear what I said? Do you want to continue this discussion in jail?"

Just then, there was a loud cry and a group of guards barged out of the market and threw a man to the ground.

"I didn't know he'd be using that stuff to kidnap the Oculate, I swear! I just sell seaweed constrictor. How could I know he'd use it on a person?" The man's shoulder-length hair had fallen like a curtain over his face, only letting through his large sniffling nose.

"And you didn't think to give this information to the Emperor's Guard after the Tiding? Give me a break, sea-scum. You'll pay for your crime."

The man's voice rose a notch, "No! Please Authentor, I beg you! I told you everything I know. He-he was a bald man, wearing a blue suit, about my age. That's all I remember."

"I hope for your sake that's not the case. If you're no longer useful for the investigation..."

"Move along, move along!" shouted the other guards, pushing back the crowd. Alessia and Kella were taken in the flow.

"I can't believe it. I'll be wearing that ridiculous kids' outfit till the end of my days!" Kella whined, her egg-shaped nose glowing ruby-red in the middle of her pallid face.

"Did you hear what he said?"

"What?"

"The shopkeeper said the guy who kidnapped the

Oculate was bald, around his age, and wore a blue suit. Doesn't that sound familiar?" Alessia asked.

Kella blinked.

"Iktor!" Alessia completed excitedly.

"I guess... But a lot of people could fit that description. You think..."

"Well, he gave me that whole angry speech about inherited powers and how the humble can beat people who believe themselves powerful. Couldn't that be about Espior? After all, he inherited his Oculate power..."

And if he could lash out like that against an innocent schoolgirl, it wasn't too much of a stretch to imagine him resorting to crime against powerful *adults* he disliked.

"I mean, he's probably not the only one that hates the 'powerful'... But I guess it *could* be him," Kella said. "If it *were* him, Triton, that would be exciting! Imagine if he got arrested!"

Alessia remembered the Emperor's threat... What might Iktor be willing to do to avoid such a fate? She might just have found the key to get the information she needed on her father – and the danger she was in.

❧ 31 ❧

They whizzed through the new town until they arrived at a neighborhood that was now oh, too familiar to Alessia. They were in Seagrass-City, the neighborhood near the cliffs overlooking the Port of Atlantis, where Ebrie, the blue girl, had said most 'non-human' species were forced to stay, and where Alessia had accidentally eavesdropped on the blue couple and grindylow on her first day.

A large round table had been set up in the middle of a group of seaweed-covered buildings. The table was laden with swirly seaweed crisps, stuffed shells, and the special chalices Nethunsians used to drink Atlantis Mead: hollowed-out, copper-colored lobster tails, that slid into purpose-built crevices in the table.

A motley crew of different creatures stood around. Grindylows were huddled in a group sneering at the nereids chatting with humans. Statuesque rusalka, including Wimmi's bandmate, floated together in a corner, their long, bedraggled hair gently swaying in an invisible breeze, like the rusalka Drifts from Gizma's Performance Arts class. And a small group of what Alessia guessed were sirens, with white swan wings and onyx black skin, hovered beside them without speaking. There was the comfort of familiarity, but no warmth between the groups.

"Hello nymphlets!" cheered a deep voice straining to get to a high pitch. It came from a broad-shouldered woman standing by the table. She had a short crop of white hair to match Kella's, and a hot pink wetsuit with baby pink swirls.

"Ugh... Vera. Pretend you didn't see her," Kella said to Alessia, trudging in the opposite direction. It was obvious enough it was her mother. She had the same bulbous nose as Kella, but it was accompanied by bulging eyes, protruding cheekbones and full lips, so it looked less striking than it did on Kella's delicate face. Also, unlike Kella, she was permanently beaming.

Alessia turned to follow Kella and accidentally bumped into a child. There was an angry high-pitched squeak.

"Oh!" Alessia stopped dead. It wasn't a child at all. It was a small, goblin-like creature with yellow skin and a head shaped like a bowl, filled with water.

The creature shook its fist angrily at Alessia, causing the bits of turtle shell from its tunic to rattle and continued on its way to the center of the festivities.

"Kappas," Kella answered Alessia's unasked question. "They're a bit sensitive about these things because they die if the water in their head spills."

"What?" exclaimed Alessia in horror. Before she could ask for clarification, she was interrupted by a loud cry.

"Yago! Finally found you!" rang out a familiar voice.

"Poseidon almighty," Kella breathed. Herior was a short way ahead of them, lifting the kappa Alessia had just almost killed, onto his shoulders.

"Watch it, young Tanushi! You almost spilled me!

Second time this evening. You humans should be more considerate!"

"Yago, you won't be angry when you see who's here!" Herior said.

"Young Tanushi, you know I could never be angry at you," the kappa answered rather incongruently in a voice as snappy as before. "But you also know it's *Yagora,* not Yago. You Atlantides made us change our Penglini names, the least you could do is use them right!"

"Ah Ya-ya, you're so funny. Come," Herior proposed, as though the Kappa had any choice but to go with him, given she was perched on his shoulders. Herior cupped his hand over his eyes, looking for someone and spotted the girls. "Oh, look at that! It's the fearsome twosome, just in front of our guest of honor."

Kella waved at Herior while Alessia turned to see the 'guest of honor' Herior was referring to. Larthuzor was there, walking beside a very old man sitting on a hoverboard shaped like a flying fish.

"Hi," Larthuzor said. The crocogull was gone, but he was cradling what looked like a sea otter... with lobster claws.

"What's that?" Alessia asked.

"This is a lotter. We had to make some repair ointment to rub on his pincers, they were all cracked. And this is Yuftor, my grandfather." The old man beside him used a harpoon-shaped walking stick to pull himself forward, like an oar on a gondola.

"Pleased to meet you," Yuftor smiled. Then he looked up at the kappa Yagora who'd just arrived on Herior's shoulders. "And my dear friend is here!"

"Yuftor! Perfect timing. I needed to see some friendly faces," Yagora said, as Herior lifted her down. "If you knew how much pressure we're under at work, to figure out the malfunction in the Orichalca mine that services the Octopus's Garden. We tell them again and again – it's not the tech! The tech is fine. There's tampering! Foreign intrusion! But who listens to us?" Yagora ranted on.

"It sounds like *you* need a laugh, Yagora!" said Yuftor with a chortle, and they started chatting away.

"So we have the honor of having our Starfish Jous-ta here!" Herior said to Alessia, flashing his dimpled grin. "Be kind, though. I'm not ready for another savage defeat at Jousting yet!"

Kella opened her mouth – no doubt to make a quippy comeback – but before she could say a word, Herior got distracted by a group of sirens walking by.

"Gotta go!" he said.

He started shouting after one of the sirens, "Niva! Niva! Don't be looking at me like that! Come on, I won fair and square. You shouldn't play Scales if you're going to be a sore loser. You can't cheat the tiles – you owe me!"

He walked off towards them, as one of them raised a wing to hide her face, pretending she hadn't seen him.

Kella flicked a dismissive hand in his direction, though it was pretty obvious to Alessia that Herior's inattention had hurt. She tried to change the subject.

"It's my first time seeing kappas! How come we don't have any of these species in our class?"

"The Emperor's Specist Laws," answered Larthuzor. "Basically they prohibit humans mixing in too much with others..." he glanced around and lowered his voice. "...as the supposedly 'superior species'. It's based on a report that said the most efficient society would give different species different roles based on their predispositions. Which most people would agree is complete nonsense... but the Emperor buys it."

"I thought there was this Ten Tackles contest to decide what roles everyone should play?"

"For humans, there is. Other species' roles are pretty much predetermined," Kella explained.

"But humans and other species are together *here*?"

"Well..." Larthuzor lowered his voice further and his sharp crescent eyes darted a glance in Herior's direction.

"Humans here aren't really seen like the rest of humans," Larthuzor began carefully. "You might hear some people call this place the Collect. They say Seagrass-City is where the Emperor 'collected' the humans that... well, that are worth *less* to the Empire. It's not true of course! They're mostly just Detached: Guppies with no parents, old people with no relatives, runaways, landfarers without guardians. But once they're in Seagrass-City, they're treated differently. They don't get to enter the Ten Tackles like other humans. They're given jobs perceived as low impact to the Empire; as entertainers, for example."

Alessia thought about Wimmi. Was he from here too? Or had he *chosen* to become an entertainer – and second-class citizen?

"There are exceptions, of course," Larthuzor continued. "My grandfather always talks about how he struck a deal with the government to let a guppy from Seagrass-City attend the Octopus's Garden, back in his day. And my parents did the same to get Herior into the Octopus's Garden after we became friends."

Alessia remembered, and now understood, why Gulusor the lemon-haired bully had said Herior had 'sub-species friends', and told him to go back 'where he belonged', before the joust. She was even more furious now.

"Look at that!" They overheard Yagora the kappa saying to Larthuzor's grandfather. "Iktor's here too, visiting Metella! I hope he's doing better, sweet finboy."

Alessia and Kella exchanged a look. Just ahead, Iktor was kneeling in front of an elderly woman and a male nereid. Iktor held the back of the old woman's hand against his forehead with such deference that it took Alessia a while to recognize her cruel professor. Then he got up and walked away.

"Do you know Iktor?" Kella asked Yagora.

"Yes."

Alessia's heart jumped. If the kappa knew Iktor, did she know Alessia's father too?

"That's great!" Alessia said. "We have so many questions about him! Can you tell us–"

"Nope." Yagora eyed Alessia with disgust.

"But–"

"You almost killed me, Tanushi! What did you think? Go ask him yourself," Yagora concluded, shuffling away with Yuftor. With a sorry shrug, Larthuzor followed his grandfather and the kappa, stroking his lotter's pincers.

"Pff.... That Yagora could have been more understanding. You just made a mistake! Kappas *themselves* are major pranksters and always accidentally endangering each other!" Kella tried to reassure Alessia.

Alessia looked back glumly at the old woman Iktor had been with – Metella. One more missed opportunity to find out about Iktor and her father.

But the longer she looked, the more she got the bizarre impression that Metella was trying to lose the male nereid with her.

"Um...Could you go and check if the rusalka group are still over there in the corner?" Metella asked the nereid.

"No need! I just caught sight of one. Why, do you want to talk to them?" he answered unsuspectingly.

"Oh... no, it's okay. It was just to know. Could you... um... get me a chalice of Mead?"

Metella was nibbling on her lip, stealing glances at a passage between buildings that lead to the cliffside.

"Kella," Alessia whispered.

"What?"

"I feel like this Metella woman's trying to slip away from her nereid friend. I wonder if it has something to do with Iktor."

"I'll distract the nereid, you follow her and shell me to say where you are in ten minutes," said Kella, glad to have an excuse to stay away from her mother.

She marched straight up to the nereid. "Can I ask you something?"

"Sure! Happy to help with any question, nymphlet," he answered amiably.

Metella didn't miss a beat. The moment the nereid turned to Kella, she backed away noiselessly.

"The man you were talking to earlier, is his name Iktor?" Kella asked.

"That I don't know," the nereid replied.

Metella was halfway across the courtyard already.

"Is he that woman's son?" Kella asked.

"I'm afraid I couldn't say," the nereid replied.

Metella reached the entrance of the passage out.

"Did he used to live here?" Kella asked.

"Good question. I'm not sure," the nereid replied.

Kella sighed audibly. "So, when you said you can answer any question, did you just mean 'how are you'?"

Alessia bit her lip to stop herself laughing out loud at

her brash friend, then followed Metella out of the courtyard.

Metella spun around as if to check she was alone. Just in time, Alessia ducked beneath some tall, red tubular grass.

She crawled behind Metella to the edge of the cliff. Metella shot a final glance back, then made her way down a flight of steps carved into the cliffside, and disappeared into what must have been a cave.

"Sea of Cortez – the Ruins," said a muffled voice.

Alessia took out her shell and directed Kella to where she was. They went down the steps, and found themselves in the cave, looking at a giant soap bubble like the one they'd used in Biomimetics.

"It must be an *illegal* one, hidden out here, like this," Kella said in awe.

"Do you think we should–" But before Alessia could finish her sentence, Kella had already pulled her wetsuit neck over her nose and swiped open the bubble. They stepped in, called out the location Alessia had heard, and a moment later, found themselves under the sea, apparently at the other end of the world.

elestial sunbeams coming from the surface danced around them, giving a spooky, sacred quality to everything, like light rays in a cathedral. In front of them stood the ruins of a giant, stone pyramid, seaweed bursting from cracks in its rocks. All around it were the remains of smaller, broken buildings: piles of rocks, lonely pillars, and square archways to nowhere. They were nothing more than a playground for the fish swimming in and out of them now.

Alessia and Kella fit their shells into their ears.

"Where are we?" Alessia asked.

"I think these are the remains of Azlanu. It was a city state like Atlantis, south of the Gulf of California. But it didn't bend to the Emperor."

A shiver ran down Alessia's spine.

"Look up there!" Kella pointed to the top of the stone pyramid. A faint glow flickered across an open doorway under the pyramid's flat roof.

Without waiting, they set about climbing the large staircase leading up the front of the pyramid to the opening. Great totems carved into fearsome creatures with heads twisted backwards, and squared serpents and crocodiles, loomed over them. The stone stairs under their feet were smooth and slippery with wear, and partially crumbled away. But they finally reached the top and peered in.

The ravages that had occurred to the rest of the Azlanu buildings hadn't spared the pyramid. Its inside had been almost hollowed out. From what had obviously once been a complex structure of chambers and tunnels, there now remained only a few broken platforms sticking out from the walls into the void that was the center of the pyramid. The floor at the bottom of the pyramid was a sea of rubble, and standing on that rubble, holding fishbowls containing glowing jellyfish, was a circle of almost thirty people, kappas, and other creatures.

Metella floated down to join them, using the remnants of the floors jutting out from the walls as stepping stones.

A friendly man at the bottom greeted her. "Welcome!" he said through a phosphorescent conch-horn, that allowed his voice to propagate through the water. "Grab yourself a walrus milk, and join us!"

Alessia couldn't tell if anybody she knew was there, since they wore their wetsuits over their noses – although one looked suspiciously like their strange professor Gizma with her perpetually changing wetsuit pattern, and another may have been Naror, the so-called 'class liar', flanked by his parents.

The attendees would lower the neck of their wetsuits just long enough to suck their drink from the tip of a sealed walrus tusk, and then cover their faces again. Some looked at each other, with shells in their ears: probably chatting in their minds.

"So who are we spying on?" an excited voice whispered

through Alessia's shell. Herior appeared beside Alessia, and Kella almost tumbled off the pyramid in shock.

"What are you doing here?" Kella's voice snapped through the shell.

"Larthu was with his grandpa and when I saw the fearsome twosome slipping out looking suspicious, I couldn't help myself. So what are you up to?" Alessia could imagine the dimples at the corners of his mouth deepening mischievously under his pulled-up wetsuit neck.

But she had no intention of telling a blabbermouth like Herior about her investigation.

"Shh – they're starting!" she said, pointing inside the pyramid.

"I'm Jor, and I am a follower of Chaco," said the man at the bottom in his conch horn, once Metella had grabbed her walrus milk. "I'd like to welcome you to our evening meeting, which I'll be chairing, and extend a special welcome to any new attendees that have come along with our regulars. If you'd like, you may introduce yourselves."

A few people introduced themselves through the conch horn, stating just their first name, and confirming they were 'a follower of Chaco'. Then the man continued:

"Let me begin the session by reminding us why we're here. We are followers of the Chaco doctrine, the teachings of the great visionary, Chaco. Through his writings – the Chaco Shield – he bestowed upon us knowledge of the Five Sensate Powers, which would one day unite the creatures of the Earth and Sea, and provide a framework for a better society. We're a fellowship aiming to keep alive the knowledge of his manifesto, despite the destruction of the scripts on which it was transcribed, and despite the perversion of its meaning into the Emperor's Shield. All those sharing our purpose are welcome among us and pledge to preserve the secrecy of this fellowship. Now, our speaker today will be Metella Authenta."

Alessia and Kella looked at each other.

"Thank you, Jor. I'm Metella, and I am a follower of Chaco."

Everyone in the crowd blew a bubble into the water in response.

"Today, I want to talk about the misconceptions the Emperor is feeding about the Chaco doctrine. A former Oculate, who was actually the mother of our current Oculate, Espior, famously said, 'The Sensate's challenge is not to fall powerless to their own power,' and it's clear that's exactly what's happened to our Emperor. Some of you know, I had first-hand experience with him. I worked in the palace, for the old king Rexol. I was there when the Emperor attacked, and I fled with a child. As far as I know, we were the only survivors."

Alessia gasped, but not because of Metella's story. Something sharp pressed against her neck. The prong of a trident as big as a garden rake. Next to her, Herior stiffened. Another prong from the same trident was wedged against his throat.

"Well, look wha' we has here," snarled a young man's voice from behind them.

"They be eavesdroppin', I reckons," said a young woman. She had suntanned skin and long, blonde, wavy hair, and was holding Kella by the point of *her* trident.

There was also something off about her that Alessia couldn't quite pinpoint. And then she realized: the woman was speaking underwater without a shell, yet Alessia could hear her with the sharpest clarity.

Herior strained to push the trident away, and the shell

in Alessia's ear transmitted his voice yelling "Let go of us!",
as he cried out something unintelligible into the water.

"Help! We're being kidnapped by pirates!" Alessia tried
to shout too. It was useless. The water garbled her voice like
Herior's.

But her captor spun her around to face him, keeping the
trident pressed into the base of her skull. He had the same
tanned complexion, and long, light hair as the woman.
"Pirates?" he spat. "What makes ye think we be pirates?"

So, they couldn't just *speak* underwater, they could *hear*
her distorted underwater voice too.

"Well...I guess because you talk like pirates," Alessia
gurgled, a little perplexed by the question. "Like those
pirates from Cornwall, in the movies."

The man gasped. "*We* be speakin' like *Cornish pirates*?
What bilge! Cornish pirates be speaking like *us*! It's them
that keeps encounterin' us and gettin' entranced by our
beautiful voices and imitatin' 'em."

If she weren't being held up at trident point, and
slightly terrified, Alessia would probably have had to choke
back a laugh.

"Ye scabby seabass," the man continued. "How dare ye
compare us to ye lily-livered *humans!*"

Compare them... to *humans?* Alessia looked down. It
turned out she'd missed a *critical* detail about their captors.
They had fish tails in the place of legs. They were merfolk.

"Now, I wonders what'em fellas down below'd give
fer some eavesdroppers watchin' their business, when it
be mighty *private* business," said the mermaid holding
Kella. She sniggered but Alessia sensed a hesitation
in her.

"Shouldn't you check with your boss first?" Alessia
ventured a guess.

"And how does ye know *we* be not the boss?" the merman sneered.

"Am I wrong?" Alessia burbled as boldly as she could in the water, hoping that she *wasn't* wrong.

The merman shoved her back around, apparently frustrated.

"Come on, we gots to take 'em to Pinca, the picaroon be right," the mermaid said quietly to the merman.

"Arr... AYE, aye. Ye be right," he huffed. "Weigh anchor."

The merfolk started to swim away with Alessia, Kella and Herior held up against them.

"Wait!" A kappa had floated up from inside the pyramid. "I know that boy from Seagrass-City. He's friends with my sister, Yagora. Leave him with me. I'm not your enemy, I'm a follower of Chaco."

The merman grunted indifferently and pushed Herior to the kappa.

"No!" Herior yelled into the sea and the girls' shells. "I'm not leaving without the girls!" But before he could make a move, the kappa pounced on him and wrestled him to the ground with uncanny strength.

"Herior!" Kella screeched, but the merfolk tightened their grip on the girls and sped off until all they could see of Herior was the cloud of sand from where he was writhing on the seafloor, in the distance.

The girls screamed and thrashed. But it was no use. The merfolk had them each in a bone-breaking hold.

Kella changed tack. She dragged her fingernails up against the grain of the mermaid's tail, scraping off four lines of glittering fish scales. The mermaid shrieked in pain, as a bright blue ink-like substance flowed out of her wounds.

Alessia tried the same but ended up doing little more

than mildly tickling the merman. Why, oh why had she bitten her fingernails to the stubs!

She tried elbowing the merman in the ribs. He grunted and lurched forward slightly. This was her chance. She wriggled downwards, but a massive smack of his fish tail sent her right back up in his grasp, with the soles of her feet smarting.

Next to them, Kella was still jerking herself around. The mermaid only had hold of her wrist now. Suddenly, Kella bit her hand. The mermaid yelped and let go. Kella leaped forward and swam away frantically.

Alessia used the moment of distraction to yank the merman's hair. But he just pressed the point of his trident deeper into her neck.

"Okay! Okay!" Alessia coughed.

"Silena! Get her!" the merman yelled at the mermaid.

The mermaid started swimming towards Kella, but howled from the pain in her tail, and stopped. Then, to Alessia's surprise, she cleared her throat, and started singing. It was a strange, ethereal sound. Deep, resounding, sad and gentle, like a whale's song. It washed over Alessia leaving her filled with an indescribable peace.

Kella stopped swimming, turned and drifted back towards the mermaid, as if she were sleepwalking.

When the girls awakened from their trance, they were firmly in their captors' grips, swimming towards the mysterious merfolk boss.

33

"We're from Atlantis. If you let us go, when we get back, we'll say you rescued us," Alessia tried. "We'll say we got lost and wandered here, and you saved us. The Emperor's Guard would reward you I'm sure! They're really worried about safety these days."

The merfolk both puffed out with laughter.

"Ye hears that Silena? The Emperor'll *reward* us!"

"Necho Authentor," the mermaid Silena said in a mock authoritative voice. "Since you have heroically saved these precious children from being lost, we hereby forgive all merfolk for their past transgressions against our great Empire!"

"Be not talkin' about what ye doesn't know, picaroon," the merman Necho scoffed at Alessia.

A faint noise came into earshot: what sounded strangely like party music. The sound got louder, and the sea brightened. Alessia craned her neck as much as she could, given she was restrained against Necho.

They were swimming towards a magnificent phantom ship. A huge vessel, with three masts and five white sails, sailing under water. And inside, a party was in full swing. Loud laughter competed with loud music, and bright lights shone from the portholes, revealing the silhouettes of people chatting and dancing.

"Pinca!" shouted Necho. "We gots a surprise fer ye!"

"She ain' gonna hear ye from *here*, Necho. We gots to bring'em in."

"But won't they die if we brings 'em in? It be only deads in there. I thought we always gots to negotiate with pris'ners *outside* Caleuche."

Alessia and Kella threw each other a nervous glance. There being the possibility of negotiation was promising. There being "only deads in there" – less so.

"Why doesn't one of you go in to get her and the other guard both of us?" Alessia suggested.

"Shut yer bubbler. Don't think we doesn't know what ye be up to," he snapped at her. "Come on we'll give it a try."

The merfolk pushed the girls towards the ship. As they approached, Alessia understood what they'd meant. The raging partygoers inside were indeed dead.

Some were merely deathly pale, with blue lips and hands – others were full-on *skeletons*. All were roaring with laughter, and singing and dancing nonetheless.

Necho thrust Alessia towards one of the ship's open portholes. Alessia screamed and kicked, and pulled to wrench herself from his grasp.

"Don't do this, *please!*" Kella yelled out to the merman and, through her shell, to Alessia's mind.

Alessia grabbed onto the window frame and pushed her body outwards from it, as Necho tried to shove her in.

A skeleton in a tattered sailor's uniform looked at them from the inside, and said something in French that Alessia didn't understand, but assumed to be a not-so-helpful suggestion that they enjoy the party.

"Let me go!" Alessia shouted at Necho.

Necho pushed harder. Her body edged closer and closer to the threshold and a cold, numbness spread in her chest. She was going to die.

"What in the seven seas be goin' on?" said a melodic woman's voice.

Necho let go of Alessia and they stumbled back from the boat.

"Pinca, yer highness," said Silena, bowing her head with deference.

"We gots pris'ners," said Necho excitedly, looking up at the porthole above the one he'd tried to shove Alessia through.

The most beautiful woman Alessia had seen in her life swam out of it gracefully. She was also a mermaid, with dark brown skin, and honey-colored locs roughly attached in a long ponytail that cascaded down her colorful, patterned tunic.

"In that case," she said calmly. "Let's negotia–" Her eyes rounded as she saw Alessia. "Be ye... who I reckons ye be?"

"Who do you–"

"Answer the Queen!" Necho said, but Pinca turned to him sharply and he stopped.

"M-my name's Alessia. I'm a landfarer. My mother died when I was a baby and my father... well, I didn't know him, but I think he was from here. Do you know him? Is that why you recognize me?" Alessia asked hopefully.

Pinca considered her carefully. Then she eyed Kella, and shot a glance around them.

"Be this a trap?" she asked.

"No! You know him? Tell me who he was... or is! Where can I find him?" Alessia blurted.

"If what ye says be true, that'd be mighty sad indeed," Pinca began. The Cornish pirate accent that had sounded comical on Necho and Silena, sounded purely regal on her. "But I jus' can't be sure." She turned to Necho. "Release 'em."

"But Pinca, we can negotiate favors!"

"Release'em," she repeated to Necho calmly but firmly. "We can't take the risk. An' if she be who I reckon, let 'er do what she be destined to do: that be their favor t' us."

"What am I destined to do? And what's sad? Tell me what you know!" Alessia pleaded.

Pinca gave her a knowing smile. Then she clapped her hands, and in an instant, the ship and merfolk vanished, and in their place, a single stone floated down to hide among the other stones littering the sea floor.

"Wow," Kella said through her shell.

"What happened? Where did they go?" Alessia shouted, rushing to the ground.

"I'd heard stories, but I didn't know they were *true*," said Kella. "The rebel mermaids, the drowned people they take in and give a second life to in the Caleuche ship, the ship turning into a stone to evade capture."

Alessia was turning over one stone after another but it was useless. There was no way to find the right one.

"Come on, it's no use. And we've got to find Herior," Kella said gently.

Alessia kicked the rocks in frustration, and they started making their way back.

"Who do you think they took you for?" Kella asked. "What was all that about your destiny?"

"I have no idea! Why wouldn't they tell me? It's so

infuriating!" Alessia groaned. Was it her destiny to be sacrificed like the anonymous note said? Did the merfolk refrain from killing her *now* so she could be killed in a different way *later*?

"You said you think your father was from here and they recognized you were his daughter. Then he must have been someone important to them," Kella started.

She was interrupted by Herior's voice ringing out in their shells. "Where are you? The kappa just brought me back to Seagrass-City for my safety. So annoying! At least he took my word when I said you hadn't seen them inside the pyramid, and didn't go warn the other Chaco followers. Anyway, now I'm with Larthu and we've got reinforcements. We're coming back to get you."

"It's okay, we got away," Kella said, the top of her nose pinkening above her wetsuit. "We'll see you tomorrow at school."

She looked up with grinning eyes, but the sight of Alessia quickly drained the joy from Kella's face.

"I know it's frustrating," she said. "At least this whole ordeal taught us *something*. Did you hear what Metella said?"

"I guess. We know Iktor's mother was a servant, and they escaped from the Emperor's Revolt," Alessia said, distractedly.

"No! Didn't you get it?"

"Get what?"

"Ah, I keep forgetting you aren't from here. You don't know," Kella thought out loud.

"Know what?"

"About the rumor."

"Poseidon almighty, what rumor?" Alessia said.

Kella snorted a laugh, then quickly covered her mouth

to hide the pig-like noise. "Sorry, that wasn't very graceful. You caught me off guard with your perfect local jargon!"

Alessia giggled. "I'm catching up. Now, tell me the story!"

"Right! Right," Kella said. "So, when Iktor escaped he'd have been a toddler, right?"

"Yeah..."

"Well, after the Emperor's Revolt, the Army High Commander conducted this major nationwide search on the Emperor's orders. The rumor says it's because they realized one body was missing after they went through the remains of the Rexol family: the king's grandson. They say that before the killings, a maid smuggled him out... And the king's grandson was a toddler at the time..."

Alessia's mouth fell open, releasing a shocked air bubble into the water.

"So Iktor would be the lost heir of the Rexol Dynasty..." she muttered, barely believing her luck.

"If *that's* not a good reason to hate the Oculate – famously the only member of the Rexol Court who switched allegiances to the Emperor– I don't know what is! Alessia, I think you were right about him being the abductor!"

Alessia finally had the means to make Iktor talk about her father! As soon as they could find proof of their theory, of course.

"Poseidon Almighty..." she said again, smiling uncontrollably under her wetsuit.

34

They arrived at Kella's home so late that they'd barely fallen asleep when it was already time to wake up and don their Inundanza costumes.

"Don't say a word," Kella warned. While Alessia wore the adult costume – similar to the princess dresses she'd seen the nereids wearing, but pearl white in color – Kella was stuck wearing the child's costume for one more year. It was an ill-fitting tunic with layer upon layer of green kelp fringes, from neck to toe. Little children looked like cute balls of moss in that outfit. On Kella, it looked like the garment a caveman might have come up with by covering himself in mud and rolling around in a pile of leaves.

As soon as they arrived at the Octopus's Garden, Herior jogged up to them shouting, "Nymphsters!"

The boys' adult Inundanza costume was a smaller variation on their everyday wear, with special breeches, cinched in after the knee, and two small emerald capes draped over their shoulders.

"So? What happened out there?" he asked. Then, his eyes fell on Kella's outfit.

Dimples tugged up the corners of his mouth. Alessia winced in anticipation. But before he could comment on Kella's questionable fashion sense, Kella distracted him by proudly announcing, "We're investigating a crime."

Alessia glared at her. The Iktor theory was meant to be a secret!

"A crime? Wicked! Which crime? Let me guess – that no-good Tamaya is behind it," Herior declared loudly, shooting Perfect Princess Tamaya a glance.

Kella's nose flushed crimson. She grabbed Alessia and stormed into the classroom.

Completely oblivious, Herior sauntered in behind them and vaulted over his hands onto the next bench.

"So?" Herior tapped Kella's shoulder. "You're not going to tell me?"

"It's a serious matter. Not for the likes of you," she snarled, slamming her bag down on the desk.

"Ouch! I'll have you know I'm great with serious matters," Herior said.

"Not this. This involves a high-profile crime *and* someone we know," Kella flaunted. "In fact..."

"In fact," came a voice that wasn't Kella's. "You are now in class and it's disrespectful to be chatting."

Iktor was standing right behind them, the vein splitting the 'V' of his eyebrows, pulsating.

"And do you know what peeves me even more than those I catch chatting?" he said through gritted teeth, turning his attention to Alessia. "Those who were chatting moments ago, and fell quiet just in time, thinking they can outsmart me; that I can be manipulated..."

"N-No," Alessia stammered. "I didn't–"

"No?" Iktor leaned back. There was a malevolent spark in his eyes.

"Are you *defying* me again, Alessia Authenta?" he breathed dangerously.

"No," Alessia snarled. "I'm not."

Kella gasped and Herior almost fell off the seat he'd been swinging on.

"What did you say?" bellowed Iktor.

"I said…" began Alessia with a cruel teasing smile, "I am NOT defying you!" she blared louder than Iktor had. She couldn't explain it. She was just *consumed* with a violent loathing. "I was NOT being rude the first day, and I am NOT being rude now. *You're* being rude to *ME*. And I'm not going to stand the unfairness."

"Enough!" Iktor yelled. His face was purple with anger, and the vein on his forehead looked like it might burst.

"You judge me but you don't know me," Alessia screamed, bitterness coursing through her. "So typical of people of your kind!"

It was as though another person's voice was talking through her mouth. What did she even mean by saying "people of his kind"?

Suddenly, she swung around the table and ran down the stairs to the center of the room, to Iktor's desk. Iktor did the same. She looked deep into his eyes and his eyes bore into hers, and – in perfect unison - they screamed: "Get out of my sight!"

An eerie silence fell over the room.

All at once Alessia was winded. She bent double to catch her breath and steady herself. White noise in her ears gave way to a now familiar cacophony of emotions. This time, though, one stood out stronger than the rest.

Iktor fell back, bewildered, against a tapestry adorning the classroom wall.

Alessia ran out of the room and down the hallway. She

knew by now what she needed to do to quiet the voices. She focused on what *she* was feeling. And she already knew exactly what that was. It was so beautifully definable, that she could pick it out from amid all the chaos of her mind like a loose thread, and simply tug to watch her episode unravel.

More than the fear, more than the anger, more than the humiliation: she was feeling the satisfaction of an epiphany.

She reached the outer fence of the Octopus's Garden and dropped to her knees in relief, letting her head fall back to drink in the soothing blue of the fake sky.

The epiphany itself seemed almost absurd... And yet, she just knew it was true.

As she'd stood in the middle of the classroom, an impulse had electrified her. An impulse of Iktor's. An impulse that she should absolutely be kept from seeing what was concealed behind the tapestry at the back of the classroom.

There was the proof she'd been looking for.

But the Inundanza procession and three-day quarantine was about to begin; and that would give Iktor plenty of time to better hide whatever it was.

She had to get it now.

35

A lessia took stock of the unusual bunch that she was now making her accomplices. Herior, the popular boy eager for an adventure; Kella, the cynic just waiting for another reason to complain about her teacher; Larthuzor, the gentle, animal-loving boy turned rebel; and herself – Alessia – accidental ringleader of a task force against an authority figure in a foreign land.

Of course, this wasn't ideal. Alessia would have preferred to keep their investigation between Kella and herself. Unfortunately, Kella had finally caved and told Herior about their theory during Biomimetics, and when Alessia had told Kella about her hunch that there was something behind the tapestry at the beginning of lunchtime, Herior had been listening in, and insisted to join in the fun.

Larthuzor walked to Iktor's classroom door with his current patient, a horned penguin (or 'pengwhal') waddling by his side like a chubby unicorn. He said something to the professor while pointing to the courtyard. Iktor followed him out, but shut the door behind him, and started fumbling through a set of keys to lock it.

Alessia, Kella and Herior exchanged a tense glance. But Larthuzor knew what to do. He screamed and dashed to the courtyard (with the pengwhal tottering behind him). Distracted by the apparent urgency of the situation, Iktor ran after him, forgetting to lock the door.

As he ran past Alessia, Kella and Herior, in a bizarre instinctive reaction, they started slapping each other's hands to mimic 'playing'. Herior caught Alessia's eye and suppressed a smile.

"Poseidon almighty, we need to get better at this," muttered Kella.

Thankfully Iktor was too focused on Larthuzor's made-up emergency to realize how suspiciously they were acting.

"Go," said Herior.

One by one they slipped into the classroom. Alessia peered back to check nobody was watching, and closed the door behind them.

"Quick, we don't have much time," Kella said. The change in atmosphere was palpable.

They rushed down the stone steps, their feet pattering like a rainstorm.

"It's behind there," Alessia pointed at the tapestry.

Herior ran ahead and yanked on the tapestry bringing it crashing to the ground along with the curtain rail that held it.

"Oops," he turned back to the horrified girls with an impish grin.

Where the tapestry had hung, embedded in the wall, was a large, smooth, night-blue rock.

"Oh no," groaned Kella.

"What?" Alessia and Herior said in unison.

"I know what this is. So typical. Of course, I should have expected this from a Biomimetics professor."

"What?" urged Herior.

"A Dead Man's Chest."

Alessia and Herior looked at her blankly.

"It's an impenetrable vault."

"Nothing's impenetrable," scoffed Herior.

"Yeah?" said Kella. "You know, sea cucumbers?"

"Of course!" Herior chuckled. "That thing you—" Alessia signaled him not to finish his sentence.

"Yeah, that thing," snapped Kella. "Well they learned how to replicate the properties of catch collagen to make impenetrable safes. This," she knocked on the rock, "is an indestructible rock, like a kind of diamond. It liquefies to perfectly fit in the hole in the wall where you want your vault – like a sea cucumber would – then, it hardens, and only liquefies again to open if the owner wills it to. So, as I was saying: impenetrable."

Alessia's stomach dropped. She was so sure this was going to be the answer. But here she was, facing another dead end. Still clueless about her family, and still in danger.

"On the plus side," mused Kella. "It proves you were right. He's *definitely* hiding something. You wouldn't go to those lengths just to keep thieves away from regular valuables or—"

"Well how do we open it?" interrupted Herior, now bouncing from one foot to the other like an impatient child.

"Did you not- I *just* said only the owner can. It's linked to his brain. The owner has to transmit his brainwaves onto the rock—"

"Cool! Let's find the brainwave-transmitter device!" Herior said, throwing open desk drawers helter-skelter.

"What? There's no device. The owner presses his head against the rock. We can't open it without Iktor willingly–"

"We don't need a device? Even better!" exclaimed Herior. He leaned his head against the rock, and closed his eyes in concentration.

"I'm telling you," Kella repeated in a voice strangled with restraint. "Our brains are as unique as our fingerprints. The brainwaves we'd send are different than the one Iktor would send, so it won't open the... Get off me! What are you doing?" Kella swatted away Herior's attempts to pull her head towards the Dead Man's Chest, after his own head failed to open it.

Undeterred, Herior turned to Alessia and before she could move away, pushed her head against the rock. Nothing. He tried angling her head differently. Still nothing. He let her go.

"You couldn't just take my word for it, you *had* to try. Are you satisfied now?" Kella nagged.

Alessia let her head drop back against the rock in dismay as a lump grew in her throat. She'd dragged her friends into this failure of a mission, all in the selfish hope of finding something she could use to get information about her father. But was she even sure Iktor knew something?

She thought about what she'd felt from behind his eyes. She remembered it so vividly: how badly he'd wanted her out of the classroom, and away from that tapestry...

"You really think the most high-security vault in existence..." Kella was grumbling at Herior, who was now scratching the surface of the rock with his fingernails.

"...a vault which has never been broken into..."

Alessia watched her friends hopelessly. She wished so much the vault would open. She wished so much she hadn't wasted all their time.

"...would be openable by the likes of us – three children just trying to–" Kella froze in her rant.

The dark blue slab turned into a gel-like substance and receded into the four edges of the square. Alessia staggered back. Herior nodded and smiled in approval. Where the blue rock had been, was a hole the size of a shoebox. And standing proudly in its center, on a blank piece of paper, was a vial filled with a bright green liquid. Her random intuition had been right. Iktor had really been hiding something there.

Suddenly, Larthuzor's voice blared from outside the classroom door, "One more thing, professor. I've always wondered about, um... Sea snails!"

"What about sea snails?" sighed Iktor's voice, exasperated after what must have been a long, dreary conversation about every animal that came to Larthuzor's mind, as he tried to stall him.

"Kelpy's hooves," Kella whispered. "They're here!"

36

Herior snatched the vial while Alessia grabbed the documents Herior had thrown around and flung open a drawer to stash them back in, tearing a chunk out of her delicate Inundanza skirt as she shut the drawer on it accidentally. They bolted up the stairs to the door.

"Get on with it boy! *Good Tirnanog*," complained Iktor.

"As I was saying, since *we are now at the door of your classroom*," Larthuzor continued in an even louder voice. "I will make one final point. Without further delay. Right this very moment. And that final point is as follows. It is a point about the... um... sea snail shell!"

Alessia, Herior and Kella were almost at the door when a key clanked in the lock. They froze.

"Did I leave this door unlocked?" Iktor barked at Larthuzor.

"I-I dunno Authentor, I–"

Alessia leaped to the hinge-side of the door, and the others followed. The door swung open, and Iktor stepped in.

The three trespassers held their breath. They were only concealed by the swung-back door.

Iktor stopped in his tracks before walking down the stairs. He was so close, Alessia could see his bald scalp prickle with goosebumps. His vault was open; the tapestry, splayed on the floor. He knew now someone had taken his precious vial.

He whipped his head back to Larthuzor, thankfully turning from the right and leaving them in his blind spot.

"Where is it..." he hissed through gritted teeth.

"Wh-where is what?"

He marched back out of the doorway. Alessia, Kella and Herior crowded behind the door hinge to watch the scene through the gap with the wall.

Iktor stood so close to Larthuzor that his chest almost touched the boy's nose. The pengwhal, apparently defensive of its 'healer' shuffled up to Iktor and rested its horn against the professor's knee to stop him getting closer.

"Don't you play the fool with me. You know perfectly well what. So, it was you the whole time? What was it – did the old man put you up to it?" Iktor spat, livid.

"I swear," Larthuzor said, slowly stepping back. "I have no idea what you're talking about."

"No idea? So it's just a coincidence that Yuftor Nolol's grandson insists I go out to the courtyard with him, and pesters me with nonsensical questions while my...my...my..." he stammered.

"We should go now," whispered Herior.

"What?" Alessia choked. "We can't!"

She finally had something she could use to get information from Iktor! She couldn't risk them losing it now by getting caught.

"It's now or never. He's far enough. Larthu's pulling him away."

"Herior's right," Kella said. "It's now or never," and with that she crept around the door, and dashed out of the classroom.

A look of admiration washed over Herior's face, dimples bursting onto his cheeks.

Larthuzor seemed to be making a conscious effort not to draw attention to Kella as she stayed by the door, gesturing to the two others.

"Herior, don't!" Alessia whispered, but without losing a moment he took five *giant* and theatrically silent steps around the open door and joined Kella.

Iktor kept ranting at Larthuzor, his back turned to them.

Alessia sighed with relief. Herior had the vial and he was out.

She wanted to tell him to leave, now. She needed the vial out of Iktor's reach. But Herior wouldn't see her signaling behind the door.

"Give. It. Back," Iktor sputtered, prodding at Larthuzor's chest. The pengwhal tried headbutting Iktor's leg with its horn, but the horn bent to the side. (Apparently, *that* was this one's ailment).

"You hear me, finboy?" Iktor continued.

"Hey! Iktor's attacking Larthu!" yelled Herior.

Alessia's heart stopped. What was he doing? After managing an almost impossibly silent escape, he was now drawing all the attention in the world to himself!

The courtyard fell quiet, except for the rippling sound of 'Scales' game tiles spilling, as a group of boys stopped playing and looked up. Students started gathering around Iktor and Larthuzor.

It suddenly clicked. *Herior was drawing all the*

attention in the world to them. The best place for a student to hide... was in a *crowd* of students. Herior was trying to offer her a safe escape. He was foolishly putting the vial at risk for her.

"You!" Iktor turned to Herior, letting go of Larthuzor. Then he faltered, distracted by the ever-growing congregation, now whispering and pointing at him. "Y-You're his friend. You helped him. You took it, just now! Give it!"

"Took what?" shouted back Herior, leaning towards the professor in defiance. Alessia started creeping around the door.

"TOOK WHAT?" Herior insisted, slamming his arm through the air for emphasis.

Alessia passed the door, and joined the others inconspicuously.

"You took my-my..." A veil of anger fell over Iktor's face and he added, "You *know* what!" in disgust.

"I was with Herior the whole time," Kella blurted, out of the blue. Surprise rippled through the crowd. Kella straightened her stance and lifted her chin. "Herior spent his lunch time with *me*. I'd know if he'd taken something."

Iktor's demeanor changed from furious, to uneasy, and back again. Without saying another word he pushed past them, marched into the classroom and slammed the door behind him.

At the same moment, Gizma appeared in the doorway of her classroom and looked at them all in horror, the moving patterns from her wetsuit going completely berserk.

"Guppies! The procession's about to start! You're meant to be in your positions! Good Tirnanog! Hurry!"

She ushered them to the Octopus's Garden gates.

"Here, you take it." Herior slipped the vial into a pocket

of Alessia's skirt, without making eye contact. "It'll be safer with you. He suspects me."

"Thanks!" she exclaimed, unable to hide her excitement. The vial was finally safely in her possession.

"Come on, I'm just glad it got you out!" he answered.

For a moment Alessia was confused, then she understood. He thought she was thanking him for helping her get out.

"Oh, yes. It was really brave of you."

"It's the least we can do! You're the brave one, always standing by us and stuff. Just returning the favor."

Alessia gawked at him. She was the *'brave one'*? That was a first! Drama queen, crybaby, attention-seeker, okay. But brave? What on earth had made him think that?

Gulusor shoved past her to get into his procession position.

Was *that* what Herior was talking about? Her snapping back when Gulusor had called Herior's friends "sub-species"? But that wasn't a *brave* moment! That was a *weak* moment when she'd let her emotions get the best of her!

"Come quick! We'll miss our turn!" said Quina and Naror, each grabbing Alessia by one arm.

As she was dragged away, Alessia thought she saw someone– a certain familiar 'senile department store owner' someone – watching her intensely from behind the Octopus's Garden gates. But a moment later, Dolia had disappeared into the crowd filling the pavement.

🦑 37 🦑

The murmur of the procession advancing towards the Octopus's Garden grew, hushing the students.

Leading the procession was a ring of men in traditional Inundanza outfits. They twirled with both arms raised so the capes hanging from their shoulders flapped out ominously, like the wings of a bird of prey, then swooped down onto one knee in perfect synchronization. In the middle of the ring, three musicians played their instruments, sitting cross-legged on a hoverboard shaped like a giant manta ray.

After the dancers, came a crowd of men and women, each holding a fishbowl with a different-colored jellyfish, like the ones Alessia and Kella had seen carried by the Chaco followers. But what *these* men and women were honoring became clear shortly after, as the Emperor Oscor floated in, in a bubble surrounded by giant crabs.

After the passage of a group of people collectively dressed as giant squid which intermittently blew jets of ink into the air, the end of the procession came into sight, cueing the Octopus's Garden to join.

Alessia's class was the first to elongate the snake. Dancers turned around her, their skirts and capes spiraling out radiantly, and Alessia excitedly whirled in turn, a small cog in the big movement.

She spun and spun until suddenly, she found herself face-to-face with Iktor. He was staring at the hem of her skirt. Alessia followed his gaze to the large tear from where her skirt had been caught in his desk. In his white knuckled fist, he was clutching a small piece of matching fabric.

She spun away at double-speed. He knew it was her. And it was all wrong. This wasn't the right timing. She was meant to tell him she had the vial when it was safely stored away, not when it was still *on* her!

She felt his eyes boring into the back of her head. Her heart pounded in her throat. She couldn't risk him stealing it back.

She twirled frantically, pushing through the crowd of students, away from him.

"Hey!"

"Watch it!"

Great. In case anybody hadn't realized it yet, she was cementing her image as a weirdo.

"Are you okay?" said Kella, jolting her out of her frenzy.

"He knows," Alessia mouthed. "Iktor knows."

"What?"

But Alessia didn't have time to reply. Iktor was nudging his way through the procession. She looked around desperately for an escape. They were in the new town now, and so many people were joining and leaving the procession here, that it had almost merged with the mass of onlookers.

She knew what she had to do. It wasn't how she'd planned this to go down, but so be it.

She pulled out the vial and held it just high enough for

Iktor to see, shaking her head at him with a reproving look. Iktor went deathly pale.

Time to run. She shoved the vial back into her pocket. But, as she did, there was crumpling sound. From a scrap of paper in the pocket. She fished it out.

"What are you still doing here? They're going to kill you!"

Great. Her mystery note-sender had struck again. And Iktor was steamrolling through the crowd now.

Alessia stuffed the note away and elbowed her way out of the current to disappear into the mass of onlookers.

❧ 38 ❧

Alessia weaved through the cheering spectators, head ducked between her shoulders. She may have been small and agile, but Iktor had more pushing force, and he was gaining on her.

And now, they were heading straight back to the deserted old town. No more people to serve as obstacles between them, and no witnesses for whatever he'd do to her.

The crowd thinned and as soon as she could, she started sprinting. Moments later, a beat of footsteps thumped behind her.

She snatched vases and statues and any object she could off the walls and hurled them back at him, but he always dodged them.

"GIVE IT BACK! YOU DON'T KNOW WHAT YOU'RE DEALING WITH, PICAROON!" he screamed.

"I KNOW VERY WELL!" she yelled. She only took a breath after every few words so he wouldn't hear her panting. "I'LL GIVE IT BACK. ONCE YOU TELL ME. WHAT YOU KNOW ABOUT MY FATHER!"

"YOU LITTLE SEAWEEDBAG!" The beat of his steps quickened. He was going to catch her.

The Octopus's Garden was ahead of her. The front gates had been left open. She had an idea. She charged through the gates but swerved left. She was almost in his reach now.

She sprinted up to the side entrance. There was a glimmer of blue as the symbol of her father's trident lit up on the mosaic doormat. Iktor's fingertips brushed against her back. She zoomed past the doormat, into the building and turned back just in time to see Iktor somersault backwards through the air. He crashed on the ground and rolled down the hill into the blue oak-leaf hedge.

The doormat had risen like a mighty wave and thrown him back as he'd tried to pass the threshold of the door – like Wimmi had told her it would in the past, to stop anyone without a trident entering. Without waiting further, she ran through the Octopus's Garden and back out the front gate. There was still no sign of movement from him. Part of her was relieved she could escape, and part of her, anxious that he'd been *really* hurt. But she couldn't risk losing the vial now, and she ran on to Junonia building.

Just as she arrived, Felthor emerged from the procession wearing his Inundanza costume, with a glowing blue lanternfish Drift floating above a pearl in his hand.

"A safe and splendid Inundanza to you, my dear!" he said, hugging in her shoulder. "Isn't it just lovely bubbly?"

They watched the parade roll on, while streams of people flowed out from it to their homes, until one of those people was Wimmi.

"A safe and SPLENDID Inundanza to you both!" he shouted, crashing into his little family with arms wide open. "Quick! Let's go up for the best part!"

They floated to their apartment, and Wimmi poured three lobster-tail-chalices of a bright blue, sparkling drink.

"Your Spirulina wines, if you please."

"Can I?" Alessia asked.

"Not to worry, it's alcohol-free," Felthor said. "Just some festive, fizzy seaweed juice!"

"Oh... yum..." said Alessia, trying not to flinch.

They spent the rest of the evening on the living room balcony, happily snacking on seasonal blue and green seaweed-based munchies, while watching the parade meander through town. When it ended, the lights that served as stars in the Atlantis sky, "rained" down magically in commemoration of the Inundanza rains of the past.

"Well! That would be bedtime!" Wimmi chimed, his orange face beaming.

With that, he scooped up Alessia to cradle her in his strong, nutmeg-smelling arms. She yelped. A glimmer of light bounced off the vial as it tumbled from her pocket. With a surprisingly fast reflex, she grabbed it and stuffed it back in.

Thankfully, Wimmi was oblivious, looking up at the last of the raining stars. And while Felthor's crinkly eyes were looking roughly in her direction, his gaze was distracted as usual.

Wimmi put her down in her clamshell bed (after their own mini-procession through the apartment) and left her with a "sweet dreams nymphlet".

Before going to sleep, she took out the vial for a final look. There were inscriptions on it she hadn't noticed before. Strange characters in squid ink. She couldn't read them, and yet, there was something familiar about them.

But by the time the fatigue of the day caught up with her and she dozed off, she hadn't figured out *what*.

𝕩 39 𝕩

Alessia woke in the middle of the night, with a flash of realization. She picked up her shell. Kella didn't answer. So she tried her second-best option.

"Hullo?" came Larthuzor's sleepy voice.

"Larthu! It's me, Alessia." It still felt odd to transmit her thoughts wordlessly through her shell, though she *was* grateful there was no chance of Wimmi and Felthor overhearing her discussion with her criminal accomplice.

"What's wrong?"

"Nothing... I'm sorry for calling in the middle of the night, I just couldn't wait. On the vial we stole, there are inscriptions. They don't look like Atlantide alphabet – or like any Selvan alphabet I know. But I've seen similar ones before... and I remember where now. On a dolphin skull, when we were in the Sulu Sea."

"On a skull?"

"Yeah, I know. It's a bit grim."

"If you saw them on a skull, I think I know where they're from. In Penglini, sages used to write important things on animal skulls. That one must have been left there by someone leaving Penglini southwards through the Sulu Sea. The good news is I can work it out."

"Really?" Alessia said.

"Yeah, my grandfather has some forbidden botanical books left in Penglini language... we use them to get recipes for our animal medicines. He kept a Penglini to Atlantide dictionary so I can understand them too. Can you describe the glyphs?"

Alessia rolled the vial around in her hands examining it.

"Well, there are two columns of glyphs. It starts with a letter that's like a diamond-shaped fish, facing head up... oh, it's too hard to describe."

"No, no, continue! I'm drawing it now," Larthuzor encouraged her.

Alessia continued, paining to describe both columns of symbols until the early hours of the morning.

"I'll shell you back once I've worked out the message," Larthuzor said.

"I thought I heard some noise here!" Felthor popped his head around her door. Alessia jumped. Thankfully the vial was hidden in bedcovers. "My dear, what are you doing up so late – or rather, so early? Is everything okay?"

"Yes, yes! Just... nothing. Going back to sleep now," she blurted, hating how suspicious she sounded.

❧ 40 ☙

The next two days of Inundanza break were deplorably anticlimactic. Iktor didn't take the bait and reach out to tell her about her father, and Larthuzor didn't shell with news on the translations.

Instead, Alessia wrote back to her stepfather George – who was still perfectly clueless, and asking her about boring things like the weather in Scotland in his letters – and she spent the rest of the time reading Wimmi and Felthor's books. Needless to say it was pretty frustrating to have nothing better to do than read about *others'* adventures when she should have been slap-bang in the middle of her *own* adventure.

Finally, on the last afternoon of the break while she was reading in the living room, with Wimmi and Felthor snacking on Inundanza Chinese-water-chestnut cookies next to her, Alessia's shell floated across the room to her ear.

"Meet me on the beams – in our tunnel," Vulcor's voice intoned in her brain.

He was reaching out to her again! And he was calling it

"*our* tunnel"! Alessia's cheeks burned, and she scampered to her room for privacy.

She suddenly panicked and wondered how the shell sorted thoughts which came to recipients as speech, from those that stayed silent. She couldn't leave it to chance.

"Vulcor!" she said out loud, keeping her voice low. Surely what she actually *said* would drown out anything private she was *thinking*.

"You went back to the tunnel?" she asked.

He huffed. "Alessia..."

"Fine, fine." She didn't want to nag again.

"So I'll see you there," he said.

"What? No, I can't, it's—"

"Come on," he insisted.

"Vulcor, I'd love to, but it's Inundanza..."

He clicked his tongue against his teeth. "You know what? Don't bother. If you don't want to see me, that's fine. No need to let me down gently... If you really wanted to, you'd find a way. Just say you don't."

Before she could answer, the line went dead.

Alessia sat in stunned silence. What on earth was that rash reaction? He was completely unreasonable! Infuriating!

She shuffled back into the living room, brooding.

"Can anybody leave home during Inundanza? If it's an emergency, for example..."

"Look at this nymphlet! Getting calls, asking to go out..."

"No! I'm not!" Alessia cut in, her cheeks burning again.

"Alright, alright! We wouldn't be offended, you know. We know we're oldies and you'll be wanting to hang out with the youth," Wimmi teased, twirling his ginger beard between his fingers.

"No! I–"

"We believe you, my dear," Felthor interrupted mercifully. "And to answer your question, if it's an emergency, you can of course. But it's traditional to stay home. It's funny you should ask though, because I actually *do* have to pop out–"

"What?" Wimmi cried. "No! Why?"

"I forgot a key ingredient for our Inundanza closing night in my office."

"You didn't... Felthor!" Wimmi sounded scandalized.

"I know, I know! Oh, you're right. Let's just do without."

"No, no, no. Our nymphlet needs the full Inundanza experience. Off with you!"

Felthor smiled sheepishly, gave Alessia a kiss on the head and said, "I'll be back soon."

"Our dear Felthor almost deprived you of the best part of Inundanza. The divine Inundanza cake is cooked twelve days in advance. It's a delight of agar caramel covering crispy arame shredded like angel's hair, hiding an aquamarine gemstone..."

But Alessia couldn't bring herself to listen. Vulcor had a way of getting under her skin. Did he really think she didn't want to see him?

Her shell flew to her ear again. Her face lit up uncontrollably and she ran to her room, only to hear it was Larthuzor, shelling the whole gang. After two and a half days of deciphering glyphs with the stolen dictionary, he finally had answers.

"So, in the first column, there's the signs for human and fish and energy – which means 'a Nethunsian person with power'."

"Like Sensate Powers you mean?" Alessia asked.

"I think so."

"Those powers that Iktor dislikes so much. Interesting coincidence," Kella reflected.

"Larthu, you starfish, you!" Herior exclaimed.

"Then, if I'm not mistaken, the last glyph in the first column is... 'rain'." Larthuzor's voice darkened.

"Rain? Do you even get rain here? Apart from the fake Inundanza rain," Alessia asked.

"That's the thing – no," Larthuzor answered. "So when they say 'rain', it has the same sense as in 'Inundanza rain' – that's to say, 'that which cleans away something toxic'."

"Throw us a fishbone, Larthu!" Herior pressed. "What does it *mean?*"

"It means that this destroys Sensate Powers..." Alessia whispered out loud as it hit her.

Larthuzor sighed in confirmation.

"Holy tridents," Herior said. "He really did abduct the Oculate to destroy his powers."

"But, can *anything* destroy Sensate Powers?" Kella asked.

"One thing can," Larthuzor said.

"What?" Herior asked.

"Green Pung. Remember, Naror mentioned it on our first day when he went on about Sensate Powers, and Rascor Authentor got angry. Green Pung was a very rare plant that grew in Penglini. I read a story about it in my Grandfather's hidden Penglini botanical books. It was about a Penglini woman who could know the full history of any object or person – with one kiss. She'd just bring something to her lips, and know everywhere it had been and everything it had seen. This woman became well-known in the surrounding villages because she was using her ability to solve crimes – the 'Kiss of Justice', they called it. Anyway, one day she came across Green Pung and brewed its flowers in a tea. After taking one sip, she lost her ability completely, and by the end of the day, she died.

"When knowledge of the Chaco Manifesto scripts spread from Azlanu to Penglini, and the Penglini people read Chaco's Sensate Powers theory, they saw that one of the Five Powers in it – the "Gustate's power"– was knowing everything about an object from its taste. They realized that 'Kiss of Justice' woman must have been this Gustate... and that made Green Pung the only substance known to extinguish Sensate Powers."

"So surely it's illegal to have Green Pung in your possession! That *alone* would get Iktor arrested," Kella said.

"Definitely!" Larthuzor answered. "What I don't get is that it's not meant to *exist* anymore. The plant was very delicate and became extinct a long time ago. Unless..."

"What?" Alessia asked.

"Well... my brother told me a rumor that a Sage from Penglini's Lin Mo Court had distilled the essence of the very last living Green Pung plant into a vial..."

"That's it then! It must be!" Herior said. "Triton... *our* Iktor managed to get the *one* existing vial of this stuff!"

"Well, there's still one thing that doesn't fit," Lathuzor said. "It's the second column of glyphs. There's the glyph I don't understand, and then it says: 'A Power Entrusted, a Power Evolved and a Power Expensive. It's like these are the conditions the power needs to fulfill for it to work."

"So what's the issue?" asked Alessia.

"Well, as far as I know, Green Pung didn't need any special conditions to destroy powers."

"Why does it matter?" Herior said. "It's pretty clear what's happening. Iktor wants revenge for what the Emperor and the Oculate did to his family years ago, so he's going to destroy the Oculate's powers with this Green Pung."

"So... should we go to the Emperor's Guard, then?" Kella asked.

"No!" Alessia yelped. Her mind raced to find a good argument. She couldn't let them go to the Emperor's Guard, not before she had a chance to barter the vial for Iktor's information on her father. "I think we should only get the authorities involved when we have something really undeniable. Right now, we have a vial of Green Pung, and it's our word against his that we got it from him in the first place."

"That's true," said Kella.

"And there's a risk they'd believe *him* rather than *us*," added Larthuzor. "He's a respected professor, and there are holes in our story..."

"What do you mean?" Herior asked.

"Well, if he wanted to destroy the Oculate's powers, and he had the Green Pung vial, why didn't he just use it to spike the Oculate's food or something? It's a lot riskier to actually *abduct* him."

"Couldn't it be so he could use Espior's 'Oculate powers' and see where the Emperor is, so they can abduct the Emperor whenever he's alone?" Herior said.

"I don't know. The Oculate had a lot of security. If they could get to *him,* surely they could also have figured out where the *Emperor* was, without the Oculate's help," Larthuzor said.

"Exactly!" Alessia jumped in. "To avoid this backfiring, let's get a more solid story before we involve the Emperor's Guard."

"Alright for me. The investigation continues!" Kella said with delight.

Just then, Wimmi gave a loud cheer.

"Gotta go," said Alessia before tapping on her shell to pull out of the call.

Felthor was at the front door, his brow knotted, and his jaw muscles bulging slightly from his moon-shaped face as he chewed on the inside of his mouth.

"Inundanza cake time!" Wimmi announced.

"I'm afraid somebody had foolishly placed a book on it and it's a little worse for the wear..." Felthor said, apologetically presenting a transparent box filled with crumbs, and one large turquoise gemstone.

Felthor looked so anxious, even Wimmi refrained from kicking up a fuss.

"Was that *someone* a professor whose name begins with 'Fel' and ends with 'Thor'?" he simply said, grinning.

Felthor gave a half-hearted smile.

"It's okay, it still looks delicious!" Alessia said.

"Yeah, don't worry, silly. It's fine!" Wimmi put his arm around Felthor's shoulder and gave him a shake as they walked to the kitchen. "We'll be serving Alessia a masterpiece of the culinary arts: the *deconstructed* Inundanza cake."

"Thank you both," Felthor said. "I'm just upset it's not *perfect*. You know how it is. When you've planned something for a while, it's frustrating to mess it up."

Alessia *did* know how it was... And as her anonymous notegiver had gently reminded her, if she messed up *her* plan, it would be more than frustrating. It would be deadly.

❧ 41 ❧

Sitting on her bed after dinner, Alessia rolled the vial around in her hands. Who would have thought she'd be in possession of something so secret and dangerous! Drama queen Alessia, caught up in some *real* drama. She uncorked the vial for the first time and a green mist escaped. The moment it reached her nose Alessia shuddered. The strong, carrot-like odor made her head spin so violently, she barely managed to put the vial down on her bedside table.

She covered her nose and mouth with her bedsheets, and waited for the nausea to pass. When she'd regained enough strength, she quickly put the cork back in the bottle.

A silhouette shifted in her mirror.

She snapped her head around. On her balcony, leaning against the balustrade was Vulcor, writhing in pain.

Alessia jumped down from the bed, tossed the vial into her schoolbag, and rushed towards him.

His clothes were torn and he was holding his side. The skin exposed in the gaps between his fingers, was swollen and stained purple and red with fresh bruises.

"What happened?" She put out her hand to touch him but saw him wince with dread just in time to stop herself.

"That doesn't matter. I just came to warn you." He was rushing through his speech as though it were taking all his strength to get it out in time, before he might collapse. "Be careful. Don't go out alone."

"So *you* sent me those notes?" Alessia jumped in, unable to contain her excitement at having this mystery solved.

"What? What notes? I didn't send you a note."

It wasn't him. He was talking about something else. *Another* danger. Great.

"Never mind," she said. "What did you come to warn me about? And what do you mean 'it doesn't matter what happened'? You're injured!"

"Ah!" he groaned in pain – or perhaps impatience. "I knew I shouldn't have come here. Enough with the questions! I'm not safe – I've known that for a while. I thought I'd managed to stay out of sight, but apparently not. So, you need to be careful in case he saw you with me."

"He? Who, he?"

"Who do you think?" he snapped. "My attacker."

"You were attacked? Where? Who attacked you?"

"Stay out of it, Alessia. I've said what I needed to. I'm going."

"What?" Alessia reached out to him as a reflex, forgetting his pain until he yelped. She quickly pulled her arm back. "Stay here! I'll get Felthor and Wimmi. They'll help–"

"No!"

Alessia opened her mouth to say something, but stopped. He'd just keep snapping at her.

She took a step back, and in the coldest, calmest voice

she could muster, said, "Alright, then I'll go back to bed now. And you should stop contacting me, if that's how it's going to be. You don't trust me – fine. You're hiding something– also fine. I don't need to be your friend. If you have nothing more to tell me, just go. I'm tired of this little game."

She spun on her heels so he wouldn't see her face, in case she started crying, but he grabbed her arm.

"Wait."

He had a pained look. He hesitated a little, then said, "You're right, I'll leave you alone."

She harrumphed. "But why? Why can't you tell me more?"

The muscles in Vulcor's face seemed to grind together in thought.

She took the risk of pushing a little more. "It's only fair that I should know as much as you do about what I'm facing, if I'm really in the same danger as you are..."

He didn't need to know she was already in some danger of her own. A little guilt-trip wouldn't hurt him.

"It's... complicated." He was hesitating. She'd never seen him so (almost) malleable. If she treaded lightly, she might finally get him to shed some light on the mystery he was shrouded in.

"I'm sure..." she said softly. "Come."

She made her way into the room and sat on the edge of her bed. He followed her in and leaned against the wall.

"Ok. I'm going to trust you with something very, *very* sensitive," he said. "Don't make me regret it."

She swallowed the patronizing comment, and just said, "I won't tell anyone. I promise."

He looked at her with suspicion, then came to sit next to her, and clasped his fingers together.

"You know the Emperor?" he said. "I'm his son."

Alessia snorted a nervous giggle. "His son?"

"That's what I said, isn't it?"

"The emperor doesn't have a son, even *I* know that," she snapped, bemused.

"He does. I'm his son. People just don't know about it."

"And why wouldn't people know about it?" Was he really going to insist on this blatant lie? "And where is the *'Empress'* your mother?" she continued sarcastically.

"There is no Empress."

"I'm glad we agree on *something.*"

"My mother was just my father's favorite in his harem. She passed away when I was a baby."

"How convenient!" Alessia burst in. She immediately regretted it. "I'm sorry, that's not what I meant. I just wish you wouldn't take me for a fool."

"Why would I do that?" he answered disdainfully. "What was the point in pushing me to tell you my secret, if you're not going to believe me?"

She gulped down her pride one more time.

"Ok, so your mother passed away and your father's..."

"The Emperor."

"Right..."

"He kept me a secret from everyone except my special bodyguard, and my tutor, the Oculate Espior. He didn't want anyone to know about me because he was scared people would realize he no longer had powers."

"What do you mean?"

"What you know about the Five Sensate Powers from the Emperor's Shield is just the tip of the iceberg. It came from a much larger book–"

"The Chaco Manifesto scripts. I know," she said quickly, to take his condescension down a notch.

"Then you know my father banned it, and has the only remaining copy. One of the reasons he did so, is to stop people from finding out what it said, specifically, that those that have powers lose them to their first-born child. He tried to kill all the Chaco followers who knew this, but to be extra safe, he also kept my birth a secret."

"So you're saying *you're* now the Manibate?" Alessia said, choosing to ignore the frighteningly nonchalant tone with which Vulcor referred to his father's murders.

"You need me to prove it to you?" he cocked an eyebrow.

"I don't *need* anything... But I'd be curious to see powers in action, yes."

He looked at her and slowly raised his left arm. When his hand was at shoulder-level, he stopped.

They stared at each other, waiting for something to happen. Alessia bit her lip to stifle a laugh. He looked at his hand and back up at her. In a quick sharp motion, he lowered his arm and pulled it up again. Nothing happened. He slapped his arm up and down, again and again, glaring down at his own hand in frustration, and finally let out a loud, angry grunt.

"*Spraints!*" he roared. (Thankfully, Kella had already taught Alessia all the Nethunsian curse words – so she knew this one to mean 'otter poo', and didn't need to interrupt his temper tantrum to ask.)

"*Spraints, spraints, SPRAINTS!*" he yelled, throwing his arms up in the air.

The objects from Alessia's bedroom shelves flew across the room and she yelped in shock.

"Did anything hit you? I-I'm sorry," he stammered, stepping towards her. Alessia backed away, the image of the

Emperor throwing people around the square burning in her brain.

"I didn't mean to break your things," he continued. "Really. When I couldn't lift you, I got angry. I thought the guy in the struggle tonight had weakened my powers or something, and you'd think I was just an idiot lying to you. On the plus side, *now* you see..." his voice trailed off as she gave him an appalled look.

He decided to go about it differently, raised his hands and gestured delicately, like the conductor of a grand orchestra. One of the books that had been laying all crumple-paged and injured on the floor slowly levitated, made its way to the shelf, and set itself down gently.

Alessia's horror turned into awe, and Vulcor grinned. Slowly all the objects floated to the shelf, in a strange haunted ballet.

When he was done, Vulcor lowered his arm, and scoured Alessia's eyes.

"Wow..." she gasped. "That was... amazing!"

"Thank you," he said.

"You really are the Manibate... That's incredible! And you can just move anything? Even heavy things? Even several things at once? Even things far away from you"

"Yep."

"Wow. If I'd had that power my whole life, I swear I'd be so lazy. I'd just stay in bed *manibating* stuff over to me!" Alessia laughed.

"Well, my power only just got to its evolved state–"

"Evolved?" Her face went slack. *A Power Evolved*. Like on the vial.

"Yeah," Vulcor said. "It was only passive before. I was just able to sense the trajectories of things, and I couldn't control *when* I'd sense something. I'd just touch something and randomly get this feeling of being thrown, or being rolled or punched – whatever had happened to that object. I hated it actually – it gave me vertigo. But I got to eleven years old, and trained, and finally evolved it. So now I can *influence* the trajectory of things."

So a Power Evolved was a power that had gone from passive to active. If she could only find out what the rest of the message on the vial meant... Vulcor was looking at her strangely. She hadn't said anything in a while.

"So, who do you think is out to hurt you?"

But now she knew he had powers, one name rang in her mind.

"The same people that attacked Espior and me last time."

"Wait... you were *there* when they captured the Oculate?"

"Yeah. They doctored the footage you saw in the Tiding... my father had me edited out. We were coming back from class. There were two attackers, but I couldn't see their faces. I managed to get away from mine, but they wanted to get me too. That's why my father stepped up security at the palace so much."

"Of course... Sterna Authenta was arguing about the crabs leaving the Octopus's Garden."

"Don't get me started. Those *leechy* crabs were EVERYWHERE in the palace. I couldn't turn over in bed without Carcinor knowing," he protested. "They want me locked up in the palace like a prisoner, for my 'safety'."

"Well, they have a point," Alessia mumbled, her gaze hovering over the purplish skin showing from under his torn top. "Someone just attacked you. And the cloaked man in the tunnels that day must have been after you too. They're still tracking you, and they've managed to find you twice since the Oculate's abduction!"

The realization shed a different light on her decision not to tell the Emperor's Guard about Iktor. Her little malicious plan to get information from him, meant leaving Vulcor's attacker at large.

"Alessia, I didn't come here for your advice. I should go."

"Go where?"

"Where I won't be found, and where I won't attract their attention to you."

"But let me help—"

"I never needed your help before. I don't need it now."

"Fine. Bye then," she sighed, barely refraining from rolling her eyes. That quick temper of his was exasperating.

Vulcor let out a cold and cryptic "Bye", threw himself over the balustrade of her balcony onto his flying fish board, and zoomed off into the darkness.

She slumped to her bed. She hated thinking she was keeping Vulcor in danger.

Her strategy needed tweaking.

She'd confront Iktor the next day as planned. But once she got her answers about her father in exchange for the vial, she'd go to the Emperor's Guard *immediately* to have Iktor locked up for possessing Green Pung, before he had a chance to use it on Vulcor. She'd have to be quick and ruthless. It was the only way.

This time tomorrow Vulcor would be safe, she'd have more of a clue about the kind of danger *she* was in – and she'd finally have the answers she'd sought her whole life.

Alessia rushed into the Octopus's Garden, her plan turning in her head at nauseating speed. But when she got to Iktor's classroom door, and reached into her bag, the vial wasn't there. She rummaged around, but it was no good.

Her heart sank. How could she be so stupid? Her whole plan depended on giving him the vial, and she'd forgotten it. She could have *sworn* she'd put it in her bag. She must have been so distracted by Vulcor's visit, she'd taken it back out and left it in her room.

...Unless, he'd taken it.

That wasn't possible, she'd have noticed him grabbing something from her bag.

Except, with his powers, he wouldn't need to grab it...

She ignored the thought, ran back out to the line of tadpoles on the street, and took one home. But when she arrived, a horde of giant crabs and Emperor's Guards were gathered outside her front door.

Her mind went straight to Vulcor. Had they followed him here last night?

Just then she realized that one of the humans in the horde *wasn't* a guard, but Wimmi.

"Alessia! What are you doing here?" he said, weakly attempting a smile. If Alessia wasn't already concerned, seeing her permanently cheerful Wimmi fail to put on a convincing smile did the trick.

"I forgot something at home..." she mumbled vaguely. "What happened?"

"There's been a break-in."

Panic sparked in Alessia's chest. This couldn't be a coincidence. She had to get in there immediately.

"She should go in there immediately to see if anything was taken," one of the guards commanded urgently, mirroring her thoughts exactly.

She passed the door she'd only closed half an hour before, her heart pounding in her chest. The scene ahead made her blood run cold.

Felthor and Wimmi's valued possessions, strewn on the floor. Clothes, in a disorderly heap in the middle of the living room. Books had been tossed from the shelves and lay scattered all over, their pages staring at the ceiling.

Alessia tiptoed through the mess to find her room in a similar state. Drawers had been thrown so violently to the floor that it was littered with broken shards of mother of pearl. But as heart-breaking as it was to see her little ecosystem decimated, another thought was throbbing in Alessia's mind: Where was the vial?

A sickening feeling rose in her stomach. She fell to her knees and sorted through the rubble, in a nightmarish daze. Her erratic breathing turned into sobs of desperation. She searched the same spots again and again in horror, but there was no denying it. The vial was gone.

❦ 43 ❦

"**Y**ou lost what!" Kella exclaimed, her face even more ashen than normal.

"Ssssh!" Quina reprimanded before turning back to listen to their Selvan Studies professor. Luckily, Moxia was so engrossed in her own lesson, she didn't notice Alessia had snuck in halfway through class – but nothing escaped Quina's eye.

"Iktor must have broken into my house and stolen it this morning," Alessia whispered.

"The singularity of the New Current's failed uprising was that the ringleaders were *not* underdogs," Moxia was saying, eyes popping out of her small gaunt face excitedly, lending her a slight resemblance to a cartoon bunny. "The ringleaders were part of the Emperor's Order. They were the 'crème de la crème'! Stellar students that the Emperor had handpicked for top secret missions to guard us from Selvans."

"I've changed my mind, Kella," Alessia said, while Moxia continued her tirade. "I know what we agreed yesterday but... I think we should tell the Emperor's Guard."

"What? Why? We said we needed a more solid story."

"I know. But now Iktor has the vial and that means he can hurt... people. Also, if we act before he has the chance to hide it, they'll find the vial on him – and then it won't just be our word against his. They'll have evidence." It was *almost* her plan coming to life... Forgetting the vial at home had just cost her the truth about her father... and possibly her life.

There was a long pause and Kella held her side glance on Alessia unflinchingly. Finally, she sighed: "Yeah, you're right. But this doesn't just implicate *us*. Iktor knows Larthuzor and Herior were involved. He'll bring them up if he gets interrogated by the Emperor. They need to agree to this first."

"So, this is where our Selvan Studies lesson about the New Current ends," Moxia concluded, completely oblivious to the important discussion that had just taken place in her classroom. "The revolutionaries were all but erased from history. All Drifts of them were destroyed, to avoid them becoming figureheads of future rebellions. We study them in Selvan Studies as a cautionary tale.

"Tomorrow we'll move back to discussing the belligerent Selvan nations, and how their many wars have been a nuisance to our peaceful empire."

Alessia's stomach was in a knot. After having been so confident in her plan the night before, now that she was about to tell the Emperor's Guard, she had the nagging feeling she was making a mistake. Larthuzor was right. There were holes in the story they'd pieced together.

Perfectly on cue, Naror trotted by, under his cloud of black hair, flanked by Quina, as always.

"Hey Naror!" Alessia called him.

"Hi," answered Naror seemingly unsurprised. "Save me a seat, Quina!"

"Okay!"

"Naror, you know about... about Sensate Powers, right?" Alessia began tentatively once Quina was out of earshot.

"I do," he answered with curious wonder. He looked like a foreigner who'd crossed paths with a stranger speaking his language.

"What are you doing? He's a landfarer. What does he know about Sensate Powers?" Kella muttered quietly to Alessia.

"*Second generation* landfarer, if you please," Naror corrected coolly, crumpling his freckly nose. "My dad is Nethunsian and a direct descendent of a line of Chaco doctrine dignitaries, I'll have you know. And just because my mom grew up in Selva, doesn't mean she doesn't know Nethunsian things. If anything, that made her all the more fascinated about them. So, as I said, I *do* know about the Sensate Powers."

"Perfect!" Alessia said. "I'm a landfarer too, so I guess I have the same fascination as your mother, and that's why I have a few questions for you."

"No, you don't," Kella said with round eyes, pulling Alessia aside. "I don't think we should be blabbing about this to randomers!"

Alessia whispered urgently, "Maybe he can help us figure out some of the holes in our story before–"

"What's he going to tell us we don't know?" Kella whispered back. "Our story's good enough. The Oculate was abducted to give information on the Emperor's whereabouts, so they could both get their powers destroyed by–"

"See, *that*," interrupted Naror, "is completely wrong."

Kella and Alessia started. They hadn't realized he could hear.

"If you have powers yourself, you're immune to others' powers. So the Oculate can't see the Emperor any more than we can."

Alessia threw Kella a meaningful look, and returned to Naror.

"You mentioned Green Pung in class once. How does it work?" she asked. "Like, you said people used Green Pung to destroy others' powers. Was there any other reason people would have kept Green Pung?"

"Well... there is one other *rumored* use, but it's a little far-fetched..." he began. "According to the Chaco Manifesto scripts—"

"Great, now we're having illegal conversations about Chaco doctrine on top of it all..." mumbled Kella, pinching the bridge of her pinkening nose. –

"There are only two ways a power is transferred from one person to another," Naror continued, undeterred. "When a power-bearer has a baby, the power goes to the child, and when a power-bearer dies, it goes to their 'next of kin' – that is, any younger person in their extended family. Well, some Chaco followers theorized that if people had tried, the properties of Green Pung could have been redirected to create a *third* way of transferring powers."

Alessia and Kella looked at each other. This was a new thought. Iktor had a chip on his shoulder about not having powers. He'd ranted about how the humble could find greater powers than inherited powers. Was this his 'humble man''s solution to get powers?

"It was just speculation," Naror added. "So I can't tell you much more about it. Except that, based on everything that's known about powers, it's likely the powers would have to be in their evolved state for a transfer to be possible..."

Alessia and Kella muttered in unison, "A Power Evolved."

"By the way, will you be staying much longer?" Naror asked.

"What?"

Just then, a pang of pain bloomed in Alessia's right cheekbone, up around her eye socket and down her jawline. A sharp pain seared in her right shoulder. Someone had shoved her into the wall. Her knees buckled and she crumbled to the ground, her wetsuit ripping as it scraped against the stone.

"Up! Get up!" shouted a furious voice. Standing square in front of her was Iktor himself.

❧ 44 ❧

"Y ou won't escape this time, picaroon," he murmured malevolently before yanking her up to her feet.

"Let go of her!" Kella shouted.

"Stay out of it," he snapped back. "Where is it?" he hissed at Alessia through gritted teeth.

"We said LET GO!" came a loud voice from behind Iktor, and suddenly Iktor's hands were pried off Alessia, and his devilish shape shrunk out of her sight.

Herior had grabbed his professor by the shoulders and thrown him off, with astonishing force.

Kella whispered something urgently to Herior, as Larthuzor ran to see if Alessia was alright.

"Get Carcinor," Alessia told him. Larthuzor whipped his shell out and put it to his ear.

"It's over, Iktor," Herior said. "We know you've got Green Pung and you abducted the Oculate." There was an audible gasp. Other students had gathered around them, watching in shock.

"How *dare* you lay a hand on Alessia? *Break into her home?*"

A familiar clicking noise sounded. Carcinor's crabs had already scuttled in through the cracks in the crowd.

"Break into *her* home? What about the break-ins to *my* home all these years?" Iktor spat. "And to my..." he stopped himself short of saying 'vault'.

"You're dangerous and rotten, and we're not letting you get away with it," Herior finished, just as Carcinor emerged.

❧ 45 ❧

What happened in the next hour felt like a dream. As professors tried to usher their classes away from the spectacle unsuccessfully, Alessia, Kella, Herior and Larthuzor told the whole story to Carcinor and a seemingly important member of the Emperor's Guard.

Carcinor's crab investigators took the four of them and Iktor to the Dead Man's Chest vault, and forced Iktor to open it. The vial wasn't there – only the blank piece of paper that the friends had seen there during their heist.

But Carcinor didn't ignore it, like the friends had. He took a pearl out of his pocket, so the Drift of a lanternfish hovered above his hand, and held up the page. In the lanternfish's glow, words appeared on it: "The New Current Manifesto".

The blank page had been an illegal revolutionary pamphlet written in invisible ink!

Iktor's face fell at the sight of it, but he didn't protest nor deny knowledge of it.

Two crabs walked him back to the courtyard, holding

his arms so tightly in their pincers that a blood stain blossomed out from their grip, on his blue wetsuit top.

The Emperor's Guard grilled him and even questioned Sterna (since she was the headteacher who'd hired him). Iktor answered their questions at first, but at some point, his demeanor changed. He raised his chin and looked at them defiantly. It was as if he knew it was over, and had decided to face his destiny. He seemed almost liberated.

Within the hour, he'd been locked up in a high-security ovehic, designed to resemble a deep-sea anglerfish, with a bioluminescent pole sticking out from its top, and long, fang-like teeth barring the opening in front.

"You'll have some explaining to do, guppies," Carcinor said coldly. He watched Alessia with particular suspicion, through beady eyes that seemed pierced in his thick, clay-like skin. "For instance, you'll need a good reason *why* you didn't turn in the suspected Green Pung vial as soon as it came into your possession. Be ready for our investigators' summons."

With that, he scuttled off towards Iktor's ovehic jail.

"Guys, we did it!" Herior exclaimed. "We put that sea-scum away! Come on, let's watch him go."

Herior, Kella and Larthuzor followed Carcinor. Alessia was trying to enjoy their victory as much as her friends were, but something was stuck on her brain like a parasite: *'Where is it?'*

That was the phrase Iktor had spat at her in his fury. *'Where is it?'*

And there was only one explanation for that phrase: He *had* been the one to break in to her home... But he *hadn't* found the vial there. He wasn't the one who'd taken it.

A lump filled her throat and she couldn't swallow it down.

She advanced towards the ovehic behind her friends, and looked at the man held captive inside.

Her episode in Iktor's classroom had given her the correct intuition about his hiding place behind the tapestry. If only she could *bring on* another episode now. But she had no idea what triggered them. All she knew is they always seemed to happen after she felt an intense emotion – like the fear in jousting.

Could that be it? Perhaps being so overwhelmed with an emotion forced her to let her guard down, and unleash her over-empathizing tendencies.

It was her best shot. She closed her eyes, and with each breath out, she imagined pushing down the barriers around her heart a little more, until it just sat there completely vulnerable.

There came an inpouring of voices and emotional noise. It was working!

Now she had to ignore the mess and focus on him; to go from hearing to listening.

She sharpened her attention – and finally, she sensed him.

She sensed his relief at his secret being out, and his fear at what was in store for him in the interrogation... And she sensed what she'd dreaded: incomprehension.

He was *confused* about them telling the crabs he'd stolen the Green Pung back. And he was desperately wondering where it was.

Alessia's breath caught in her throat. It was true. Someone else had taken it. She'd been wrong, and now she'd put in motion a deadly machine she couldn't stop.

Iktor leaned forward on his seat, pressing his face against the fang bars of his ovehic. He looked straight at her, and his face twisted into a demented V-shaped smile.

"Tell me, were you in it with them from the beginning? Or are you just a foolish nymphlet that led them right to it without knowing it?" He snickered an eerie laugh that pricked the hairs on the back of Alessia's neck. "I guess it doesn't matter."

He fell back grinning to himself. There was something tragic about his grin – as though he could break into tears at any moment.

"He's lost the plot," scoffed Herior. "Don't listen to him, Alessia."

"This is why I wanted *nothing to do* with your family, ever again," Iktor mused. "I *knew* it would bring me trouble. But you just wouldn't let me go."

He paused.

"It's almost funny. He was always such a *loyal lackey* to Oscor. It's only fitting his daughter should make the same mistake. If your father could see you now..."

Carcinor gave the signal and Iktor's ovehic shot off into the distance.

❧ 46 ❦

"It just doesn't make any sense," Kella broke the ice. In perfect unison, Larthuzor and Herior leaned forward and slurped from their cockle shells of hot whelkee, keeping their eyes fixedly down. Even the hermit crab Larthuzor was caring for that day, retreated into his shell.

The friends had been sitting in silence at an Etruscan crockpot cafe since they'd left the Octopus's Garden, with none of them knowing how to raise the topic. Kella had apparently finally decided that the best way to do it, was bluntly.

"So Iktor knew your father and didn't like him because he was loyal to the Emperor. But then the *merfolk* we saw, who were famously part of the rebellion *against* the Emperor, seemed to like him! They released you and even said they'd help you fulfil your destiny and stuff!"

"The merfolk that attacked us? You didn't tell me they said that!" Herior complained.

Kella shrugged, taking pride in the independence she'd shown by keeping things from him.

"Yeah, I dunno." Alessia looked down at her whelkee

glumly, twirling her crocodile tooth stirrer. Nothing made sense.

And whatever this mysterious "destiny" was, that she was meant to fulfil – there was no sign of it happening. Just like there was no sign of someone trying to "sacrifice" her, like the anonymous notes had said. In fact, no one had tried to abduct her since that first grindylow. Were the notes just a prank? Was Iktor locked up because she'd taken *a prank* too seriously?

Tears pricked Alessia's eyes, and Kella and Herior exchanged a helpless glance. Larthuzor, however, was ruminating on something.

"He was the Emperor's *loyal lackey*..." he said slowly. "That's quite intense."

"You can say that again! Suddenly revealing he knew your father the whole time. What a seaweedbag," Herior shook his head.

"No... I mean, it's quite intense to call someone the Emperor's *loyal lackey*, right? You wouldn't say that about just a common person – even if they're a 'good subject' who follows the Emperor's rules and does their regular duties to serve the Empire. *Loyal lackey* sounds almost like..."

Alessia looked up at him.

"... it sounds like what you'd say of someone who served the Emperor *closely*," Larthuzor completed. "Look, they found a New Current pamphlet in Iktor's vault. So we can assume Iktor was part of the New Current revolutionaries. That group was led by deserting members of the Emperor's Order. What if Iktor and your father knew each other because your father was a member of the Emperor's Order?"

"Your father would've been a member that *didn't* defect

to this 'New Current', and that's why Iktor had it in for him," Herior continued.

"Or he *pretended* to defect, and that's why the mermaids thought he was a fellow rebel – but Iktor knew that in reality he'd stayed faithful to the Emperor!" Kella exclaimed.

"Now we just have to find another Emperor's Order member, and ask who he was," Herior said. "That can be our next mission!"

He and Kella were sat upright like the perked-up ears of a dog whose attention has been caught.

"Alessia," Larthuzor said, more cautiously. "What do you think?"

"I think..." Alessia started quietly. "I think if my father *was* part of the Emperor's Order, that could explain how he met my mother: on one of his missions spying in Selva.

"And if he chose to leave us and return to Nethuns, out of loyalty to the Emperor's Order... my mother's death, and my being essentially orphaned, could be the reason Iktor called his decision a mistake. I think it makes sense."

Herior's large, bronze-colored hand came down heavily on Alessia's shoulder, causing some of Alessia's almost untouched whelkee to spill onto it in a large beige pearl.

"Starfish Jous-ta, we'll find out."

Alessia hesitated. There was another question smoldering in the pit of her stomach, that they had yet to discuss.

"What about Iktor? If *he* didn't take the Green Pung vial, who did?" she said, quietly willing them to suggest another plausible name, so she could stop wondering about Vulcor.

Herior brushed it off: "Iktor's a liar. I'm sure he has it. Everybody *says* they're innocent."

Alessia opened her mouth, but shut it again. How could she explain her episodes, and the intuition she'd gotten?

They left the café, and Alessia and Kella got into a shared ovehic and directed it to drop them both home.

"How are you feeling?" Kella asked.

"I'm happy I have you guys. I've never had anyone care that much about me before."

"Of course! And we'll find your father," Kella said.

"I dunno. Maybe it's not possible."

"What do you mean? We have so many clues now!"

"We have clues, but no way to get to the *truth*," Alessia said.

And then it struck her.

"To Seagrass-City," she ordered the ovehic. "Fast."

"What? Why?"

"The Whirlpool of Firnor. I heard Minchans talking about it when I first arrived! Saying you could find the truth there. I can ask my Minchan friend Ebrie to take me."

"Then I'm coming with you," Kella said.

"No. It only accepts you if you go alone," Alessia said. She didn't know this for a fact, but didn't want to put Kella in danger.

"I can't let you go by yourself!" Kella exclaimed.

"If you want to help me, you should go home. That way... you can get help more easily if I shell you!"

"But Alessia, do you even know if it's safe?"

"Yes! There's nothing to worry about. I'll be fine, I'm sure," she lied.

❧ 47 ❧

"E brie!" Alessia shouted in the Seagrass-City courtyard. "Eee-brieee!"

'If I can ever help you with anything, you know where to find me,' Ebrie had said, when Alessia had dropped her off at Seagrass-City. But Ebrie hadn't exactly detailed *how* to get in touch. So yelling her name it was.

"Ebrie!" Alessia screamed. Then, she slammed into something.

"Ah! Watch it, young Tanushi! You almost tipped me over *again*!"

It was Yagora, Herior's kappa friend. The one who'd called Iktor a 'sweet finboy'.

"I'm so sorry... *again*," Alessia said.

Yagora brushed down the tortoise-shell pieces on her tunic and continued on her way.

"Wait!" Alessia called after her. "I'm actually very glad I saw you again. To apologize for last time."

"Apology accepted," Yagora answered flatly.

"And," Alessia added. "Well, I'd be so grateful if you could tell me a little about Iktor."

"I have better things to do. Bye."

"No! Wait! Please!" Alessia bit her nails. She needed to get back into Yagora's good books, and apologizing wasn't enough.

She shut her eyes, emptied her mind, and opened up to let in Yagora's feelings, as she'd done with Iktor.

At once, she was flooded with anxiety. Her head was spinning and her body started shaking. It was like her mind was compressed, about to implode. Crammed with problems to solve. Not least of which was the constant worry that water would spill from her head, and she'd die. She was craving for an outlet by which to escape... even for a bit.

She came back to herself. Wow – it was terrible being Yagora! And to think Kella had said kappas were fun-loving pranksters! There wasn't one free nook in Yagora's mind to think about fun things.

That was it.

"I've got a joke for you," Alessia said. "If you have time."

Yagora stopped in her tracks.

"It's not too long. And... it's the best joke in the world," Alessia baited her.

Yagora turned to her. "I bet I know a better one."

"Only one way to find out," Alessia said.

A cheeky grin tugged at the corners of Yagora's yellow lips. "Go on, then."

"A human and a kappa walk to a pastry stall in the market," Alessia started, transposing the old Scottish joke to her new context. "The human slips a manatee cheese pastry into his breeches. 'See how clever we humans are? You could never steal like that!' he boasts to the kappa. The kappa signals to the nereid at the stall. 'Could you give me a pastry, I'll show you a magic trick,' he says. The nereid's suspicious, but gives him one. The kappa eats it. The nereid's furious. 'Hey! Where's your magic trick then?' the nereid screams. The kappa says, 'Look in the human's breeches.'"

To Alessia's relief, Yagora shared the same sense of humor. She burst out laughing, the water in her bowl-head splashing around alarmingly as she shook.

"Ah, that's not bad for a human," she said, when she recovered.

"Glad you liked it," Alessia said.

"I haven't heard a joke like that in a long time. I needed that."

It was true. Although the kappa's stress was still there, that small comic relief had undeniably quieted the storm.

Alessia opened her mouth to ask about Iktor, and shut it again. Now that she knew how anguished Yagora was already, it somehow didn't feel right to grill her about her Iktor-problem.

"Anyway, I'll be off," Alessia said. "Sorry again."

"What did you want to know about Iktor?" Yagora asked. "I can spare a minute."

"Really?"

"Don't make me change my mind. I don't have all day."

"Okay, okay," Alessia answered quickly. "Well, what made you say 'he's a good finboy' at the Inundanza feast? He doesn't seem that good. You know he's been arrested now for kidnapping the Oculate."

"Oh, he didn't do that. He avoided politics like the plague. Poor finboy, they're going to hurt him."

"But he had Green Pung on him."

"Of course he had Green Pung on him. Yuftor gave it to him," Yagora answered simply.

"Yuftor, Larthuzor's grandfather? How did *Yuftor* have Green Pung?"

"Green Pung grew in Penglini, where Yuftor was working for the Lin Mo royal family. But it was a delicate species. When the last remaining Green Pung plant was dying, Yuftor picked it to save one vial of its essence, before it was too late."

"He was *that Sage*? But why would he give it to someone cruel like Iktor?"

"Iktor isn't cruel! He was a terrified Detached Boy living in Seagrass-City not far from the kappa reserve where Yuftor would come visit me. Yuftor smelled the fear in him. Fear can turn dark in a place like this. Yuftor wanted to help..."

Alessia suddenly realized, "Iktor was the original Herior... the Seagrass-City boy Larthuzor's grandfather made a deal with the government to get into the Octopus's Garden."

"That's right. Getting him into the Octopus's Garden wasn't enough, though. The finboy was paranoid. He was completely terrified of the Emperor and Powers. That's why Yuftor told him about the existence of the Green Pung vial, to reassure him that powers *could* be stopped. But then, it became an obsession for the boy. He begged and begged for it. So on Iktor's fifteenth birthday, Yuftor gave in."

"On his fifteenth birthday! You mean... Iktor had the vial for *years?*"

"Not years," Yagora answered. "He had the vial for *decades.*"

A crushing pain spread in Alessia's chest. Iktor had had the Green Pung for *decades,* without trying to use it on the Oculate. It wasn't him. She'd put an innocent man behind bars.

A phrase seeped into her mind from the corners of her memory, 'the break-ins to my home all these years'.

With sickening speed all the pieces fell into place. *Someone else* had been trying to steal the vial from Iktor for years before Alessia and her friends did. That explained why the Oculate was abducted rather than his food being spiked. Whoever took the Oculate, didn't have Green Pung yet. Alessia had been the one to put it into their hands.

Yagora shuffled away, muttering 'look in the human's breeches!' under her breath and chuckling. Alessia reached for her shell, to deliver the news to her friends when she was interrupted by a deep, calm voice.

"Hello again!"

Alessia looked up to a familiar long, blue face.

❧ 48 ☙

"Ebrie! I need your help," Alessia said.

"Sure! After what you did to help *me* escape from those crabs– anything!"

"How do I get to the Whirlpool of Firnor?"

Ebrie's face dropped. "Okay, anything but that."

"But I really need to find out the truth about something and I heard–"

"The Whirlpool of Firnor is not some cheap fortune-telling device you can ask if the boy you have a crush on likes you back," she interrupted with regal coolness.

Alessia's spine straightened.

"That is *not* what I want to use it for."

Ebrie turned away shaking her head. "I'm sorry, I can't help you."

"Hey, I trusted you when you told me it was a life-or-death matter I needed to take you to Seagrass-City. Why can't you trust me that I need this?" Alessia cried.

"You don't know what you're getting yourself into," Ebrie said. "I'm trying to protect you! These are powerful forces. People *die* in the Whirlpool."

Alessia remembered what the grindylow had said. 'Everyone I know got stuck there'. So 'stuck there' meant 'died there'!

"I know that," Alessia lied, setting her jaw. "I wouldn't be asking if I weren't desperate. Please. I don't need you to protect me. Can you just tell me how it works and take me there?"

Ebrie considered her carefully. Her stoic face didn't let transpire whether she was sympathetic or disdainful. But after a long silence, she said, "Come with me."

They walked to the edge of the cliff, where Alessia had followed Metella to the 'Chaco follower' secret meeting, and then down the cliffside stairwell to sea level. There, Ebrie stopped, held up both of her hands to the sea, and chanted:

"Go your way, oh Selvan child,

To the waters and the wild,

If Chief Shony's rhymes you match,

The truth of Firnor you can catch."

Just then, the giant seahorse head of a black Marcaval popped out of the water in front of Alessia.

"This will take you to the Council of the Minchans, where our leader Shony will test your worthiness to enter the Whirlpool of Firnor," Ebrie began. "If he doesn't find you worthy... they'll execute you."

"Mm-Hmm," Alessia managed, while trying to keep the surge of panic inside her from showing on her face.

"If you make it past there," Ebrie continued, "you'll be thrown into the whirlpool. That's where you'll see the truth you seek. Only, the longer you stay and watch, the deeper you'll sink into the vortex. That's how people get lost and never make their way out."

"Are you coming or not?" the voice of a nereid howled

from inside the Marcaval... rather less politely than Alessia was accustomed to, for nereids. "When you're a clandestine traveler, speed is appreciated."

"I'm a what?"

The seahorse head almost seemed to roll its eyes and it turned to leave.

"No, wait! I'm coming!" Alessia exclaimed. Trying to channel her mother's bravery as a sailor, she stepped towards its snout.

"Is there *any* way I can make it out alive?" she asked Ebrie.

Ebrie thought for a moment, and then answered: "When you feel that you're getting stuck in the spiral, there's always a way out. You just have to look for the light."

"Look for what?" But before she could hear more she was sucked into the Marcaval's snout.

❦ 49 ❦

The Marcaval finally drew to a stop, and Alessia paid the nereid and prepared herself to be ejected from the Marcaval's snout. What she was *not* prepared for, was the Marcaval ejecting her in the middle of the sea, with no land in sight.

Alessia plunged into the dark, icy waters. Everything slowed and went deadly quiet, like the first time she'd found herself unexpectedly submerged. A glacial cold sunk its teeth into her. She kicked and punched and burst out of the water, to the heightened noise of her panicked breathing. She yanked her wetsuit collar over her nose. But to her horror, it filled with water as soon as she sank again. When Iktor had pushed her at the Octopus's Garden, the top of her wetsuit had torn– and now the turtleneck she relied on to breathe wasn't keeping the water out.

She pulled it back down and kicked herself to the surface. Her cold, wet hair slapped her face as she turned from side to side. The Marcaval was nowhere to be seen. She was going to drown before even meeting this famous Council.

Something touched her feet. She screamed just as a wave engulfed her, and she gulped down a disgusting mouthful of brine. Suddenly, her whole upper body was thrust out of the water, and in front of her, was a black horse's head. She screamed again and the horse whinnied. Something shifted beneath her. She was sitting on the horse's back. Somehow, it had come from the depths of the water to her rescue, and was holding her above sea level.

"Good boy, *very* good boy, Trigger!" she wheezed, patting his head. He snorted in acknowledgement.

She let out a laugh of relief – that turned into her coughing up the last of the water in her lungs – then tossed her head back and gratefully inhaled. The air tasted like salt and the breeze puckered her skin. Overhead, gulls were squawking and the sun shone that much brighter in the sky than when she was in Atlantis. She was back in Selva.

Or almost. This far out at sea, among the seagulls flew sirens, women and men wearing feathered tunics, with large, white wings, dark skin and black tresses. The surface of the sea wasn't Selvan territory. It was the frontier between the two worlds.

"Now where's this Council..."

She looked behind her. No sign of the Council, but something else got her attention. Instead of hind legs, her horse had one massive fishtail, beating from side to side.

"You're no ordinary horse are you, Trigger? You know I'm normally scared of horses, but I'm a BIG fan of *you*! Yes, a *very* big–"

She fell silent as she spotted a strange blue rock beside her, half submerged in the water. And another similar one ahead. She whipped her head around. There was another behind. She was surrounded by them. Then, the one next to her moved; uncurled itself. A blue head emerged from the water behind it.

They weren't rocks. They were the chests of Minchans, curved backwards and just poking out of the water. Within a few seconds they all uncurled to bring their heads above water, and she found herself surrounded by nine blue men and women, bobbing up and down.

One of them wore a small crown made of starfish legs, and he addressed Alessia.

"Lady of green, what have you to say

As your Marc'val cleaves the brine?"

Alessia opened her mouth to answer, but then shut it again. Ebrie had said, *'If Chief Shony's rhymes you match, the truth of Firnor you can catch.'*

Her answer needed to rhyme with his question. She sighed in dismay. Where was Mr. McCrum's 'Rules of Poetry' poster when you needed it?

She paused to think.

"To my father's truth I seek a way," she began, counting the syllables on her fingers.

"Please help me, Council of nine."

The blue people looked at each other. Alessia couldn't decipher the glance they exchanged. She curled her fingers over the prongs of the trident tied to her wrist, and waited for their verdict.

"Many before have come, brave and bold,

To lie in watery graves," Shony continued.

Alessia thought carefully.

"Yet I stand sure, though I am not old,

That I'll emerge from these waves," she lied.

Chief Shony whipped his head around to the other blue people. He was aggravated. He would have relished in her humiliation, and she was doing better than expected.

"And if we drown you *before* you go,
To the Whirlpool of Firnor?"

Alessia's breath caught in her throat. But she couldn't let him scare her into failing.

"Well, then that would only go to show
That blue men have no honor."

Shony's hands came crashing down on the surface of the water with a colossal splash that sent a tidal wave out into the distance. Alessia's horse was pushed up and down by the force of the swell, but she held tight to its mane.

Shony threw his head back, and plunged into the sea. The others looked equally enraged but stayed put.

When Shony emerged from the frigid waters he was holding an enormous spear that appeared to be made of bone. He raised it above his head and pulled it back like a javelin, aimed straight at her.

Alessia shrieked and cowered. Jump off and drown, or stay on the horse's back and be speared? As usual, she had great options.

"The truth you seek, is yours to find, in the Whirlpool of Firnor," Shony intoned.

"But beware, for what you see there, you may wish had stayed obscure.

I hereby perform the duty bequeathed by blue men of yore.

Wisdom of Ancients – be shown!

Kelpie – begone!

She must take this journey alone."

The horse reared up on his tail, tossing Alessia off his back. The freezing waves felt like a stone wall as she crashed into them. They softened to let her sink into the water and she saw her noble steed gallop down into the depths of the sea, before she sprang back up to the surface with a raucous gasp for air. She thrashed her arms around as the cold smited her flesh. She was so focused on trying to stay above water level, she only half-noticed Shony releasing the spear into the sea in front of her.

It hit the crest of a wave, and the water beneath opened up into an enormous whirlpool, as deep as a skyscraper is high. Like an icy hand, it grabbed her and set her in motion. The deadly race to the seafloor had begun.

"What do I do?" she screamed out, looking for Shony as she was yanked around the hellish maelstrom. But all she could see were blue mounds bobbing up and down in the waves, like dolphins' backs. The Minchans were swimming away. She was alone.

50

S he reached beyond the whirlpool to pull herself out. There was a blood-curdling snap. A raw pain shot up her arm and she grabbed her hand back in with a howl. Two of her fingers throbbed as if they had heartbeats of their own. They must have been broken by the force of the whirlpool. She wailed. But the tearing noise of rushing water swallowed her cries.

She needed to stop panicking.

"Breathe. Think. Breathe. Think," she said to herself.

The surface wasn't visible any more. Before her was just a great, glistening wall of water. She was spiraling down the whirlpool.

She had to gain time. Maybe if she could jump across the middle of the whirlpool to a higher point on the other side of it?

"One... Two... THREE!"

She threw her weight forwards to detach herself from the grip of the water.

It was no use. A colossal force was pushing against her, holding her in place on the edge of the whirlpool.

She let out a puff of air. It was hopeless. She should have listened to Ebrie.

She sank deeper and deeper in her crystalline cage, her revolutions getting dizzyingly smaller as the funnel narrowed. The water spun into a dazzling blur. Kaleidoscopic colors broke out within the shimmer, like shards of a stained glass. Her mind was turning into a giddy mush; as though a spider were crawling around inside her head, tickling her brain.

And then, the scintillation of the water became glints of light reflecting off a golden throne. The wavelets took the shape of a beautiful, young woman.

Little by little, the whirlpool around her morphed into a throne room, with a young woman in it, cradling a baby and looking at Alessia.

Could she see her? Alessia tried to say 'hello' and move forward but she couldn't.

Instead she found herself uncontrollably reaching a hand out to the woman. A man's hand.

She was in a man's body. And she didn't have any control over it. She was watching a scene unfold from his viewpoint.

"I don't know, Authentor," the woman said to her, or rather, to the man. "Are you sure about this? Espior the Oculate warned me to hide. He thought Oscor might not take the pregnancy well."

Alessia heard the voice of the man say to the woman, "Lutecia, the Emperor couldn't possibly harm you! You *know* how attached he is to you!"

The woman apparently called Lutecia smiled, her large, worried eyes sparkling.

"Our Emperor's just eager to meet this little one!" the man said, giving his finger to the new-born baby in Lutecia's arms to grab. "Emperor Oscor told me himself. He's yearning for a normal family life. Trust me, I know the feeling. I recently found out my partner's expecting our baby, and I can't wait to be a father!"

"Really?" Lutecia said. "Congratulations! I'm so happy for you."

The man laughed, brimming with emotion.

"Thanks! I'm thrilled. That guppy's not even born yet, and I already love him or her so much!"

Suddenly from the dark depths of the sea beyond the whirlpool, a shadow emerged and joined the throne-room scene.

"His Imperial Majesty," Alessia heard the man she was inside of announce happily. "Here's his majesty's beloved, safe and sound, as requested."

A younger Emperor Oscor walked up to Lutecia, and flung his arms around her. She gave a giggle of relief, and he loosened his hug to look down at the baby, who was cooing softly. The Emperor stroked the baby's head lovingly, and then looked back up at the mother.

"May I?" he asked her.

"Of course!" she answered sniffling, and handed him the baby.

The Emperor looked down at the child in his arms, bouncing it gently.

"I love you, Lutecia, you know that," he said.

"Yes," she said, smiling.

His face fell into an empathetic frown.

"That's why you have to believe, I'm genuinely sorry," he said in a voice tinged with feeling. "People can't find out about this... and I just can't take the chance."

Before Alessia could understand what was happening, the Emperor was behind Lutecia, and Lutecia had fallen to her knees. The Emperor winced and looked away, bouncing the baby in one arm while he wiped blood off his blade onto his breeches. A puddle of blood grew around Lutecia. He'd slit her throat.

"Lutecia? Lutecia!" yelped the man Alessia was inhabiting, and he slid down to Lutecia's side.

The baby was bawling. With a few more hollow choking noises, Lutecia finally collapsed in Alessia's man-arms.

"NO!" the man yelled. Alessia could see his tears dropping onto Lutecia's face.

The man delicately placed Lutecia's head on the ground, and jumped up to his feet, but the Emperor was gone. All Alessia could see before her was a shadow growing against the wall, engulfing her. Someone was behind her; behind the man. A sharp pain in her chest yanked her out of the scene.

51

It took Alessia a moment to understand where she was. She was still in the whirlpool, though around her, everything had grown much darker. She was deep in the sea, spiraling in a narrow tunnel to the abyss.

What had she just seen? If that was the Emperor Oscor, the baby must have been Vulcor. Had she seen the wrong person's truth? How did it relate to her father?

Her throat tightened. *She* had been in her father's body.

He *was* a part of the Emperor's Order. He *was* loyal to the Emperor. He'd followed instructions and brought Vulcor and his mother to the Emperor, believing they wouldn't be harmed, but he'd been mistaken.

'*I recently found out my partner's expecting our baby*'. Her father knew about her!

Tears filled Alessia's eyes again. She'd felt first-hand how excited her father had been. He *wanted* to meet her, to care for her. He *loved her* before she was even born! She curled her fingers over the prongs of his trident, and squeezed it as though she were squeezing his hand.

Why had he not stayed with her and her mother? Had something happened to him?

Her stomach lurched. Now that she was so close to the point of this infernal underwater twister, spinning so fast, the dizziness was unbearable.

She couldn't get stuck here, not now that she finally had some answers.

'Look for the light', Ebrie had said.

But she'd sunk so deep, there was *no* light. When she tilted her head up to where the sky had been, if anything, it seemed even *darker*.

Darker?

She looked down. She was right – it was less dark below her. That meant there was light there, even if she didn't see it now. She must have been turned upside down.

She jerked her body around until she was the right way up again, then cupped her hands, trying to ignore the ache from her broken fingers. She'd have to 'swim' up the whirlpool. (Or do her best imitation of it, at least.)

She kicked, and pulled herself up, gasping in pain. She wouldn't be able to go on like that for very long. But she had to try. She bit her lip, and kept going. It was almost like climbing up a watery wall. Pulling and pulling with shaking arms, pushing and pushing with her feet. Little by little, she made her way out of the narrow tunnel. She could see the whirlpool opening up above her now. The light was there, and that meant the surface was there. It was working.

She kept climbing, completely breathless, her broken fingers throbbing. Suddenly her hand cramped up. She couldn't keep it cupped anymore. Water flowed through her fingers.

She stopped. She screamed, furious at herself. She

wasn't just going to watch herself spiral back down the funnel after all the progress she'd made!

But she was exhausted. It was only a matter of time before her legs didn't have the strength to kick her up anymore either.

"Help!" she screamed breathlessly. Her lungs burned from the effort, and shouting felt like scratching at scorched flesh. "Help!"

She broke into sobs. Who was even there to hear her screams?

"Alessia!"

Was she dreaming?

"KELLA! OVER HERE!"

"There, Niva! I see her!" Kella's voice shouted again, barely audible over the crashing water. "Alessia, we're coming!"

Something obstructed the light from above. There was a soft, but violent noise, like a bedsheet smacking the air. Alessia looked up to see two sirens swooping down to her, their large, majestic white wings flapping to brake as they came to a halt just above her. Kella was dangling under one of the sirens, held up by the siren's hawk-like claws.

The other siren wrapped her claws around Alessia's shoulders, flapped her wings vigorously, and lifted Alessia out.

"Kella," Alessia managed, panting, as both girls hung above the vortex. "Thank. You. So. So. Much"

"Don't thank me, thank Niva and Noora!"

The siren holding up Kella tossed her head back to get the tresses out of her face and answered, "The pleasure's mine. Now my debt from losing that last game of Scales with Herior is settled, he'll finally be off my back!" She chuckled.

"How did you find me?" Alessia asked.

"I thought this whirlpool thing was suspicious," Kella said. "So I went to Seagrass-City after you, and started shouting after this 'Ebrie' person you mentioned."

Alessia had to choke back a laugh imagining what Seagrass-City inhabitants thought about all these weird humans going around screaming 'Ebrie' at the top of their lungs.

"Well, this Ebrie was pacing around there, all worried, and seemed super relieved to see me! She told me that Minchans can't save others from the Whirlpool of Firnor – but that *I* could. Since the clandestine Marcaval still wasn't back, we decided the best way would be to find a Siren to fly me out there. So I shelled Herior, told him you were in trouble and asked him if he had siren friends that could help us. So he rushed out to find Niva and Noora."

"We went to the spot Ebrie told us," added Kella's siren. "Good thing you called out for help! We'd never have found you otherwise. Nothing sounds more like rushing water, than more rushing water, and Triton, the waves were rough today!"

Alessia couldn't believe all the people who had mobilized to help her!

Below them the vortex slowly closed up and she shuddered to think where she would be without them.

"Well, it's me who owes you a debt now. You saved my life. All of you." She looked at Kella with tears in her eyes. If she'd only known in that first Biomimetics class, that that small gesture of empathy would be the beginning of such a precious friendship.

"Where do you want us to drop you?"

Alessia opened her mouth to answer, but then hesitated. This was her chance. She was dangling over the ocean, in the middle of nowhere. This was no-man's-land. She could ask to go back to Scotland, to her boarding school, to her life in Selva, and forget everything that had happened. After all, she'd fended off a grindylow attack before, maybe she'd survive the next one too. And what benefit did staying in Nethuns have? It wasn't like she was safe there either, the notes made that abundantly clear. What if she couldn't get any more answers about her father? What else did she have to stay for?

The waves had calmed, now that the vortex was shut. Everything was quiet but for the squawking of seagulls, and flapping of siren wings. Alessia looked up at Kella again; her first real friend.

"The Port of Atlantis, please."

52

"**D**id you find out the truth about your father?" Kella
asked her, when they were alone again, at the port.

"I think so…"

Alessia was as brief as possible. The adrenalin had worn
off, and the pain from her broken fingers was unbearable.
She recounted what she'd found out from Yagora and from
the Whirlpool of Firnor, leaving out the part about the baby,
to protect Vulcor's secret.

"It helped a lot, but I still don't know the most
important piece: where my father is now," she concluded.

"Yeah…" Kella said. "And there's still something that
doesn't quite make sense. I get what Iktor meant about your
father making a mistake by trusting the Emperor. Your
father was part of the Emperor's Order and the Emperor
tricked him into bringing in this random innocent woman to
be killed.

"But is that really the only reason Iktor was so
distrustful of *you*? Because your father, who you clearly
don't even *know*, was Emperor's Order? So many students'

parents work for the Emperor's Guard, or the Emperor's communication. Why would he single *you* out?"

"Well, if there *is* anything else about my father that made Iktor wary, there's one person who might know," Alessia said.

"Larthuzor's grandfather! I still can't believe what Yagora said! Who'd have guessed that sweet, old man had such a huge secret? We should go and talk to him and- Whoa!"

Kella grabbed Alessia's hand and Alessia screamed in pain.

"Sorry!" said Kella, carefully letting her friend's horribly bruised and swollen hand go. "What happened to your fingers?"

"I think I broke them in the whirlpool. Let's talk to Larthuzor's grandfather tomorrow, now I really need to go home and rest," Alessia said.

Kella agreed and let her go. Sadly though, resting and tending to her fingers still had to wait. Alessia had to find Vulcor to tell him what she'd found out about Iktor, and ask his help to get the Emperor to release him.

~

Alessia jumped off her ovehic at the Octopus's Garden and made her way through Vulcor's hideout. She strode down the corridor lit by ghostly glowing fish Drifts, each of her steps echoing loudly and craned her neck to check the wooden beam above.

"Vulcor!" she called out. "Vulcor, come out, it's me. It's Alessia!"

Her fingers were stiff, and she wondered if she shouldn't have gone home after all. At the end of the corridor, Vulcor jumped off the beam to the ground. The poor light of the corridor cast shadows that further warped his face, already contorted with rage.

He marched towards her, his trousers billowing dramatically and his eyes like smoldering coal. The little baby cooing in his mother's arms flashed through her mind and she felt a pang of sadness. How different would he have been if he'd stayed with her instead of being brought back to the Emperor?

"What was that?" he snapped at her. "You can't be *a little* careful for once? I tell you I'm being hunted. And *you* think it's a good idea to barge in and shout after me. You're not a stupid girl. So why would you do this? Do you not care? It's all the same to you whether—"

"Vulcor!" Alessia interrupted. The pain in her fingers flared. "I came to ask you a favor. It's about your dad."

"What about him?" he answered with a belligerent bark that failed to disguise the fact he'd been destabilized.

"He caught the wrong guy," she answered, sucking air through her teeth. Her fingers ached unbearably now.

"They caught someone?" Vulcor said.

Alessia painfully recounted everything about the Green Pung, and the arrest, and why she thought Iktor was innocent.

Vulcor listened attentively, then his face eased into a skeptical smirk. "Well, of *course* he *says* he didn't take the Green Pung."

"What? No, it's not like that. He *asked* me where it was."

"So he's good at playing the fool."

"No!" How was he not getting this? "I could just *tell*, Vulcor. Trust me for once. I made a mistake. He was inno–"

"Alessia," Vulcor interrupted. His tone shifted and he

approached her kindly. "I know you feel guilty. I can imagine being responsible for someone going to jail is tough."

"That's not it! He's an innocent man. You have to help, Vulcor, please!"

"Look, I couldn't help even if I wanted to. You think my father could be convinced to release this guy because I tell him about your 'intuition'? He won't let him go. And it will only make things worse for you!"

"But–"

"It's okay," he continued. "It's good news! I may not be totally safe, but at least one power-hating guy is out, and my father will ease the crab guard around me so it'll be livable back at the palace."

Alessia groaned in frustration. He was so obstinate. And the worst thing was that that only reinforced his point. If it was this hard for her to convince *him*, there was no way they'd manage to persuade the Emperor. She needed a lot more to fix the mess she'd made.

She dropped her head back against the tunnel wall. Her fingers were back down to a dull ache, but she didn't have the energy to keep arguing.

"Alessia, don't be angry," he said. "All I'm saying is I'm a little relieved. This is already something! And it seems it's thanks to you."

She winced. As if she didn't feel guilty enough already, now her mistake had earned her Vulcor's admiration... and she couldn't help liking the feeling.

She opened her mouth to correct him, but stopped short. There was something different about the way he was looking at her. He seemed suddenly nervous. His normally cold marble-white face was pinkish, and he was shifting from one leg to the other, hesitating. Then, he steeled himself, inched closer and gulped.

She got startled and averted her gaze, and he immediately looked away too, and stepped back.

Alessia's heart leaped in her chest. Had he been about to *kiss* her? If he had, he'd obviously felt the same shyness as her! And that made her feel closer to him than ever yet.

"I'll be returning home then," he said, looking at his feet and rubbing the nape of his neck.

Alessia looked at him, trying to seem 'normal' but forgetting what 'normal' looked like.

"Yeah," Alessia said. "Stay careful though. I'm telling you the *real* bad guy is still–"

"I will," Vulcor interrupted to placate her.

She wanted him to know that she wanted to keep seeing him, but she swallowed the words before they came out of her mouth and started to walk away.

"Alessia," Vulcor called out, his voice slightly shakier than normal. "Are there other Selvan games you know? Like that hide and seek one you showed me."

She could have burst with glee.

"Yes! Loads!"

"Then let's meet tomorrow evening?"

"Okay, but be ready. They'll get tougher!" she said unable to control the smile growing on her face.

"Bring it on!" he said. "I'll pick you up tomorrow evening at your place."

She struggled to get herself to turn away from him.

As she stepped out the tunnel, she swatted away the thought buzzing at the back of her mind like an irritating fly: *Could it be that he wasn't worried about the still-missing vial of Green Pung, because he was the one who took it?*

53

"**M**y grandfather? What are you talking about!" Larthuzor said, biting off each word. Alessia had never seen him so outraged. Even the eelrus (eel with walrus tusks) around his neck cowered.

"Don't blame us! It's what the kappa said," Kella defended. "And considering your grandfather has all these forbidden Penglini botanical books you told us about, it's not so far-fetched he made the forbidden vial too."

Until that moment, the next day had come as a welcome injection of normalcy. The night before, Felthor had treated Alessia's fingers with a gel made from coralline red algae, so her fingers were already straighter and hurting less. That morning, Iktor's classes were cancelled, but apart from that, it was 'business as usual' at school – from the daily recitation of the Emperor's Shield in the morning, to the whizzing around of the sole-fish tablets at lunch. It's only when they were about to go home that Kella caught the boys alone, and confronted Larthuzor.

"Watch what you say," Larthuzor threatened. "You could get him killed with an accusation like that!"

"We *have* to go and talk to him."

"Out of the question. If my parents find out you're talking about illegal stuff, they'll never let me see any of you again."

"Aw, come on Larthu! It's for the investigation!" Herior said.

Larthuzor's crescent eyes shot daggers at him, and Herior stepped back in surprise.

"Okay, okay. Let's drop it for now," Alessia said to ease tensions. "We have plenty of other things to investigate. Like... Um..."

Herior kicked the fence. "If only they hadn't destroyed the Drifts of the Emperor's Order when they were erasing the traces of the New Current."

"What difference would that make?" Kella said.

"Well, she must look a lot like her father if everyone keeps recognizing her. If we had a Drift, we could probably have identified him on it."

Kella opened her mouth to argue, but shut it when she realized he had a point. They were distracted by a shriek coming from Sivaria and Perfect Princess Tamaya as they walked by.

"Seriously! She was downright *chasing me!*" Sivaria was complaining while fingering her chestnut plait, clearly proud of having been at the center of whatever drama they were talking about. Kella wrinkled her round, red nose in disgust.

"Oh, Herior! Larthu! Don't mind us. We're just talking about crazy ol' Dolia," Sivaria said. Apparently her teasing didn't spare elderly, bereaved store-owners. "Always a conspiracy theory with her. '*My daughter! They said she was the crème de la crème, then they took her!*' I swear I thought I was her daughter, back from the dead!"

"Aw... I almost feel bad for her!" Tamaya giggled. "Poor, crazy old lady."

"Wow, Tamaya, what a heart of gold," Herior applauded sarcastically.

"Of course," Tamaya said sweetly, curtsying.

"'*Crème de la crème*'..." Alessia murmured. She signaled Kella to step aside with her.

"'*Crème de la crème*'. She said Dolia called her daughter the '*crème de la crème*'," Alessia repeated.

"Yeah, so what? Dolia always says that. As much as I hate to agree with those girls, that Dolia *is* a bit loopy. I mean, you know it – she's your upstairs neighbor isn't she?"

"She is, but that's not the point. Moxia Authenta said the students picked for the Emperor's Order were the '*crème de la crème*'. I remember because I thought it was an unusual expression to use: a Selvan French expression, that's not even that commonly used in *Selva*."

Kella paused to reflect. "Now that you mention it, it is a *really* unusual expression. If Moxia used it, it must have been how the Emperor talked about his Emperor's Order at the time. So you think Dolia's daughter... was in the Emperor's Order?"

"It fits. Wimmi told me that the Emperor made Dolia the owner of the Iceberg department stores completely out of the blue. That could have been the Emperor rewarding Dolia's daughter for her service in the Order. And then her disappearance could be linked to the New Current."

"I have an idea," Kella said. "Come with me."

They took an ovehic to Alessia and Dolia's olive-seashell-shaped apartment building. Somehow its red glow, which normally seemed warm and inviting to Alessia, struck her differently this time. She found herself thinking about the red beacons at sea, that warn sailors of the limits they could go. She shook the feeling and they 'Fluita-ed' up to a wavy door on the top floor.

Kella knocked, but the cold, thick shell barely made a noise under her knuckles. She went to knock again, when the door flew open to reveal Wimmi's nereid friend, Ballina.

"Alessia! What are you doing here?"

"We wanted to see Dolia Authenta. It's for a class project," Kella lied.

"Dolia Authenta isn't well," Ballina said. "And guests can be quite upsetting to her. It's better you do your project on someone else."

Alessia felt the intensity of Ballina's compassion for Dolia. This was never going to work. Her heart sank – she wanted to be inside so badly. Since Larthuzor had refused to ask his grandfather, Kella's idea was their only lead.

But just as Kella opened her mouth to protest, Ballina surprised them with, "You know what, I really want you to meet Dolia. Come in, come in!"

Kella whipped her head around to Alessia, her eyebrows curled like question marks.

"That was weird..." Alessia mouthed.

They followed Ballina into an immense, round vestibule, darting looks at each other. The high ceiling spiraled up to a point like the roof. Beneath it, the room had all the trappings of aristocratic Selvan living rooms from around the world, from antique Chinese lacquer cabinets, to chesterfield sofas. But it was as though all of the mismatched items had just been positioned at even intervals with no purpose other than to fill some of the vast, empty space. This wasn't a living room to be lived in. It felt more like a doctor's office, with stiff sofas that were just meant for waiting.

"She'll be in the young Authenta's room."

Between the various items of furniture were doors apparently leading to other rooms, and Ballina signaled the girls to the one that stood between the superimposed Ottoman tea tables and a velvet fringed couch of non-descript color (either a rich green, turned yellow with time, or a luxurious gold, turned khaki with mildew).

Alessia opened the door slowly enough to give warning that they were coming in. Unlike the austere anteroom, this space had clearly been lived in. And yet, there was something even more grim about it.

The scrumpled covers on the clamshell bed were coated evenly in a thick layer of dust. Sitting on the dressing table across the room, was a hot whelkee cockle which must have been left half-full years ago, and was now overgrown with thick mold which had spread over the desk and was no doubt responsible for the putrid smell filling the room. The room had been frozen in time, *years* ago.

Dolia was sitting on the small stool next to the dressing table, looking in the direction of the bed without really seeing it.

"Dolia Authenta?" Alessia said hesitantly.

For a moment, the old lady didn't react. Then, she peered up at them through her straight grey bangs, and her face contorted with a strange mix of alarm and hope.

"Cariesa," she muttered, and had a sudden impulse towards Alessia. Alessia cowered, and just in time, Ballina stepped forward and caught Dolia.

"Dolia Authenta, this isn't Cariesa," Ballina cooed calmly, as if by habit. "Remember, we talked about this? Sometimes you miss her so much, you see her in other girls?"

Dolia looked frightened and confused for a moment. "No, no! Cariesa, tell them–"

"Dolia Authenta," interrupted Ballina. "This isn't Cariesa, this is *Alessia*. You only recognize her because she lives downstairs."

Dolia's eyes darted frantically from Ballina to Alessia. Finally, she let out a sigh and her head dropped in resignation. Ballina gently accompanied her back to her stool.

"Dolia Authenta, do you have any Drifts of the Emperor's Order?" Kella blurted. People could say what they would of Kella, at least she was direct.

"What are you talking about?" Ballina yawped. "You know it's illegal to have their Drifts. I hope this isn't what you came to disturb her over!"

She glided across the room to the girls, and started shooing them out, when Dolia's weak voice said: "Wait, let them stay."

Ballina looked at her boss with pity. "Dolia Authenta—"

"Let them stay, please. I want to speak with them," Dolia replied.

"As you wish, Authenta," Ballina answered. She left the room, shutting the door behind herself, after giving the girls one last warning glance.

"Why do you think I have Drifts of the Emperor's Order?" Dolia asked Kella.

"We think your daughter Cariesa was part of it; and we think you'd have wanted to keep Drifts of her after losing her, even if the Emperor forbade it," Kella answered simply.

Dolia eyed them carefully. "Why?"

It wasn't clear which of Kella's outrageous accusations Dolia was reacting to.

Alessia stepped forward, and accidentally kicked a hairbrush lying on the floor. Dolia rushed across the room to it. On the floor underneath where the hairbrush had been, there was a darker hairbrush-shaped mark. Dolia placed the hairbrush carefully on the exact marking, before taking her seat again. She was purposely keeping this room exactly as Cariesa had left it.

"You kept Drifts of her because you love her," Kella answered, "as obsessively as my mother loves me."

Dolia gave her a sad knowing smile. Then, she removed a hairpin from her hair, and opened the top drawer of the dressing table which was strangely full of old cosmetics with packaging printed in Russian alphabet. She ran her hand along the underside of the drawer and stopped at a point. Keeping her finger there to mark the spot, she pushed the hairpin up against it. The hairpin seemed to vanish up the bottom of the drawer and all the Soviet cosmetics tumbled to the back.

The drawer had a false bottom, and the hairpin was pushing it up through a small hole. When she had pushed it up enough to grab it, she lifted the false bottom out altogether to reveal the secret compartment below. There lay a hidden pile of books.

"They wanted to take away all the Drifts of my baby," she said with emotion. "I couldn't let them. It's all I have left."

Alessia and Kella exchanged an excited look as Dolia's dry fingers carefully reached into the middle of the pile and extracted a small notebook.

"This was her diary," Dolia said, opening it delicately to show a handwritten page. "And if you wanted to see the Emperor's Order, this was Cariesa's own album where she'd captured her Emperor's Order friends." Dolia handed them a small brown book.

The moment Alessia opened the cover, a mini-Drift grew out of the book like a pop-up card, above a small pearl glued in it. A dozen people the size of dolls, stood on the page.

Alessia scoured the Drift from left to right slowly when something caught her eye. The third person from the left. Her heart skipped a beat. She pulled the book up to her face to be sure. She frantically flipped through to find another Drift, a larger Drift, a confirmation. One after the other, the Drifts started growing before being whipped down by another page turn. She finally stopped on a page where the Drift was a close-up of three men. 'Silor and the guys' was scribbled on the page, below the glued pearl. There he was again. The familiar face that had no place there, looking up at her with an almost mocking grin.

Alessia's hands dropped and the book slipped out of her fingers.

"You okay?" asked Kella.

Alessia barely heard. She was in shock.

"Sorry, I've got to go," she muttered, and she ran out.

～

Alessia stormed into her apartment.

"Felthor! You were in the Emperor's Order? Why didn't—" she stopped dead in her tracks. Vulcor was unconscious on the floor, hands tied behind his back. Before she could do anything, Alessia came crashing down with a thud.

54

Grey stone tinged with a teal glow fluttered in and out of sight through Alessia's trembling eyelids. She finally managed to pry her eyes open. It was as though she'd woken from a deep sleep, and it took a moment for her to remember where she'd been just before, and understand the area now around her.

She was in a dark cave, lying on her stomach on a rough stony tabletop. All around her were pillars of the blueish green light that connected to a huge glowing mass hovering above her.

She'd seen that before – that strange 'squid' of light with its oblong head stretching up to a point in the ceiling, and tentacles reaching into the ground.

Suddenly, it clicked. She was in an Orichalca-conduction mine. Like the one they'd 'visited' in Rascor's power class. In the far corner of the cave was the miner's entrance, with a closed door, just big enough to fit a kappa or a child. And the blue 'squid' was a reservoir of Orichalca, the liquid crystal through which the heat from the Earth's core was being transferred to be used as power in Atlantis.

Only two things were different than she remembered. A huge transportation bubble was shimmering near the miner's entrance. And strange shadows were floating across the reservoir.

A wet stony footstep pattered softly behind her, light but loaded, like a pad of papers dropping.

She dragged her arms to her side to push herself up and see what was making the noise.

"Stop," shot out a man's voice. "Don't move."

Alessia froze. She didn't dare look. Had he pulled a gun on her? Did they have guns in Nethuns?

The voice softened: "My dear."

Her heart dropped. The thought she'd been avoiding without realizing it bubbled up to the surface of her mind: Felthor. There was no denying it. The voice was his.

"Why are you doing this to me?"

"Oh, it's not something I'm doing *to you*," he answered softly, bending over to get closer to her level. "It's so, so much bigger than you. I'm terribly sorry but it's necessary, I'm afraid. It's for the cause."

He spoke in the same voice he'd used to teach her, to help her. Hearing that tone of voice was the spookiest part: he wasn't possessed, or angry. He was *himself*.

Then she noticed it. On another stone altar like the one she was on, stood the vial of Green Pung. A strangled cry swelled in her throat.

Of course. Felthor had seen it slipping from her pocket during Inundanza, and had simply taken it from her room, at his leisure, the night before school. No fuss, no break-in. She'd basically handed him his weapon.

He followed her gaze to it, then rushed to a corner of the cave to get something. Before she could react, he threw a quilt of black seaweed on her. The same kind she'd seen used on Espior the Oculate in the Tiding.

She screamed, and tried to lift her arms to throw it off, but it was too late. Like a boa constrictor, the seaweed slithered around her body, extending from all sides to wrap her in its embrace.

"Let me go!"

But Felthor had already walked back to the table with the Green Pung. He held up a large trident, and looked back at her, closing one eye as if to check something was in alignment.

By now, only Alessia's head, shoulders and feet stuck out from the tight, dark cocoon of seaweed. The more she struggled to free herself of its grasp, the more it tightened around her. She yelped in pain as it squeezed her not-fully-healed fingers. She needed to figure out another way to get free. She craned her neck to look at the reservoir again and suddenly realized what the shadows floating across it were.

One was an elderly man, his chest seemingly attached to the hovering blue mass by purple lightning bolts, and his head hanging backwards unconsciously. His face was gaunt, and marked with exhaustion, but she recognized him from the Tiding. It was the Oculate Espior. And the other shadow...

"Vulcor!" She couldn't stop his name escaping her lips in a shocked whisper. It all tumbled through her mind like a house of cards falling. Inundanza. She'd said out loud in front of Felthor that Vulcor was in the tunnels, when he shelled her. Felthor had left that evening and come back flustered. Someone had attacked Vulcor. It was Felthor chasing him all along. And she'd led him to him.

Vulcor's head lolled to the side drowsily and he slowly opened his eyes.

"Alessia," he wheezed. He'd been beaten badly, and was fighting to regain consciousness. He groaned with effort and a spark of life finally flashed into his dead, dark gaze. "Alessia!"

He let out a roar of fury, and pulled his head around to the side. It was the only part of his body he could move. Both he and the Oculate were wrapped in the same dense, black seaweed as she was.

"What kind of monsters are you?" he bellowed. Monsters? So someone else was there with Felthor.

"How could you hurt her?" Vulcor continued. "She had nothing to do with this! You're going to pay..."

A woman's laugh resounded loudly against the cave walls. It was a graceful laugh, the laugh of a glamorous woman, not that of a villain.

"Oh finboy! You are a funny one."

Something struck Alessia about the voice. It was *familiar*. She wracked her brain. Whose voice was it? A few stones crumbled off the wall.

"That's not very polite, Vulcor!" the woman said. "I take it from that feeble attempt to throw rocks at me that you can't yet control your powers without your arms. How disappointing! Should've studied harder."

"Let Alessia go! It's me you want!" he yelled.

"Ah, you're just like your father – so absorbed in your own power, you miss the whole point," she answered in amusement. He let out another furious grunt and more rocks fell from the ceiling.

In a slow, deliberate, teasing voice, she finished, "Alessia has *everything* to do with it."

Alessia's stomach turned. Was this about the sacrifice from the note?

"Who are you? What do you mean?" she shouted at the

woman she still couldn't see. She turned back to Felthor. "Felthor, please! You have to tell me what's happening! Why are you doing this? Is Wimmi in this too?"

Felthor was taken aback and dropped the trident he'd been holding up.

"What?" His moon face melted ever so slightly into a sad expression. "No, no! Of course not! Wimmi's... he would never–"

A cloud came over his face and his eyes turned cold.

"Stay quiet, now," he said and picked up the trident again.

She'd touched a nerve. Maybe she *could* make him see reason. She had to trigger an episode to understand how. She closed her eyes, let in that familiar rush of emotions, and finally, felt *him*.

Frustration. Shame. Rage. He was torn between his pity for her, and his anger and determination, but the latter was undeniably stronger. It was toxic. It obsessed him. He was fanatical. Whatever his plan was, he'd see it through.

Goosebumps popped down her neck. She hadn't expected this; feeling her *own* trusted Felthor, so decided on hurting her. She didn't want to feel this anymore, she wanted to pull out. Now.

She swung back to what *she'd* been feeling to stop the episode short, like he'd taught her. She focused on her physical pain, leaning on the spot where he'd knocked her head. It ripped through her and replaced the hold his furor had on her brain.

There was a scream. But not from her.

Felthor was bent double, groaning through gritted teeth and pressing his palms on one side of his head so hard that veins bulged on the back of his hands. Alessia's jaw went slack.

The spot he was pressing was the *exact same spot* where *her head* was throbbing.

"Stop!" Felthor barked, all the warmth gone from his voice now. "Don't do anything. It'll be over soon. Just try to relax."

"What's going on?" the woman snapped at him. "Throw on some more seaweed constrictor, I see her moving."

But Alessia hardly noticed what she said. Something had happened; something Alessia barely dared to consider because it was so absurd. And yet... it also didn't feel that surprising at all. Like being sure you don't know a piece of trivia, and then being told what it is, and realizing that you *had* known it all along.

If her episodes were letting her feel what others felt, were they also transmitting to *others* what *she* was feeling, when she focused back on her own emotions?

Fragments of the past year flashed through her mind.

When she'd become so violent with Iktor in class. She'd felt *his* hatred at first, but when she'd focused back on her own mortification, *he'd* suddenly looked ashamed and scared.

When she'd run into Dolia. She'd first felt the old woman's delusion of recognizing her daughter, but when she'd focused back on her own desire to run away, *Dolia* had randomly run too.

When she'd wanted so passionately to be let into her home after the break-in. Out of the blue, the investigator had insisted she be let up.

When she'd wanted Ballina to let them speak to Dolia. Ballina had suddenly changed her mind and invited them in.

Even the Dead Man's Chest vault, that was meant to

open only when its owner wills it to, had inexplicably opened when *she'd* wanted it to. Had she willed Iktor to open it from a distance?

It was impossible... but it was even *more* impossible that these were all coincidence.

The episodes she'd thought were an illness, were looking almost like... a power. Just as Vulcor could move objects, she could manipulate *minds*.

And judging from how Felthor just reacted – instantly blaming her when his head had hurt – he knew. She remembered how he'd insisted on her first day that she tell him about any 'unusual sensations'. He'd known all along. And he'd led her to believe she had some weird condition landfarers got, and was imagining things.

She closed her eyes and was about to plunge back into Felthor's mind, when another pile of black seaweed was thrown on her. It crept around her already enveloped body, and tightened.

She screamed in agony as it crushed her fingers.

"Take it off! Please! I promise I won't move. Please Felthor!" she cried.

"Let her go!" Vulcor yelled, and a few more stones tumbled down the cave wall.

She needed to focus her mind back on Felthor, to use her power. She closed her eyes again. It was no use. All she could think about was the excruciating pain in her hand.

Felthor came, but only to turn her on her back. She was lying like a sacrificial animal, looking up at the glowing blue-green reservoir helplessly.

"Don't. Do. This," she grunted. Her seaweed straitjacket constrained her so tightly now that she couldn't even move enough to wriggle off the altar.

A figure in a dark purple wetsuit emerged from the

shadows of the cave, approaching with large, confident strides. It must have been the woman, though her face was half-covered by the neck of the wetsuit.

She uncorked the Green Pung vial, and mist spread rapidly out of it. Alessia went into a fit of coughs that became increasingly guttural until she was retching.

The woman paid no attention. Without hesitation, she threw half of the vial's green liquid contents into the hovering reservoir, before recorking it and placing it back down.

As soon as the Green Pung hit the Orichalca liquid crystal, there was a blinding lime-green flash. Moans of pain came from Espior and Vulcor, and the reservoir glowed emerald.

Then, to Alessia's surprise, the woman gave Felthor a nod and jumped up into the reservoir too.

Unlike Espior and Vulcor, she seemed to suffer no pain from coming into contact with the Green Pung-laced Orichalca. She floated effortlessly in the middle of it, with Vulcor and Espior writhing in pain on either side of her.

A mechanical clang resounded. Felthor cranked back a lever and Alessia's altar was raised halfway to the reservoir. The four of them had been positioned to form the shape of a trident. That was the alignment Felthor was checking. The leg of the altar was the stick, the three figures in the Orichalca were the three spikes, and as soon as she'd be raised to the level of the Orichalca, she would be the base of those spikes. Some sort of ritual was about to occur, and they were almost in place.

She had to get into Felthor's head now. She had to focus. But all she could think about was her pain. And it wasn't like other overwhelming feelings, that *helped* bring on an episode by distracting her, and making her let her guard down. The pain was pushing her guard *up*; blocking her. She couldn't open herself to his thoughts.

Felthor gave the lever one final crank, and a purple spark from the reservoir reached the tip of her nose. The floodgates were open. The single purple spark grew to a massive lightning bolt, wrapped itself around her head and pulled it up towards the reservoir.

She instantly felt faint, and cold. Her thoughts slowed. Her senses melted away. Patches of darkness spread before her eyes, and white noise grew louder and louder in her ears. It was as though all the energy was being sucked out of her, up into the Orichalca.

Like... a transfer. That was it! It was exactly like Rascor had taught them. For a transfer of power, you need a conductive material and an imbalance of power to trigger the shift. The Orichalca was a conductive material... and Vulcor and Espior suddenly having their powers destroyed by the Green Pung would create a huge void: an imbalance.

Felthor and this woman were trying to get *Alessia's* power transferred up to the woman.

Vulcor was a floating shell now. The Green Pung was *killing him*. Alessia had to stop this. She needed to stop thinking about the pain in her fingers. She took a deep breath in, and back out. In, and back out. In, and back out. Her chest was so compressed, even breathing was difficult. But she kept going. Focusing on her breath, to forget the pain.

Her mind was emptying. It was working. She took another deep breath and opened herself to receive Felthor's mind. His frenzy poured in immediately, and once she had him, she flipped the switch.

"Free Vulcor, let Vulcor go, free Vulcor, let Vulcor go," she urged in her head.

Felthor looked at her suspiciously. He knew what she was doing. He marched towards her. He was going to stop her.

"Come on, free Vulcor, let him go, you want to let him go." Tears filled her eyes as she begged and pleaded silently, all the while feeling weaker and weaker.

Felthor was almost in front of her now. He was carrying a large rock. He was going to knock her out. There was a blip in her thought process as her mind instinctively raced to find any means to escape. She shook off the thought. She couldn't lose focus.

"Let Vulcor go!" she yelled in her head just as Felthor reached her altar.

And then, he walked right past her. He paced to the cave wall behind her, pushed down another lever and they were plunged into pitch black darkness. The purple sparks vanished, and with them, the Orichalca reservoir that had been shining above their heads. The Green Pung that had been in it splatted on the floor, and Vulcor, Espior and the woman dropped with a thud.

55

"Vulcor!" Alessia cried.

"*Spraints!*" cursed the woman.

"Vulcor! Are you okay?" Alessia shouted again.

"Alessia..." he answered weakly.

"Oh thank Triton!" she exhaled in relief.

"She knows about the power, Felthor. Shell the rusalka for reinforcement," the woman ordered.

"I swear she didn't know," whimpered Felthor. "Everything happened like I told you – she believed the episodes were a sickness and I was coaching her to control them. The moment I saw it had evolved, when Dolia ran away from her for no reason, I told you immediately that she was ready."

"You disobeyed me," the woman answered. "You're almost as bad as the Gavrols – helping with the first abduction, but then turning their noses at the operation when they realized sacrifices would need to be made."

The Gavrols? Where had Alessia heard that name before?

"Being part of the New Current means getting your

hands dirty!" the woman continued. "When you don't, we fail! You waited to abduct the boy. They became friends, and seeing his power, she understood hers."

"I didn't wait!" Felthor protested. "I tried to get the boy when I saw them go into his secret hideout after class, and again when he contacted her during Inundanza. He got away from me! I only managed to get him today when he came to our house."

"Alessia, psst," Vulcor whispered. He'd rolled over to the foot of the altar where she lay.

"Vulcor! Use your powers, take off the seaweed," she whispered back.

"I can't control them with my hands tied, we have to get it off ourselves," he answered in a strained voice as he squirmed to get free.

Alessia wondered if she could use her powers again on one of their captors to get them to take off the seaweed. It was too risky. Manipulating one of them would only attract the other's attention.

She twisted her body again but the seaweed only tightened.

"It's no use!" She grunted in frustration. "It's like it's doing it intentionally!"

And then it hit her. This seaweed was a living thing – it *did* have some form of intention. Was that enough for her to control?

She took a deep breath and opened her mind. She immediately felt Felthor's shame, and the woman's fury, but deflected them. Finally, she found what she was looking for. It was fainter than human emotions, less tangible: like how the light aroma of an herbal tea might compare to the full flavor and consistency of solid food. It felt foreign, but she could still empathize with it: the seaweed's unconscious instinct to wrap. She held the feeling in her heart, then shifted back to her own longing to be released to transmit the urge to the seaweed.

Suddenly, it loosened around her. She heard Vulcor's seaweed binding flap to the ground too.

"Alessia, the seaweed–"

"Ssh. I know. Come, the miner's entrance is just in the corner. Let's go," she muttered.

"Not before they get what they deserve."

Vulcor jumped to his feet and a cascade of rocks came crashing down the cave wall. He was randomly throwing his arms in this direction and that, in the pitch black of the cave, hoping to hit their abductors. Alessia rolled her eyes. Vulcor and his temper. So much for not attracting their attention.

She slipped off the altar. If they weren't going to escape, at least she had to prevent them from getting drained again. She crept towards where the Green Pung had been.

"Turn that light on, seascum! I want to see your faces when I beat you up," Vulcor howled.

"Look who found use of his powers again," the woman teased.

"That's right!" he yelled, tearing rocks from the cave walls, and sending them all over the place. "And now you'll pay for this!"

The woman laughed naturally. As though she had no intention of being vicious, and was genuinely *amused* by his feisty reactions.

"It's useless to fight, finboy. Calm yourself! You can't win this. You've never met anyone as accustomed to the dark as me, I promise you that."

She was right. Every sentence she said seemed to be

coming from somewhere else in the cave. She was moving around in the dark with uncanny dexterity.

"Who are you?" Vulcor yelled, thrashing around furiously.

Alessia felt the edge of the Green Pung altar with her fingertips.

"I'm sure you've figured that out by now," the woman answered in the gentle, no-nonsense tone of a schoolteacher. "I'm your father's worst nightmare, finboy. I'm the Instigator."

The Instigator of the New Current rebels? That was a woman?

Alessia felt a suction of the air near her head. Something being swung at her. She shot her arm forward to block it, but the strike was so powerful, she was thrown to the ground.

"No touching," warned the Instigator. "I'm going to need that."

"Instigator, we're here, at your service," came a new man's voice from the dark.

"The reinforcements arrived, Instigator!" Felthor announced. "Shall I turn on the orichal–"

"Shh!" the woman answered, but she was too late. There was a grunt and a thud and the blue-green squid reappeared, blindingly bright. Alessia winced as her eyes adjusted to the sudden flood of light.

Vulcor had apparently heard where Felthor's stationary voice was coming from, and hurled him up against a cave wall. Felthor had fallen from there onto the lever and turned back on the Orichalca reservoir, so Espior was back up floating unconsciously inside it.

"Get the kids," the Instigator said.

Two rusalka, ghostly silver and hovering like Wimmi's

bandmate, appeared out of nowhere, and grabbed Alessia and Vulcor. At least a dozen creatures stood around them: blue Minchans, humans, rusalka and grindylows. There were even merfolk, sat with their fishtails coiled on the floor like eels. At the back of the cave, the large bubble glistened. They must have used that to get in.

Alessia pushed against the rusalka's translucent arms but she couldn't get free. She couldn't even *really* push them. It was as though they were made of water. They were holding her tight but were too slippery to cling on to or push against. It was like trying to keep her head above water in the sea, with a relentless tug pulling her down, but nothing consistent enough to press down on. Rocks were racing across the floor as Vulcor tried to use his powers without being able to raise his hands.

"Quiet him down," the Instigator told the rusalka holding him. She threw her floor-length hair over him. It tangled all over his face, arms and neck, and suddenly Vulcor seemed to be drowning in it.

Alessia had to get into the rusalka's mind before she hurt him. She tried to focus on her, but there were so many people in the room and as soon as she opened herself, the hodgepodge of their emotions crashed in.

She couldn't focus. The Green Pung had taken its toll on her, and the effort she'd just made with Felthor and the seaweed must have depleted the little energy she had left. She couldn't control her power anymore.

Vulcor wrestled frenetically to get out from the rusalka's hold, like an animal fighting for its life.

"Calm down, Vulcor! You'll exhaust yourself!" Alessia shouted at him.

His fighting dramatically slowed, and came to a stop.

Alessia sighed with relief. Then, he collapsed unconscious on the floor.

"Vulcor! What did you do to him?" Alessia yelled at the Instigator.

"Put him up there," the Instigator said to the rusalka, ignoring Alessia.

The rusalka threw him up on the reservoir, and he hung there limply, like Espior.

"Now put her back in place. We're starting again," ordered the Instigator. The rusalka dragged Alessia towards the altar flanked by a Minchan man and a grindylow.

"How can you all do this? She's about to kill that boy!" Alessia cried.

"Yeah? So what, after all the Empire's taken from us?" grunted the grindylow.

"There must be another way! How can you just accept that people have to die?"

The rusalka was lifting Alessia off the ground to place her on the altar when something stopped her. A light was growing, opening like a book against the cave wall. With three shadows cut out against it. Three people were coming in through the miner's entrance.

"Look, Larthu's grandfather says you'd need a conductive material to transfer powers with Green Pung. Orichalca's a conductive material. Yagora and the other kappas are complaining this Orichalca reservoir's been tampered with. It's worth a shot, isn't it? I'd rather wait for Alessia and do it together *too*, but she's unreachable! It's not my fault," came Herior's voice.

"Herior! Help! It's me, it's–" Alessia screamed before she was gagged by the grindylow's long, sinewy fingers.

"Alessia!" shrieked Kella, when they came into view.

"Holy Tridents..." muttered Larthuzor.

"Get them," ordered the Instigator. Three merfolk slithered to the mine entrance on their tails, dragging themselves with their arms. Alessia bit down on the grindylow's fingers.

"Hey!" the grindylow snapped. "I didn't know we were on *biting* terms..." He came an inch away from Alessia's face and bared his horrific, yellow pointed teeth in a wicked grin.

"Leave her!" the Instigator ordered. "We still need her. Get her back on that altar."

The grindylow stepped back and the rusalka lifted Alessia again. She screamed and started a fruitless struggle against the rusalka's grasp, just as Vulcor had done.

"Don't!" shouted Larthuzor as the three friends ran towards Alessia. "Don't fight them! Remember what Gizma Authenta said."

Just then one of the mermaids grabbed his ankles, tripping him. When he was on the floor, the mermaid held a trident to his neck, and stuck a starfish on his mouth so Larthuzor was left mumbling indecipherably. Alessia wracked her mind, wishing she'd paid more attention in Gizma's class.

Meanwhile, Herior reached behind his back and whipped out a stick. With a swift movement from side to side it extended to be the HeriOAR. He swung it across and brushed away two of the merfolk coming at him while Kella ran on to help Alessia, narrowly dodging the grasp of two rusalka.

Alessia's rusalka lifted her up to the altar. What had Gizma said? There was something about drowning... and it not being the rusalka's fault... Suddenly she remembered. Being tense was the worst thing she could do. She needed to relax. She stopped resisting and became a complete dead weight. Just like water, when she didn't fight them, the rusalka's arms softened, and she slipped through them.

She immediately rolled away. The grindylow pounced. She cowered in anticipation, but just when he was about to land on her, Kella grabbed her wrist and yanked her away.

"Thank you," Alessia panted, jumping to her side.

Herior was rolling on the floor near Larthuzor, with a merman trying to wrench his HeriOAR from his hands.

"Let's help Herior get Larthu back and go!" Kella yelled.

"You go, I'll get Vulcor!" Alessia answered.

"What? No! We can't split up! There's too many of them! We don't even have weapons!"

"We can't leave Vulcor! They'll kill him!" Alessia said, and without waiting for Kella's comeback, she dashed towards the lever on the far wall, to bring the Orichalca down.

"What are you doing? There's only three of them left! Get them!" the Instigator shouted at her minions.

A grindylow leaped over Alessia's head and landed between her and the lever. She took a step back. His long green arm shot out to grab her when he was thrown off and crashed against the cave wall onto Felthor. Standing beside her was Herior with his HeriOAR still brandished to whack any other creature trying to get her.

Before she could even thank him, he yelled, "Watch out!"

Coming at them from her other side was a group of Minchan men, backward-flipping like they'd done underwater at the Whirlpool of Firnor.

But one by one, they seized up in mid-air and came crashing down to the floor to thrash about under seaweed constrictor blankets. Alessia and Herior whipped their heads around to see Kella in the corner where Felthor had kept the seaweed blankets. Two rusalka that had chased her were at her feet, covered in seaweed. She'd found her weapon.

"Seaweed constrictor. I *knew* I should've chosen that instead of sea cucumbers for that shipwreck of an assignment about escaping," she said to herself.

"You Biomimetics Starfish Kella!" Herior shouted back at her just as two grindylows pounced on him.

He whacked one of them, but the other stuck out its huge tongue and it landed right on Herior's free hand.

"Eww!" Herior shouted.

The grindylow dragged Herior towards him. Herior flicked the antennae on his HeriOAR so they threw out a spark of lightning. That did it. In an instinctive panic, the grindylow's tongue recoiled, and he was free.

Alessia ran for the lever again. A human man was in front of it now. He ran straight for Alessia. She prepared her fists, when a muffled scream of her name came from Larthuzor behind. She turned to see a mermaid leaping to strike at her, like a snake. She threw herself on the floor, and the man and mermaid crashed straight into each other.

"Nice one!" Kella shouted.

"Kella, watch out behind!" Alessia screamed back

A human woman was about to attack her. Kella threw the last seaweed blanket onto her and she fell backwards, wrapped in the tightening black net.

Then, the fight froze. A strange sound had grabbed all their attention. A ghostly hum, "Ooooh Ooooh... Oooh ooh ooh oooh... ooh oooh Ooooh."

The children, and remaining creatures all turned to where a merman sat coiled, singing his song of the abyss. An emptiness and deep relaxation grew inside of Alessia, and her head lolled to the side. Just as it did, a pang of pain from where Felthor had hit her head slowly reverberated through her skull, and drew her ever so slightly out of her stupor.

"No... Block your ears..." she mumbled sluggishly, sleepily raising her hands to her own ears. Immediately she came back to her senses.

"Block your ears!" she shouted louder. Kella turned back to her in a daze, and her hands slowly drifted up to cover her ears. As soon as she'd done so, she seemed to perk up too.

"Herior! Block your ears!" they cried out in unison, just as the Instigator drowsily shouted, "Enough, Ayco," to the merman.

But Herior was closer to the merman than Kella and Alessia had been, and had succumbed to the sound faster. He'd already dropped his oar and walked straight into captivity by the time the merman Ayco stopped singing. The merman stuck a starfish on his mouth and held up a trident to his throat, like his companion had done to Larthuzor.

The remaining rusalka shook off the trance they'd also been under, and glided towards Alessia and Kella. The girls were outnumbered. And with the seaweed constrictor blankets used up, they didn't have any weapons left. They'd never be able to save Vulcor *and* Larthuzor *and* Herior, *and* fight the rest of the creatures off. There was only one thing Alessia could do.

She ran straight towards the rusalka, dodged them as they tried to grab her, and lunged for the Green Pung vial on the altar behind them.

Before the rusalka could do anything, she grabbed it and swung her arm back, ready to propel it against the wall.

"NO!" cried the Instigator. In a flash she was by Alessia's side.

"DON'T get any closer. I'll throw it. I will," cried Alessia.

"Okay, okay. I'm backing away, see? Don't throw it." The Instigator said.

A rusalka was approaching Alessia's back arm from behind. Alessia clasped the vial up against her chest, took a deep breath, and threw off the cork. Immediately she felt nauseated and stumbled.

The Instigator screamed as she did, her eyes locked on the now open vial of Green Pung.

"Nobody touch her!"

"That's right," Alessia coughed. "Any sudden movement and I spill everything."

"Alessia, you don't know what you're doing. Give me the vial. This is much, much more important than you think."

"Enough!" Alessia shouted, between a fit of coughs. "Let go of my friends! Now! And get out of my way if you want this back."

"Alright, okay," the Instigator said gently, holding up her hands in surrender. She turned to her followers: "Move!" she ordered, and the rusalka nearest Alessia and Kella backed away, and merfolk dropped their hold on Herior and Larthuzor.

"And him," Alessia ordered, indicating Vulcor. A grindylow reached up his tongue, plucked Vulcor off the reservoir, and placed him, unconscious in front of Alessia's feet.

"Come with me!" Alessia called after them, and Kella, Larthuzor and Herior all hurried to her side, the boys hissing with pain as they detached the starfish stuck to their faces.

Alessia walked into the giant bubble, coughing into one arm and holding the uncorked vial high up in the other. The others walked in beside her, dragging in Vulcor.

"Seagrass-City," Alessia said, hoping that would get them to the illegal bubble in the cliff. There they'd be able to get help. They'd find Yagora or Niva or the other Sirens, or *somebody* that wasn't an Emperor's Guard or New Current fanatic.

The Instigator's brow was furrowed nervously above the wetsuit still pulled up to her nose. Just as Alessia was closing the bubble, the Instigator dropped to the ground, rolled in beside her, and with a sweeping kick, threw the four others out.

56

Alessia materialized, alone with the Instigator, in the cave in the cliff by Seagrass-City, overlooking the port of Atlantis. She ran out of the bubble.

"I told you to release my friends!" she yelled, stretching her arm to hold the Green Pung out above the water.

"No! No, I beg you!" the Instigator said. "Your friends won't be hurt. Please put it down. You don't know what this means, you don't know who I am."

"I know who you are. You're Dolia's daughter, aren't you? You're Cariesa. You didn't disappear, you went into hiding."

The woman seemed slightly taken aback.

"Yes. You're right. I *am* Cariesa," she paused, "but you knew me under my cover name. You knew me as Cecilia."

Alessia's blood ran cold. The Instigator rolled the wetsuit down from her mouth to reveal her face. Alessia's arm slackened.

"Alessia, I'm your mother," Cariesa said, brushing her short pixie-cropped hair out of her face.

Alessia stumbled back. Cariesa gasped in horror and

instinctively extended a hand towards the vial, but Alessia quickly snatched the vial back against her chest.

"You're not," Alessia shouted, but looking at her, she knew it was true. Her large, deep-set green eyes, the square shape of her face, her jaw, her straight mouth, her hairline... It was like gazing at herself twenty years from now.

"I am. I'm your mother."

"Don't say that."

"Alessia, you have to listen to me—"

"That voice..." Suddenly Alessia realized where she knew it from. "The voice from my recurring dreams..."

"Yes, that was me! You see?" Cariesa smiled urgently. She stepped closer, staring at Alessia with desperation. "You remember! I've been with you your whole life Alessia, I never really left you. I faked the sailing accident and hid out in the far reaches of Nethuns, and I came to you almost every night. I used to fill your room with Slumber Smoke. It would put you in a stupor so I could contact you but be remembered only as a dream. I'd talk to you and teach you our language and our ways, so we could be here together when it would be safe again. It was me that sent Jimmy Greenteeth, the grindylow, to get you, and then convinced a renegade siren to help me with an unofficial siren's song, when that didn't work. And I went down there myself to make sure you'd follow it."

Alessia made a guttural sobbing sound she didn't even recognize, and turned to face the cliff edge. She remembered George complaining about the smoky smell in the house, and Felthor telling her landfarers could contact people in Selva through their dreams. She remembered peoples' surprise that she spoke the language upon arriving. It all fit. Her chest was heaving.

She turned back to study Cariesa. That petite woman,

with athletic arms and cropped, mousey-brown hair that cut sharp edges into her face. She looked like a warrior... not like a mother, at least not the one Alessia had always imagined.

"Alessia–"

"Quiet."

Her mother had been her role model, a perfect woman she was *barely* worthy to be the daughter of. How could she be this vicious, cold-blooded criminal that was prepared to *kill* Vulcor and Espior? A terrible sadness washed over Alessia. For her whole life, she'd have been so happy to imagine her mother was still alive and was with her, talking to her every night as she slept, like a guardian angel.

Now the thought was horrifying.

"I know what you're thinking," Cariesa said. "You must think I'm some kind of monster. I'm not, Alessia. I promise you. I'm just one of the many poor souls the Emperor tricked into believing they were spying to defend Nethuns against the Selvans. He betrayed us, Alessia. We were spying to help him build his attack, without even knowing it. We were helping his self-interested attempt to take over the world as the Sensate Supreme."

Alessia backed away from the cliff edge and into the cave, shaking her head as tears streamed down her cheeks. Cariesa followed her in.

"We thought we were doing good. We thought we were special... the *'crème de la crème'*. We thought he cared about us. He used us! Used us and disposed of us when we became inconvenient. He killed your father Alessia. Stabbed him because he knew about baby Vulcor, because he knew too much."

"Stop it!"

"Alessia, I know it's hard to hear. But it's the truth. Isn't that what you came here for? To find answers? To find your family. You've got it! You've got me," she said excitedly, taking another step closer to Alessia.

"No!" Alessia yelped, jumping further back into the cave. "My mother would never have abandoned me. And my mother was nothing like you. She was b-blind and–"

The words kept catching in her throat as she sobbed.

"Alessia, I *had* to stay away, to keep you safe. Your father and I had met George during our mission in Scotland, and it was the only place I could think to take you. I acted blind when I went to him, so that slippery picaroon Espior the Oculate couldn't see you through my eyes. I no longer had my power to make me immune to his. To lessen the risk, I faked my death, hiding out under water thanks to my Nethuns outfit just long enough for them to call off the search party. Then, every time I came to see you, I came 'blind'. I stayed 'blind' for the better part of *twelve years* so Espior wouldn't tell the Emperor where we were. But that's all in the past now. If you join me, together we can destroy them, and we will never have to hide again! We can go back to living like mother and daughter."

Alessia turned away, biting her nails. A million thoughts wrestled in her mind and she couldn't make sense of them.

For a moment, neither of them talked. Then Cariesa said, "You're just like Silor, you know."

Alessia looked back at her.

"Your father. Quietly thoughtful. With a strong sense of justice. I can see that in you as clear as I saw it in him. He'd be so proud of you."

Alessia remembered feeling the kind heart and excitement of the young father-to-be in the Whirlpool of Firnor, and held the wrist on which she'd attached his trident up to her chest. Now she knew what that vision had been; the moments leading up to his murder by the Emperor. If it hadn't been for that fateful day, would they have had a happy, normal family life together?

"If my father was so great, why did Iktor hate him?" Alessia asked, trying to stop herself idealizing him and being disappointed again.

"Iktor? Iktor didn't hate him. Iktor was our friend since we were all at the Octopus's Garden! When I told him I suspected the Emperor of your father's death, he felt so sorry for us. He even told me about his secret Green Pung vial to make me feel safer. For a moment I thought I'd convince him to join me in the New Current, despite his debilitating fear of the Emperor and all things political. He humored me long enough to read my pamphlet! *That* was how much he liked your father," Cariesa said. "Of course, he started hating *me* when he caught me using powers to convince someone of something one day. He never did get over his hang-up with powers. Understandably, I guess. And he became downright unpleasant when I came back years later to ask him for the vial."

That explained why Iktor was so defensive around her – he'd recognized her *mother* in her, not her father. He'd understood she had powers, and thought she'd been sent by her mother to get the vial from him, by appealing to his affection for her father.

"But Silor..." Cariesa paused, as a few tears rose from her eyelid. "Silor was a great man. The best. You have to believe me on that."

Alessia looked down. She did believe her.

"That's how it all started," Cariesa continued, getting closer. "They announced he'd died at the hands of the enemy on a mission, and it destroyed me. In my grief, I went to see the Emperor to find out more, and that's when I first sensed his guilt. My powers kicked in. I didn't even yet know what they were, but I just *knew* what I'd felt was right. It's hard to explain."

She didn't need to. Alessia knew intimately what she meant.

"I went home, to the outrageously lavish new lodgings the Emperor had given my mother in Junonia building just before, and suddenly it all made sense," Cariesa said. "He'd *planned* it. He knew he'd have to kill Silor, and knew how devastated I'd be, so he'd tried to secure my loyalty in advance by giving my mother riches. My whole world fell apart. I grabbed a trident and headed to the palace. I was going to kill him, but Espior the Oculate intercepted me along the way. The Emperor had told him to watch me, and he'd realized he *couldn't*, which meant I must have a power. He told me about it, to get on my good side. He thought I might come in handy in the future."

The shadow of a smile flickered on her face. "I used that power to start the New Current."

Alessia looked down at the vial in her hands. "And now you want to start it again."

"Yes! And you can help me."

Alessia paused in thought. She could be with her mother. It was what she'd always wanted. She could help avenge her father, and take down the evil Emperor, while uniting what was left of her family.

"But when my powers were transferring to you, it was killing Vulcor and Espior," Alessia said.

"A necessary sacrifice. I need my powers back to take the Emperor down, like I did before."

The fetid Green Pung scent wafted towards Alessia, carried by the ocean breeze.

"Alessia, we should go back to the Orichalca mine now.

The Emperor's Guard will be scouring the city. We need to act fast if–"

"You didn't though," Alessia murmured.

"What?"

"You said you can take down the emperor *like you did before*. But you *didn't* do it before. You *almost* did. Why was that?"

"Alessia," Cariesa smiled. "Dear, we–"

"Answer my question. You had the power before. And you had the New Current behind you. Conditions were perfect for you to take him down. What went wrong? What aren't you telling me?"

"Alessia, there's nothing I'm–"

"You forget *I* have the power now. I can empathize with what you're feeling," Alessia closed her eyes and took a deep breath. She was still too weak to use her powers, but Cariesa didn't know that. And she still had her natural empathy to go on. "You're not doing this for the emperor's victims, are you? If you were, you would have found another way to help them, instead of just waiting *twelve years* to get your powers back. Maybe it was about revenge and justice before, but it's not anymore. You want to rule."

"Only to prevent the Emperor from doing more harm–"

"What did you mean when you said the Emperor wanted to take over as 'the Sensate Supreme'?"

"Alessia, don't make things more complicated than they are," Cariesa said gently, edging closer. "I've been watching you all my life and I *know* how much this empathy's been crippling you. How it was making you too sensitive, and how you made a fool of yourself because of it. How desperately you were trying to suppress it and ignore it. If you give me your powers, it'll lose its hold over you! You can finally be normal!"

Alessia paused.

"The empathy wasn't crippling me, though," she said. "Maybe I didn't see it at first, but... it was my greatest strength all along. And not because it gives me the power to manipulate others, like *you* want to. But because I can understand people, and I can be a good friend to them. And that's how I got my friends. And that's why I'm not going to let you hurt them."

Before Alessia realized what was happening, Cariesa lunged forward and yanked at the vial of Green Pung. Alessia tried to push her off with her free arm but Cariesa was shockingly strong. Alessia's palm was sweaty, and the vial was slipping out. She tightened her clutch as much as she could and punched and kicked. Cariesa barely flinched. Finally, a kick landed on her stomach and Cariesa stumbled back.

Alessia ran towards the cliffside staircase. But before she'd gone two steps, Cariesa shoved her to the ground and pinned her down. Alessia writhed and kicked but could barely budge. She was only gradually shuffling the two of them backwards.

Cariesa started pulling on Alessia's fingers, one by one, to uncurl them from the vial. She plucked two fingers off, and bent them backwards. Alessia yowled with pain but clenched her remaining fingers even harder around the Green Pung.

Then suddenly, Alessia's head fell back. It was flopping off the edge of the cliff. If she shuffled back any further, she'd fall off.

Cariesa tugged at Alessia's last two fingers on the vial.

Alessia had to get into her head again. She winced as she tried. It was no use. She was still too weak, too distracted. And now she was dangling off the cliff, off-balance.

The joust at the Octopus's Garden flashed in her mind. Herior losing balance and Gulusor toppling after him.

She put down her feet and rammed herself backwards, towards the precipice. Her shoulders slumped off the edge. Cariesa snatched away the arm she had holding down Alessia's upper body, to stop them both tumbling over.

Alessia swung her freed arm across, grabbed the top of the vial, and with both her hands, slammed the vial on the ground. It shattered

"No!" A furious groan tore out of Cariesa's throat.

A musty, rodent-like smell, with fetid notes of urine and aniseed, filled the air, as a green vapor emanated from the liquid spilled on the ground. Alessia felt immediately light-headed, and the skin on her hands became numb.

"What have you done?" Cariesa roared.

In one abrupt move, Cariesa stood, leaving Alessia lurching backwards. Alessia grappled desperately at the ground, sending pebbles around her cascading into the abyss. Finally, she got a purchase on the rocks around and heaved herself upright.

Cariesa stepped back and stayed very still. The shadows from the cave cloaked her right side. But the artificial moon had now appeared in the Atlantide sky, and it reflected in a tell-tale shimmer below her hand. The blade of a dagger.

So pushing her off the cliff wasn't enough. Cariesa would stab Alessia to death, to be sure the job was done.

The side of Cariesa's face Alessia could see was perfectly neutral. There wasn't a wrinkle on it to betray any emotion.

She blew out a breath.

"You ruined everything," she muttered, shaking her

head. The heat of the gaze of her hidden eye burned through the shadows.

Alessia shut her eyes. She found herself saying her last words calmly. Words she didn't know she had in her. Remnants from what she had overheard Metella say at the Chaco's followers meeting in Azlanu: "I understand now what it meant. That previous Oculate's quote. 'The Sensate's challenge is not falling powerless to their own power'. Whoever you are – Instigator, Cariesa, Cecilia... mum – it seems you did."

There was silence, only cut by the sound of her own breath pumping out of her mouth, and the roar of the water far below. She waited for her doom. She couldn't sense Cariesa's reaction. There was no sound, no movement, nothing. Then, nothing happened for so long, that Alessia slowly opened her eyes. She couldn't see her. She eased herself up to her feet ever so gently, and walked into the shadows where Cariesa had been. She was gone.

❧ 57 ❧

Light smeared the darkness, as Alessia blinked open bleary eyes. Muffled voices came into focus.

"Look, look! She's waking up!"

A pale blur sharpened to become Kella's large, friendly, oblong nose, hovering above Alessia's face.

"Alessia! Alessia, do you hear us?" came a voice from her side.

Alessia turned her head slowly. Her neck felt stiff, but any pain had been numbed. Herior lay on a bed beside her. They were in a light blue room with vibrant-colored furnishings, made to resemble a tropical coral reef.

"Wh-where are we?" she said, her voice cracking from not having been used for a while.

"Thank Triton," muttered Wimmi, kneeling by her bed and holding her hand in his. His eyebrows loomed heavier than normal over eyes puffy with tears, and his carrot-colored beard shook with his trembling lip.

"You're in hospital Alessia," Kella answered, realizing Wimmi wouldn't be able to. "Both of you are. You and Herior." Her deep voice sounded so soothing.

"Alessia! Starfish Jous-ta!" Herior tried to say enthusiastically, but his smile was too pained to even form dimples.

"Oh Alessia," Kella cried out with uncharacteristic emotion. "When the Instigator came back to the cave, we thought for sure she'd killed you!"

"She went back to the cave? What happened? And w-what about Vulcor?" Alessia asked hazily. The last she remembered she was scrambling up the staircase along the cliff edge, hoping she'd make it to the top before she finally collapsed with exhaustion.

"Well, Larthuzor had the idea to fake Vulcor and the Oculate's death, so they'd leave them alone!" Kella said.

"I slammed on the switch to turn off the Orichalca conduction, so Espior fell next to Vulcor, then I screamed 'Guys, I think they're dead!', and Kella and Herior played along," Larthuzor explained, as a kind of octopus with giant flapping dumbo ears sat contentedly perched on his head. "Herior cut his hand with the HeriOAR and squeezed some blood onto Vulcor's head."

"And I gave a very convincing scream and held up Vulcor's bloodied head and cried about how they'd killed him," Kella added.

"Seriously?" The scene was beyond Alessia's imagining. "Wait, you did all that to protect Vulcor? You don't even like him!"

"Well, *for some reason* he's your friend, so..." Kella shrugged.

"When the Instigator came back, and told her guys they needed to flee and take the prisoners, they told her the prisoners were dead," Larthuzor said proudly.

"Yeah, and then there was a marching sound from the miner's entrance. So with all the urgency, the Instigator and her guys rushed to take the bubble to wherever they're hiding out, and left the prisoners' bodies behind."

"Marching? Was it the Emperor's Guard?" Alessia asked.

"Not exactly," Larthuzor smiled.

"While the Instigator's followers were distracted by the little fake death spectacle, Larthu here *also* had the bright idea of shelling Yagora to tell some of her Kappa friends to come for reinforcement."

Alessia dropped her head back in awe. "You guys really are incredib–"

For the first time she noticed someone else in the room, half-hidden behind Kella.

"Naror? What are you doing here?"

"He insisted to come with us after class, when I said you'd been injured," Kella answered for him.

"I felt so bad and I had to tell you... I'm the one who sent you the notes," said Naror, the freckles on his nose magnified by tears. "I'm so sorry, I couldn't tell you earlier."

It all came back to Alessia. What her mother had told Felthor in the cave. The "Gavrols" – as in Naror *Gavrol's* parents – had helped with the Oculate's abduction, but backed out of the plan when they found out about the sacrifice.

"Your parents told you to warn me that I'd be sacrificed?" Alessia asked.

"No. They couldn't bear being part of a plan that meant sacrificing two children – but they also couldn't stop it. They were too scared that the Instigator would hurt me to get back at them if she got any inkling that they were interfering with her plan. And they couldn't tell the Emperor's guard or we'd be locked up for them having been part of the New Current in the first place."

"Triton! Your parents are Chaco's followers *and* New Curr–" Kella stopped herself when Alessia shot her a 'not now' look.

"But I heard my parents talking about it, and I just *had* to warn you," Naror continued. "Only, I couldn't tell you directly because you wouldn't believe me on account of–"

"You being the class liar?" Herior completed clumsily.

"Well, ex-liar, but yeah..." Naror said. "And I couldn't put too much in writing in case it fell into the wrong hands, and they traced it back to my family."

"Wow... You put yourself on the line like that, for me? How can I even begin to thank you?" Alessia said.

"What about you Starfish Jous-ta? Tell us what happened," Herior said. "We only found you because the sirens were flying around and Niva saw you on the cliff unconscious and brought you into Seagrass-City! You know a cliff edge isn't the best place to take a nap, Ali."

Alessia gulped. She owed it to them to explain everything. And so she did.

～

For a moment, they all froze, and the only movement in the room came from the fluttering dumbo ears of Larthuzor's octopus.

"Poseidon Almighty," muttered Kella in shock.

"Ho-ly Triton," echoed Herior. "Well, we suspected the part about her being your mother, to be honest. Even before meeting the Instigator, Kella had shown us a Drift of Cariesa she got at Dolia's after you left. She really was the spitting image of you. But you having a power?"

"A sixth Sensate Power no one knows about!" Naror added.

"Can you read my mind now? Or make Kella want to massage my shoulders?" Herior asked.

"Leave her alone! She's recovering!" Kella swatted at him.

"We'd figured out the power transfer piece too," Larthuzor explained to Alessia, ignoring Herior's antics. "While you and Kella were at Dolia's, I decided to confront my grandfather about the Green Pung, after all. He confirmed what Yagora told you. And also said a power transfer like Naror had suggested *would* be possible, if the laws of an ordinary power transfer, and the instructions on the vial were followed."

"That's when I got the idea for the Orichalca mine as somewhere conductive!" Herior added proudly.

"And we finally deciphered the vial," Larthuzor continued. "Power Entrusted, means it can only go to someone of kin: so being your mother, she could only get *your* power transferred to her. Power Evolved, means it can only be transferred if it's evolved from being passive to active. So it makes sense they waited till you could *affect* others' emotions, not just *sense* them. And Power Expensive, means the person from whom the power is transferred dies, so..." Larthuzor's voice trailed off.

All three of them stared at her uncomfortably and the big-eared octopus on Larthuzor's head squirmed, its tentacles twisting into his hair. The famous "sacrifice" from Naror's note. Despite having kind of guessed it already, the thought still grasped Alessia's mind like an icy cold hand. The whole time, her own mother had been prepared to kill her to get her power back.

"I mean, we're not *sure*," Herior tried weakly.

"You're not?" Alessia said.

"Well, no. We are. We asked my grandfather. He made

the vial and wrote that based on his experiments back in Penglini... I'm sorry," Larthuzor said, lowering his eyes.

"The Instigator told my parents and Felthor about it just after they kidnapped the Oculate Espior, so they all definitely knew," Naror added.

"And they didn't just *wait* for my power to be evolved," Alessia said. "Felthor *taught* me how to do it, pretending he was teaching me how to treat an episode. And my mother taught me the Atlantide language so I'd be able to come here and learn from him fast when I reached the right age, like Vulc–" she stopped herself just in time. "They *trained* me to be sacrificed."

Wimmi inhaled sharply, bit his lip to swallow back his sobs and raised his face to the ceiling, as though trying to draw in his tears again.

"I'm so sorry Alessia," he exhaled quickly. "I'm just so, so sorry. I had no idea, I swear. Seven years..." He was overwhelmed by a violent sob, at the thought. "We were together s-*seven years* and I had no idea. I should have been there to protect you. I wanted to be *such* a good guardian to you. And under my nose, the whole time, *the whole time...*" He winced at the words.

"Wimmi, don't," Alessia reached out her hand and placed it on his bulky chest as it shook with his sobs. He pulled her in and hugged her tightly, and she hugged him even tighter, sniffing his comforting nutmeg scent. Kella, Larthuzor and Herior shared a sad glance.

"It's okay, Wimmi," Alessia said. "I think even *he* doesn't fully realize what he was doing." Alessia had only said this to appease Wimmi, but as the words came out of her mouth, she knew they were true. Felthor didn't know Cariesa was doing this for her own personal domination now. *He* was fighting for freedom and equality. For good things. She was using him, like the Emperor had used her before.

"I won't let you down again," Wimmi said fiercely, wiping his tears. "I promise."

A nereid Alessia assumed was a doctor opened the door. "She's back with us!" she exclaimed. "Now I'm going to have to ask the non-patients to leave the room. And Herior, if you can come with me too. You have a visitor waiting outside."

Kella quickly took something out of her belt and discreetly placed it under Alessia's pillow before leaving the room along with the others.

The doctor made a series of reflex tests on Alessia. They were different from any she'd experienced in Selva, and each weirder than the last, but Alessia was too distracted to give it much notice. She felt totally numb to her surroundings. The day's revelations were turning over and over in her mind. She was squeezing them for extra details, for further implications.

When the doctor finally left the room, Alessia reached for what Kella had placed under her pillow. It was a Drift pearl attached to a page from Cariesa's journal:

"Castlemount Bed & Breakfast, St. Andrews, Fife, Scotland, Selva,

Silor and I arrived for our mission on Selvan land in Fife three days ago. Posing as Cecilia and Sam, local tourists this time. The accent took some practice but I think we got it! We made friends with a Scottish student called George here, who's visiting the university for a conference – and he seemed to buy we could be Scottish (he said we spoke 'funny', but so did everyone who wasn't from Inverness).

We're to check out a secret nuclear bunker hidden deep in the countryside, accessible only through a passageway that leaves from a fake little cottage. We're hoping to find the Regional Commissioner's documents there and those might contain information about their nuclear arsenal and even plans to bomb Nethuns. They stopped exploding underwater nuclear warheads in the late 6os, after our Emperor retaliated by sinking some of their ships. But the Emperor thinks we may need to defend ourselves again soon. The work we're doing is so important. It's clearly a recognition that we're the best in the Emperor's Order, and I'm so proud."

The drift showed Cariesa with a man holding her waist, and a nerdy-looking George standing a little bit further, looking at them with admiration. The man had a large, kind face and sandy gold-colored skin. His big, brown eyes were crowned with long eyelashes, giving them a sleepy, relaxed look, and his thick lips opened to reveal slightly parted teeth in a frank, jovial smile.

Suddenly, the world didn't seem so bleak to her. She may not have found the mother she'd wanted, but she'd found who her father had been. And she had Wimmi and her friends, and they each loved her in their own particular ways, and she loved each of them. That was a kind of family in itself.

✿ 58 ✿

"We'll have a little bit of everything in the middle to share," Wimmi asserted to their chubby waiter whose face seemed frozen in a broad smile, and as a result, had to nod to signal his understanding. "For me a double seal milk, and a pickled gulfweed juice. And for the guppies, pickled gulfweed juices all around."

The waiter disappeared and barely a moment later, five waiters were already back at the table, laying on it plates of the typical Atlantide dishes Alessia loved: stuffed crab meatballs, shrimp fritters, crispy salted dulse flakes, and countless other nibbles.

Wimmi had planned a good old "Fish & Seal Milk night" for her first night out of hospital. The concept – as he'd explained it to her – seemed fitting.

"In Atlantis, when everything is going to *spraints* – or on the contrary, when you celebrate; when someone you've missed comes to visit, or when someone you love goes away; for better or for worse: there's Fish & Seal Milk. It's been the staple meal of generations. The world's problems get solved around Fish & Seal Milk tables... or at the very least, heavily discussed. And my dear, I think you have more than deserved your first Fish & Seal Milk night." He'd sold the concept like a politician on campaign. "Of course, the seal milk will be for me – we call it milk but it's really a pretty hard liquor... Fear not, though! *You* will also have a fine beverage: our delicious pickled gulfweed juice!"

Alessia had grimaced unintentionally and both of them had laughed – and then laughed again in relief because that had been their first laugh in a long time.

"What's key at the Fish & Seal Milk table is to have the people you love present. So, invite your friends and let's make a night of it!" Wimmi had told her.

And so Alessia found herself at a restaurant terrace near the Port of Atlantis, overlooking the vast expanse of water that stretched between them and the end of the Atlantis airpocket, and watching the Marcavals surface as they made their way into the port. Across from her sat Larthuzor, excitedly showing Wimmi and Naror how well his newt was getting along with its new prosthetic leg. Kella walked back to the table from the bathroom, shuffling her feet, and plonked herself down by Alessia's side.

"Alessia, something happened, I have to tell you," Kella mumbled, pouting grimly. Alessia's heart froze in her chest. She didn't know how much more bad news she could bear.

"There's a rumor," Kella continued. "I heard it from Quina, whose brother knows a nereid working at the hospital. Apparently Perfect Princess Tamaya came to visit Herior and they kissed and now they're going out!"

"No way. Herior with PP Authenta?"

"Well, it was obvious enough he liked her..." Kella shrugged, failing to hide her dejection.

"But they have nothing in common! He's so adventurous and open. I mean, would *she* ever have done this whole hectic project with us? No, it won't last," Alessia dismissed.

Kella moaned. "And next week you're going to Scotland to visit your stepfather! I'll be alone with them."

"Yeah... But I'll be back in a couple of weeks," Alessia offered weakly.

As if on call, Herior walked by the terrace, holding hands with Tamaya. He was abnormally quiet, subdued, and clumsy, as he tried to act like an adult now that he was laden with a girlfriend.

Herior and Tamaya mumbled something to each other, then he awkwardly craned his neck and gave her the shortest peck on the cheek in history. Kella's already white face blanched and she slouched on the table.

Alessia took a sip of her pickled gulfweed juice.

"Triton, that's awful!" she coughed.

"It's an acquired taste," Wimmi mimicked poshly, stroking his tangerine beard. "It helps the seal milk go down"

"So seal milk is *worse* than this?"

Just then, she felt a hand on her shoulder.

"Hi everyone," mumbled a familiar voice.

"Vulcor!" Alessia exclaimed, and before she could stop herself – she'd stood up and flung her arms around his neck. "I didn't think you'd come! How were you able to get away from the palace? Your father must be even more cautious after what happened!"

"It's a long story. I'll explain," he answered, darting a glance at the others.

"How are you, anyway?" Kella asked in her most uninterested voice.

"Good," he said. "And I owe that to you." He lowered

his eyes, and continued: "I mean it. I'd never have imagined you'd save my life. I don't know what to say."

"Well, telling them 'thank you' would be customary," said Wimmi, smiling.

"Thank you," Vulcor said to Kella and Larthuzor. Then he turned to Alessia. "Can I speak to you in private?"

"Sure. Excuse us for a second," she said as she followed Vulcor out, pressing the backs of her hands on her cheeks in an attempt to cool them down. "So, how are you?" she asked when she and Vulcor were far enough from the group to speak privately.

"Okay. My powers were a bit fuzzy for a couple of days but I trained them back to normal. What about you? Espior explained your powers to me, now he's recovered too. A Sixth Sensate Power. Who'd have thought? He invented a name for you, you know. He calls you 'the Corcillate'."

"Wow. Sounds fancy!" Alessia said. "I feel better now too. What happened when you got back to the palace?"

Vulcor fell silent, his face inscrutable.

"I've got news," he said eventually.

"What?" Alessia asked.

"I've deposed my father," he answered simply.

"WHAT?"

❦ 59 ❦

V ulcor shot a glance around them. "Keep quiet! You're drawing attention to us."

He turned and led her away a little further still, where they sat on a seaweed-covered wall.

"But how did... And why aren't the Tidings... What happened?"

"When I'd recovered enough strength, he came to my room to ask me what happened with the Instigator. He always comes to see me alone, since I'm a 'secret'. I threw seaweed constrictor on him, then used my power to float him down to the palace dungeon and chain him there."

"Triton! But won't the guards free him?"

"Nah," Vulcor said nonchalantly. "I called in the Imperial Council: Espior, and the six Ministers. I told them I was the Emperor's son, showed them my powers, and explained to them that my father no longer had any.

"I then proposed myself as the new Emperor, and promised to give them more power and autonomy under my rule. They unanimously agreed. We're preparing a speech, to reassure people, and we'll declare it across Nethuns tomorrow morning."

"Really? They accepted to make a thirteen-year-old *Emperor*?" Alessia shook her head. "They just told you that so you wouldn't use your power on them, there and then. Don't you think they want to take power for themselves the moment they get a chance?"

"Of course they want to." His words were clipped. "But I've got Espior watching them, and I've got my powers to defend myself. If they betray me, they've got another thing coming."

Alessia drew a long breath and let it out in a gush. She didn't know how to tell him that *she* also wasn't convinced he'd make the best leader.

"I don't know, Vulcor. This is so sudden. Are you sure you've thought it through? I mean, trust me, I'm *thrilled* if your dad is out of power, but striking him right now, just like that, without really planning what happens next—"

"HE KILLED MY MOTHER!" Vulcor screamed. Alessia's spine straightened at the violence of his reaction. "He killed my mother, and he lied to me my whole life." Vulcor's eyes were gleaming, but he turned his face before she could see tears.

She reached out a hand to touch him but he shrugged it off.

She waited a beat, then said, "He killed my father too, you know. And a whole lot of other people. Look, I know how it feels to realize your parents aren't much to be proud of. You know the Instigator, Cariesa? She's my—"

"Your mother," Vulcor completed. He seemed calmer now. "I know. Espior told me everything."

"Alright, well if you're in power, can you free Iktor?" Alessia said. "He's innocent. He shouldn't be rotting in jail."

"Innocent? You mean the guy who was hoarding the Green Pung that's deadly to us?"

"Vulcor, please. You've got to trust me."

Vulcor gave her a skeptical look, and changed the subject.

"Look, that's not all I came here to tell you. There's something else you should know. I just found out from Espior.

"So I told you my father banned opposing ideologies so people couldn't read the Chaco manifesto scripts and find out he'd lost his powers to me."

"Yeah."

"Well," he continued. "Apparently that wasn't the *only* thing he wanted to keep hidden. The last volume of the Chaco Manifesto scripts contains a prophecy: 'The creatures of the Earth and of the Sea will, one day, be united and the Sensate Supreme will exercise its rightful control over them.'"

"The Sensate Supreme," Alessia muttered. "My mother said your father was secretly using the Emperor's Order to make himself Sensate Supreme."

"I know."

"And I'm sure that's what she wanted too."

"That's what Espior thinks. That's why the New Current failed. She needed to spend more time in Nethuns, using her power to convince people to join the cause, but she'd set her sights on being the Sensate Supreme."

"So she spread herself too thin between Selva and Nethuns. The power was so fragmented in Selva, it took more of her time than expected," Alessia completed. "Obviously, she convinced the Eastern Bloc and Western Bloc to end the Cold War, but she lost her power to me before she could fully unite and take over Selva."

"In the meantime, she left her former New Current friends in Nethuns to be cannon fodder for my father," Vulcor said.

"She probably tried to continue with her plan, but realized she couldn't make it happen without her power – so she left me with George, and hatched the new plan to get her powers back."

They fell quiet, as they both thought about the terrible things their parents had done.

Eventually Alessia broke the silence. "That prophecy corrupted both our parents."

"I know. I thought about that too. And then I realized, that's exactly why we *won't* be corrupted. Our parents showed us what *not* to do. And that's why I came to tell you this.

"As long as we're on the same side, and being truthful with each other, we'll keep each other in check. I never thought I needed anybody's help, but then you and your friends... Well, I guess it's okay to get help sometimes. We can help each other be better than them." His face slackened with a sudden realization. "So I *should* listen when you tell me Iktor's not a threat. Fine, I'll free Iktor."

"Thank you," Alessia said. "You're right. It's up to us to finally do something *good* with these powers, together."

He smiled and edged his hand closer to hers on the ground. His coal black eyes didn't seem so intense and scary now. They were more peaceful, like a pure night sky.

"Alessia!" Kella shouted out from the restaurant. "Ebrie's here now and Herior's about to finish the crispy salted dulse flakes. Get back here if you don't want to go home hungry!"

Alessia laughed. "We better–"

"Yeah. Don't want to miss on those," Vulcor added, though she couldn't be sure if he was being sarcastic.

~

"Finally!" Kella sighed empathically as they arrived back at the table.

Alessia went straight to hug Ebrie. "I'm so glad you could make it!"

"Of course! It's thanks to Wimmi, who picked a restaurant that 'looks the other way' on the Emperor's specist laws," Ebrie said in her velvety timbre. "Besides, we're not too far from Seagrass-City, and I know from experience you're willing to smuggle me there if the need arises." She winked at Alessia and they exchanged a conspiratorial grin.

"Now hurry up and get a dulse flake, Alessia! Herior's eating them by the thousands!" Naror said. Suddenly, his face dropped with fear. "That was just an exaggeration, not a lie. You got that right? I don't lie anymore. I really don't!"

They all laughed. "We know!"

"He's right, Alessia, we had to fight tooth and nail to keep some for you. The hardest thing we've ever had to do," Larthuzor said. Then, upon reflection, added, "Well, maybe second hardest."

"The hardest is getting Kellsypops to stop being grumpy with me today!" Herior grumbled.

"Kellsy-what?" Kella exclaimed in outrage, her nose, crimson. "This guy's going to get himself slapped with a HeriOAR one day."

"See!"

If Alessia ignored the fact Vulcor was about to become Emperor, life had pretty much gone back to normal, and she couldn't have been more delighted. How she *craved* for their biggest woes to be about unrequited crushes, and friendly bickering from now on.

"Can't you make her nice with me again, Ali?" Herior asked. "Come on, what's the use of these powers if you'll never show us!"

Vulcor shushed him urgently. But Alessia shut her eyes and took a deep breath... and Wimmi grabbed the last crispy salted dulse flake straight out of Herior's hand and gave it to her.

"Hey! What d'you do that for?" Herior protested.

"I don't know, I wasn't going to– Wait. Alessia!" Wimmi mock-scolded.

Alessia shrugged as she chomped on the flake.

Well, life had gone *almost* back to normal.

ACKNOWLEDGMENTS

To Patrick Laine, for getting as excited about this as I was, and for reading and editing the *countless* drafts. (It's an honour to be able to say *this* is the book you've read most!) You were as important to this book getting done as I was.

To Isabelle Laine, for the unconditional love and encouragement, for making me feel that I'd done something special, when I was riddled with self-doubt, and for being my sounding board for ideas during those long seaside walks.

To Jenny Chau-Laine, for your endless well of creativity that I used and abused in many a brainstorming session, and for our magical childhood together, playing and inventing.

To Sertaç Turgut for being my first beta reader, for the excitement and confidence you gave me, live-whatsapping your impressions as you read, and for your eagle-eye observations, and thought-provoking builds.

To Taylan Ersan for making me laugh like a kid, for the surprises and adventures that make life fun and inspiring —

and for your love, patience, and help when I go into full nerd-mode and forget to eat anything other than pasta.

To Dara Essien, Chloe Pesesse, Maria Broniek and Jan Broniek, my incredible young beta readers, for your priceless insights to improve the story! I was blown away by your level of critical thinking and communication skills.

To Anna Bowles, Jenny Bowman, Margeaux Weston, Nathan Bransford, and Rebecca Weber the fantastic editors and critique partner who saw this manuscript at various stages of completion and each took it to the next level with mind-opening suggestions.

To Alessandro Brunelli, my brilliant cover artist — I'm so proud that your magical design is the cover of my book!

To the amazing friends who had faith in my crazy project: Nina Lazic, Giacomo Reali, Christy Essien, Nhân Phạm Nguyễn Hoài, Chloe Rolland, Didem Özdemir, Victoria Delhoume, Charlotte Laurent, Sophie Loup, Sveta Kirnos, Meltem Küskü, Arthur DB, Rabia Ceran, Sara Ekman, Amandine Bezard, Thibault Colle, Aninh Souidaray, Michal Broniek, Neha Pesesse, Eleonora de Marchi, Ilker Arditi, Ayşegül Karslı, Dilay Kurtuluş Elçiseven, Ceyda Günaslan Yüksel, Carolina Rogoll Christophersen, Mert Babayiğit, Sabri Kaya, Özlem Tetik, Samet Güney, Alım Ekşioğlu, Gaël Ledun, Benan Gedikoğlu & Damla Uygur.

To that random stranger who told me one day that we know less about the depths of the ocean than we do about space, and got my imagination racing after years of hibernation.

ABOUT THE AUTHOR

Nathalie Laine lives a safe distance away from the ocean, in Paris, France, where she works in marketing.

She enjoys: poking her finger into the mini whirlpools that form above bath drains, randomly understanding words in a language she doesn't know, wrongly guessing the double-agent in cold war spy stories, sharing a Turkish meal of "Lion's milk", fish and turnip juice with her fiancé and friends, and getting spurned by grumpy cats.

She may have snuck some of the above into *Alessia in Atlantis*.

www.nathalielaine.com

CPSIA information can be obtained
at www.ICGtesting.com
Printed in the USA
LVHW091153250321
682245LV00004B/1

9 781736 170427